GONE
BY
DAWN

BOOKS BY H.K. CHRISTIE

A Permanent Mark

The Neighbor Two Doors Down

MARTINA MONROE SERIES

Crashing Down

What She Left

If She Ran

All She Wanted

Why She Lied

Secrets She Kept

What She Found

How She Fell

Her Last Words

Who She Was

How She Escaped

Lies She Told

Echoes of Her

SELENA BAILEY SERIES

Not Like Her

One In Five

On The Rise

Go With Grace

Flawless

H.K. CHRISTIE

GONE BY DAWN

Bookouture

Published by Bookouture in 2024

An imprint of Storyfire Ltd.
Carmelite House
50 Victoria Embankment
London EC4Y 0DZ

www.bookouture.com

ISBN: 978-1-83525-622-0
eBook ISBN: 978-1-83525-621-3

For Karen. Your strength both amazes and inspires me.

PROLOGUE

SCARLETT

Surrounded by towering redwoods, I perched on the edge of the sparkling blue lake and admired its stillness. It was peaceful and quiet. I couldn't help but wonder if this was what heaven would be like. It was the best I could hope for considering over the past few months I'd had neither peace nor quiet. I knew my mom and dad were going to freak out once they realized I was gone. But I needed some time by myself with no one hovering over me, constantly poking and prodding, asking me if I was okay. Could they even conceive of the notion that I had set my alarm early to sneak out and walk halfway around the lake just to get away from them? The intention was to go all the way around but my body told me I would have to settle for half. Truthfully, I was lucky to have made it this far.

Part of me felt guilty for tricking them. They only wanted what was best for me, and I understood that, but what they didn't understand was what was best for me was to have a little time alone. To be alone with my thoughts without them trying to entertain or cajole or ensure I had everything I needed.

Maybe I was a coward. Too chicken to tell them I wanted them to give me some space. I could see the mounting sadness and concern in their eyes when they looked at me. I didn't want to upset them any more than they already were.

Over the past week, I had given up on my last hope of being normal, or thinking I would ever get better. The prom dress hanging in my closet with the turquoise sequins that shimmered in the light as I twirled around—I'd never wear it. But I was sure I had convinced Mom I would be in great shape and that I'd be dancing the night away with my besties.

Clasping a small stone in my hand, I chucked it across the lake and watched the ripples across the glittering water. It was as if the water was opening up and welcoming me in.

Maybe that was the answer.

No, I couldn't.

They would blame themselves.

But it had been one of the best mornings I'd had in I didn't know how long. Throwing another stone, then another, I continued to marvel at the natural beauty as the sun rose, feeling its warmth on my skin.

It wouldn't be a terrible end.

Shouldn't I have a say in how I die?

My therapist told me not to focus on death because none of us knew when our last day would be. She went on and on about the power of positive thinking and all that mumbo jumbo. Obviously, it hadn't stuck. Death was all I could think of. Would it hurt? Would the last thing I see be white coats and bright lights as they tried to save me? Would I die a virgin? The idea that my last moments would be in a sterile hospital room made me want to hurl. Again.

The doctor was hopeful and had assured my parents I would recover and live a full and happy life. He'd insisted in a way too chipper tone, "She's young and strong. Time to plan her recovery and her future. It's never too soon to tour colleges!" I'd felt like smacking him, but the anesthesia hadn't completely worn off and I lacked the physical strength.

How could he be so sure? I was so tired of all the cheerleading. Couldn't I just be openly miserable for five minutes?

Although their intentions were to raise my spirits, I couldn't stand another bouquet of flowers or a card signed by all my friends and classmates, wishing me to "get well soon" or telling me how much they missed me. At first, the attention had been nice, but it had turned into a sick reminder I wasn't like them. I didn't get to have a carefree life.

Perhaps I was too cynical. Maybe I should believe what everyone kept saying to me: there's always hope until there isn't.

The trees rustled.

Perfectly still, I watched. I heard muffled voices, but I couldn't make out what they were saying. I didn't think it was anyone I knew. The voices were deep, low.

A man wearing a baseball cap emerged; he was old, like my dad's age. His face was weathered as if he spent a lot of time outdoors. Another figure emerged behind him but was thinner, taller, and younger. He was wearing a similar get-up. Father and son? Focusing on the men's features, I thought I knew them from somewhere, but I couldn't place them.

I lifted my hand to wave, but they didn't wave back. They stared and whispered something I couldn't make out. A wave of foreboding washed over me before beads of sweat formed on my forehead and my mind spun.

The older one yelled, "Get her!"

I opened my mouth to scream, but nothing came out.

ONE

VAL

His lips were moving, but I was tired of listening to his words. Why he thought repeating himself would gain my agreement was beyond me. He was being overly cautious, and it was unnecessary. He must have noticed my lack of interest in the topic because he whisper-yelled, "Val, you're not Superwoman."

"I never claimed I was," I retorted. "The doctor said I'm fine. I just have a few bumps and scrapes here and there. In a week—*tops*—I'll be at full speed."

Kieran's dark brows furrowed and his lips curled into a frown; he was clearly fed up with my protests. Just because he was my supervisor, he thought he knew what was best for me. He thought he understood my strengths and full capabilities. But how could he have possibly known? Yes, we had worked together for a decade and we'd worked on dozens of cases together. But he wasn't me. He didn't know my thoughts, my feelings, or my energy level. His concern was likely because of my exterior shell contradicting how I actually felt. The nurse had shown me a mirror, so I understood I looked worse for wear, with a large Band-Aid on my cheek surrounded by colorful bruises that matched those on my wrists, and, of course, the little souvenir from the Bear.

Admittedly, I wouldn't be entering any beauty contests anytime soon, although if there were a zombie beauty pageant for middle-aged women, I might have a chance.

"Look, when you're feeling better, we'll talk about you rejoining the team. When you're back, we want you at one hundred percent."

One hundred percent? What did that even mean? On most days, I gave one hundred percent. Maybe I was knocked down to eighty-five percent, but that was still above average. "I've been worse. I'm ready to get back out there with the team."

"We can't have you working from a hospital bed, Val. You know that."

Kieran was a great leader and he had become a good friend. But I wasn't about to let him sideline me in the search for the man who had put me in said hospital bed. "I'm being discharged in a few hours and I don't want to lose momentum. As of right now the Bear has a two-day head start."

Kieran stepped closer, making the lines on his face even clearer and the scar on his cheek pronounced. He wasn't stupid. He'd been in this job a long time, and if I was thinking rationally —not high on painkillers and filled with rage at the situation— maybe I would have heeded his warnings sooner. He had experience, something I should trust.

"The team is working to locate him. You didn't think we'd just pack up and leave, did you?"

No. But I wanted to be involved in taking him down. I had more than earned it. I had faith in the team, but I knew the Bear better than anyone. They needed my help.

He gazed down at me with those wise brown eyes like a big beefy owl and said, "Val, you know this guy better than any of us. He's never gone after any of his escaped victims. You don't need to worry about it. All you need to concern yourself with is getting better. Once you are, we'll talk."

"They call us survivors, sir." It was petty, but I was frustrated and sick of being confined to a hospital bed. Two days was far too long to be stuck in a frigid room reeking of industrial-strength cleaner with too many people fussing over me.

"You know what I mean."

I did know what he meant, but we had only found one other survivor, and she couldn't provide a physical description because he had blindfolded her. The only reason we knew she was one of his conquests was because she'd received the same souvenir I had. "Like you said, I know him better than anyone. Obviously, I won't be involved with tactical matters yet, but I should be part of the profiling team to help catch him before he hurts someone else."

"They've been processing the scene and gathering evidence. We've got this."

Even so, I was the one who had connected the murders and found him. Staring out the window, I couldn't look at Kieran anymore because I feared I might crumble. The tough gal demeanor was wearing thin.

Kieran softened his voice. "Why don't you take some time and spend it with Harrison? I saw him outside with your mom. When's the last time you took a vacation, Val?"

It wasn't a terrible idea. A silver lining? I could take a few days off, and then I'd be ready for action. "I took time off for Harrison's graduation."

"And before that?"

"I don't know, Kieran. But you're right. I guess I could use a few days' rest. I'll take some time and visit Mom and spend some quality time with Harrison before he leaves for his trip." *Why not?* Harrison and I were already on the West Coast and it would only take four hours to drive to my mother's. Harrison and I could spend a few days hiking and visiting my old stomping ground before he left for his big trip to Europe.

"Great. I'll be in touch."

I wouldn't have it any other way. "Sounds like a plan. Plus, with a little down time, I'll have plenty of time to up my training," I said, feeling rather cocky now. If it wouldn't rip off my bandages, I would have puffed out my chest too.

"Take care, Val. I'll talk to you soon."

I mumbled, "Thanks," and waved as he left the room.

It was nice he worried about me, but I was a grown woman, a seasoned FBI agent who hunted serial killers, yet he spoke to me like I was a second grader who didn't understand wound healing or the psychological impact of being held captive.

As much as I'd fought it, I supposed a few days off might do me some good. But I didn't like being off the case. The Bear was still out there, and I was damn sure going to catch him.

A few minutes later, Mom and Harrison walked in. Harrison's baby blues were full of concern as he clutched a bouquet of tulips. "I know they're your favorite."

"Thanks, honey," I replied, looking at my little boy, all grown up and not so little at six feet tall with defined muscles due to his latest strength training routine.

We were both in a transition, it seemed. My first major failure at work, getting caught by the person I was chasing, and Harrison was about to start at the Massachusetts Institute of Technology, MIT.

"How are you feeling?"

"I'm all right. A little woozy. They have me on painkillers, but I should be off them in a few days."

At almost seventy years old, my mother, with her shoulder-length shiny gray hair and wide brown eyes, didn't look a day over fifty. But the concern in her eyes reflected years of worry and heartache that only a woman of her age could hold. "I spoke to Kieran outside, and he said you want to come for a visit."

Nodding, I said, "Yes, I figured since Harrison is here too, we could go back with you. That is, if Harrison wants to?"

My son was eighteen and I could no longer make decisions for him. With a perfectly white smile, he said, "I packed a bag that'll last at least a week. I'm in!"

As much as I tried to maintain my tough exterior, the idea of spending time with my mother and son sounded wonderful. After what I had been through, spending time in the home I grew up in with my two favorite people was perfect. Plus, Harrison was about to embark on the trip of a lifetime, a graduation present from his father. I supposed that was what some kids did—kids from privileged backgrounds, off on vacation with their friends, gaining life experiences as they backpacked around the world, staying in hostels and learning other cultures. After that, he'd be on his own at MIT. "It's settled."

"I'm excited to have you home again. You can stay in your old room, and Harrison, you can stay in Aunt Maxine's," my mother said with a smile.

"Cool," replied Harrison.

"Speaking of which," Mom continued, "I was able to get a message to Maxine. She wants me to tell you she's doing well, and she's happy to hear that you're okay. She'll come home as soon as she can, but it won't be for a few months."

My younger sister, Maxine, was a major in the United States Army. I never knew where in the world she was other than commanding a group of helicopter pilots. I always worried about her working in war zones, even though I knew she was more than capable of taking care of herself. "How's she doing?" I asked.

"She's fine. You don't need to worry about her. We could also have some of your old friends over. When's the last time you got together?"

The old gang hadn't gotten together in twenty years, not since I'd married Harrison's father. Most of my high school friends had gone to college all over the country. I didn't know of any who had moved back home. But considering I'd skipped all the high school reunions, there may have been a few who had made the journey back to Rosedale. "I'm not sure any of them are still around."

"Brady moved back a few years ago and is working at the sheriff's office now."

"No kidding!" That was a surprise. We hadn't seen each other in years, but last I'd heard he and his wife had moved to the Bay Area. It would be good to catch up with him.

"No kidding. He transferred in from SFPD. And—" Mom cleared her throat. "You know, he just got divorced."

Ignoring any insinuations regarding my high school pal, I said, "I would love to spend some time with my son and my mother. I'm in."

My mom's eyes didn't look as clear as I remembered. She would be celebrating her seventieth birthday soon, and the look in her eyes was troubling me. My mother had always been the pillar that propped us all up. The years of loss and worry must have taken their toll, but she always held it together in front of us, especially Harrison. But I knew her well enough to know she worried constantly about my sister and me and our natural instinct to charge headlong into danger.

Mom only had herself to blame. She had been a tough-as-nails single mom and was a retired sheriff of Red Rose County. Where did she think we got our fearless nature from?

TWO

VAL

The walls were a vibrant shade of purple, the twin-size bed positioned just where I'd left it before heading off to college. In my sophomore year of high school, I had insisted that purple was everything, so Maxine and I had spent a weekend painting it ourselves. Mom had stood in the doorway, watching us get paint in our hair and on our clothes, but not on the carpet. She'd insisted on putting plastic down and told us everything else was for us to figure out.

Mom was wise in her approach, letting us learn things on our own, often the hard way. She believed it was a surefire way to not forget those lessons: the deeper the scar, the easier it was to remember.

My room had been converted into a guest room, complete with a new dresser that wasn't covered in stickers of my favorite bands. The walls were adorned with paintings of the Red Rose Forest by local artists, and matching nightstands graced either side of the bed. Yet, it was still my old room, and it felt like home.

After the four-hour drive from the hospital in Nevada to my childhood home in Rosedale, California, it felt good to be somewhere safe, familiar. I didn't know why I had resisted so hard against Kieran. He was only looking out for me. Not that I was in terrible shape, other than the bruises and wounds that felt like fire on my skin. Still, if I were in his shoes, I would have told the agent to rest up too.

It wasn't my first scrape since joining the FBI, but it was the first time I'd been held captive for nearly two days by a serial killer. One who didn't care if his victims were men or women, old or young—earning him his nickname, the Bear. Bears were known to be indiscriminate eaters. He enjoyed making his victims suffer for days on end—starting with his first cut, his signature, and then continuing to the finale. His signature was a curly "S," which he carved into their skin.

With fifteen known deaths and only one other survivor across four states, only two of the four medical examiners had picked up on his handiwork—the "S" resembling a curved slash, like one Zorro might have drawn with his sword. Thankfully, one of the homicide detectives in Oregon had reached out to the FBI, and my first impression had been that it wasn't a nonde-scriptive marking; it was the letter "S." A calling card or more likely a brand, a claim of ownership of his victim. From there I entered the details of the kidnapping and murders into VICAP, the FBI's Violent Criminal Apprehension Program, and discov-ered the Bear's pattern. He had killed four people, and then seemingly disappeared. But what I found was that he'd moved on to a new state, likely to evade law enforcement. With the FBI hunting him, we discovered three victims with his signature in Nevada, so we hit the road to Nevada, fairly certain he wasn't done with the Silver State.

When his knife pierced my skin, carving that familiar mark, I knew exactly what he was doing. It was his first cut, and I knew it wouldn't be his last. After hours of studying the autopsy photos of the fifteen victims, and photos of the one that got away, I knew his work was extensive.

He wanted me to feel pain. It was what he liked, what got him off.

He had managed to surprise me by knowing exactly who I was. The look in his eyes when he said, "Agent Costa. Isn't this going to be fun?" sent a chill down my spine, despite the warm weather.

I had been hunting him for six months, working on a hunch he might be at an abandoned property. It was his preferred location to bring victims to, to be tortured then killed. Even though I knew I shouldn't have gone alone, my inner drive wouldn't let me stop. I should have waited until the next morning and told the team, or at the very least I should have told someone where I was going. But it was the middle of the night and I didn't want to wake anyone up with a hunch. It was only after I came round from a blow to the head to find myself cuffed to a support beam inside an old barn and looking straight into the eyes of a killer who I knew couldn't wait to inflict maximum pain that I fully understood how reckless I had been. Thankfully, my unit had found the address after they had failed to contact me for twenty-four hours. They had gone through my computer search history and worked out where I'd gone. I had never been so happy to see my team, but I'd also never felt more helpless. Or stupid. One moment, I was hunting a murderer, and the next I had been caught by him.

Talk about a blow to the ego.

Now, I changed into my pajamas and headed over to my old bed. Once tucked inside, I hoped my brain would switch off because I desperately needed the rest. I didn't want to take any more painkillers; they made my head foggy, and I knew I needed to be alert. The Bear had never gone after his other surviving victim, but the glee in his eyes when he'd stared into mine made me certain he wasn't done with me yet. And I wasn't done with him.

I turned off the light and closed my eyes.

A moment later, my eyes wide open, the darkness closed in on me. My heartbeat sped up and my breathing was labored. Silently, I reassured myself he couldn't find me. I had never been afraid of the dark before, but then again, I had never been held captive by a killer, either. I reached over to the lamp on the nightstand and turned it back on. Disregarding my previous plan to go off the medication cold turkey, I climbed out of bed, fished out the pain meds from my bag, and took one before crawling back into bed. With the light on, my eyelids grew heavy, and I drifted off to sleep.

THREE

VAL

A loud banging on the door woke me and I jolted upright.

"Mom, are you okay?" Harrison's voice called out.

"Yeah, yeah, I'm fine," I managed to say as sweat trickled down my temples.

"Can I come in?"

"Give me a minute, honey." I stared down at my soaked pajama top. I couldn't let him see me like that. I grabbed my hair band from the nightstand and tied my hair up in a messy bun before hurrying over to my suitcase. From inside, I picked out a pair of black sweatpants and a navy blue FBI T-shirt. Taking another shirt from the pile, I wiped my brow, neck, and underarms before slipping on the fresh clothes. Stepping over to the door, I opened it with the best smile I could muster. "Good morning. C'mon in."

Harrison, wearing striped pajamas and his dark hair mussed in all directions, stepped into the room. "I heard you screaming. You sure you're okay?"

"I was just... I must've had a bad dream." Flashes from the dream shot through my mind. His eyes. The tear of my flesh.

After a moment, he asked, "Is there anything I can do?"

The worry on his face nearly killed me. I had to get over this whole thing and return to who I was before the Bear got the better of me. It had been three nights since my team had rescued me; it was time to move on. "No, I'm going to be fine. It may be rough for a few days while I'm healing. Try not to worry, honey."

The clock said it was 9 a.m. I couldn't remember the last time I had slept so late. "What do you say we have breakfast?" I proposed.

"Sure. I was gonna shower first."

Glancing down at myself, I realized I desperately needed one, too. "I'll rinse off and take a quick shower, too. I'll meet you downstairs?"

"Okay. Grandma said she would make pancakes."

"That sounds incredible. I'll meet you down there," I replied, reminiscing about how my mom used to make pancakes when I'd had a bad day at school or some stupid boy had hurt my feelings.

Down the hall, I ran into Mom, who was at the linen closet putting away sheets. "My gosh, you must've had a rough night?"

Thanks. "I don't remember. I took a pain pill to sleep."

She handed me a towel from the closet. "Good. I didn't like your idea of going cold turkey. Give it a few days, let your wounds heal, the physical ones anyhow. You got this, Valerie, I know you do. But even the strongest of us need to take a break once in a while. There's no shame in that, you hear me?" Mom was wearing a black headband across her silver hair. It was as she'd always worn it, even on duty as the sheriff.

"I hear you, Mom," I said, heading back to my room.

Mom was right. I'd get through this. I just needed to give it time, and my first step would include a hot shower.

. . .

Refreshed and clean, I padded down the carpeted stairs toward the kitchen. Mom was at the stove mid-pancake flip and Harrison was pouring himself a large glass of milk. I leaned on the granite countertop and admired the oak cabinets that had been in our kitchen for as long as I could remember. "Smells great."

"Will be ready in a few. There's coffee."

Turning my body toward the drip machine, I reached into the cabinet and pulled out one of my favorite mugs from child-hood, featuring Rainbow Brite in all her colorful glory. It was one of my must-watch cartoons as a child. I had been in awe of the character's magical powers and desire to make the entire universe bright and beautiful. I supposed, in my own way, by hunting killers, I too tried to make the world a brighter place. But instead of a dress featuring all the colors of the rainbow, I wore mostly black with a white or blue button-down.

Chuckling to myself, I picked up the carafe and filled up my mug with the fragrant brew. After a brief sip, Mom said, "Why don't you sit down and I'll bring over a plateful?"

I could get used to this. I took a seat and watched as Harrison grabbed three plates from the cupboard and set the table. He took a seat across from me. "Feeling any better?"

"I've got a big cup of coffee and my two favorite people."

Harrison eyed my mother, as if he wasn't buying it. The night terror didn't help my case any. Mom walked over with a heaping platter of fluffy pancakes and a pitcher of warm maple syrup. "Good to hear it. Now eat—it'll keep your strength up and help you heal."

Without hesitation, I plopped two pancakes on my plate.

Harrison said, "What did you want to do today?"

"Maybe a hike or something."

Mom tipped her head. "How about or something? I spoke with your doctor, and you should be resting. Why don't we have a movie marathon?"

"Do you have popcorn?" Harrison asked.

"Of course. Butter too."

Defeated but relieved to not have to endure a hike, I said, "Sounds great. Ooh, we could watch Harry Potter."

Harrison picked up the syrup and doused his pancakes. "Yes! I haven't seen the movies in years."

My phone vibrated in my sweatpants. With a mouth full of pancake, I set down my fork and checked the screen. I swallowed. "That's Kieran. I should take it."

Mom nodded, and I excused myself before stepping into the hallway. "Hey, what's up?"

"How are you feeling?" Kieran asked.

"I'm a little sore, but doing okay."

"Good to hear. How are you sleeping?"

He didn't need to know that I needed pain medication to sleep. "Like a baby." *More like a drugged baby after watching a horror film.*

"That's good to hear," he said, slightly hesitantly, as if he didn't believe me.

"Has the team learned anything new? Any leads on the Bear's location?" As of the day before, when Kieran had visited me in the hospital, they hadn't gotten any further in the search, but we were pretty sure he would still be in the state of Nevada.

"Not yet, but we have forensics processing evidence from the scene."

"Is the team still in Nevada? I'm only four hours away, so anything I can help with, I'm here."

All I could hear was his breathing. Was he avoiding my question? "Kieran?"

"They're still in Nevada. I'll keep you updated, but you know you can't be involved until you're cleared to come back for active duty."

Shaking my head in disbelief, I said, "When will that be?"

"It's under discussion with the director."

Hopefully, the discussion would be concluded soon. Glancing back at the kitchen, I knew I was busted. "Okay, keep in touch."

"Take care of yourself."

If one more person said that to me, I thought I'd burst. "Will do. Give my best to the team."

"And from me to your family."

Ending the call, I headed back into the kitchen and sat back down.

"Any news?" Mom asked, hopeful.

"No, he was just checking in on me. The team is still in Nevada."

"Do you think they'll catch him?" Harrison asked, concern in his eyes.

I hated that I worried him. He was only eighteen with a world of possibilities in front of him. He shouldn't have been worrying about the things that went bump in the night. That was my job. "I know we will."

If it's the last thing I do.

FOUR

VAL

A knock on the door interrupted the start of the second day of our Harry Potter movie marathon. Although I had originally suggested a hike, my body appreciated the lounge time curled up on the couch with my son. Considering I had fallen asleep during *The Prisoner of Azkaban*, the third movie, it was a clear sign I needed rest over exercise. Mom, wearing denim and a white button-down and looking like she was ready for a lunch date, said she would answer the door.

"No, it's Kieran. I'll get it," I said, climbing off the couch. I didn't want Kieran thinking I couldn't walk to the door. The fact that he wanted to talk face-to-face troubled me a little so I didn't want to give him any reason to doubt my abilities. He needed to see I was fit for duty—or that I would be in a few days. Harrison was enjoying the time at my mother's and I had promised him we'd have a full week together before heading back to the East Coast in time for him to catch his plane to Europe.

At the heavy oak door, I peered through the hole and confirmed it was indeed Kieran. I opened the door with a smile and said, "Welcome to Rosedale!"

He studied me from head to toe. "It's beautiful here."

It was. As a youngster, I hadn't appreciated how lucky I was to grow up surrounded by the greenest trees and miles of hiking trails with several lakes to swim or boat around in. "It's hot out there. C'mon in."

He wiped his feet and stepped over the threshold. Mom and Harrison were in the hallway ready to greet him.

Mom said, "Hello, Kieran. Can I get you anything?"

"Hello, Elizabeth. I'd love some coffee."

"Coming right up," she said with a chipper tone.

Harrison said, "Hi," and Kieran walked over and shook his hand.

"Good to see you. You must be excited for your trip and to start at MIT. Congratulations, by the way."

"Thanks. It's going to be awesome."

Kieran grinned proudly at him.

"Why don't we go into the kitchen?" I suggested.

Kieran nodded, and as we entered, I gestured toward the round table with four chairs. Mom set a coffee mug in front of him and one in front of me. She knew me well.

"Thanks, Mom."

"Thank you, Elizabeth."

"You're very welcome. Harrison and I are going to start our next movie and give you some privacy."

"Thanks, Mom."

Once she left, I turned to Kieran. Enough with the niceties, why did he feel the need to see me in person? "Give it to me straight."

He sipped his coffee, keeping his eyes on me. With his mug planted on the table, he said, "I spoke with the director. He feels it's best you take some more time off."

"I am taking time off. I'll be here until next weekend."

"He feels you may need more."

I shook my head. Why didn't he just say it already? "How long?"

"Four weeks. During that time, you will need to have sessions with the therapist."

My heart was racing. *Four weeks. You've got to be kidding me.* "Seriously? Four weeks! I'm fine."

Kieran raised his thick, dark brows and said, "With all due respect, you look terrible. You're moving slower than usual. You're not ready. Take this time. Talk to the therapist. And we'll reassess in four weeks."

My cheeks burned. "Reassess in four weeks? So, I could be off work for longer?"

"That depends on you, Val."

Focusing my energy on calming myself, I countered, "Two weeks."

He shook his head. "This isn't up for negotiation. Four weeks' mandatory leave, weekly sessions with the therapist. At the end of the four weeks, if you have completed the sessions and you've been cleared for active duty, you can come back."

A sinking feeling came over me. "What about the Bear? What about the team?"

"The team is packing up. We think he's gone. We're not sure where to."

It felt like the wind had been knocked out of me. They let him get away. *I* let him get away. "There's no way he's moved on. He has to complete the pattern. Why does the team think he's moved on?"

"There have been no sightings or missing persons reported in the area we mapped out. We've done a thorough check of abandoned farms and homes and there is absolutely no sign of him."

It didn't add up. Would the Bear really change his MO because the FBI had found me? "What's next? What is the team doing to find him?"

"We're keeping close tabs on reports of missing persons in the surrounding states. This isn't something for you to worry about right now. We've got it, Val."

It didn't seem like enough. I needed to be tracking him, not lying around watching young witches on the small screen. But if the director said four weeks, it would be four weeks, and I wouldn't be rejoining the team before then, at the earliest. We exchanged a few niceties before, exhausted from the conversation, I walked Kieran back to the front door.

As he left, he said, "I'll be in touch."

"Sure."

"Val. It's only four weeks. You can do this."

"I know. Thanks."

Kieran waved to my mom and Harrison before making his exit.

Back in the living room, Harrison said, "How did it go? Did you get an update?"

Oh, I did. "There's no progress on the manhunt. And I'm on mandatory leave for the next four weeks."

Mom couldn't hide the shock on her face. She knew what that would do to me. I hadn't had that much time off since I gave birth to Harrison. Harrison and the FBI were my whole world. Harrison was leaving in a week, flying the nest, and the FBI had benched me. It was a lot to take in. Not to mention the fact that the Bear was still out there possibly stalking his next victim.

"I'm sorry to hear that," she said.

Harrison crumpled up his beautiful face. "Sorry, Mom."

"It is what it is. I'm going to grab my coffee. Do you need anything?"

Mom said, "I'll have a cup."

Harrison said, "I'm fine."

With the best smile I could muster, I said, "One coffee

coming right up," as I struggled to suppress the anger rising within me.

In the kitchen, I grabbed a mug from the cupboard and turned toward the coffee maker. My attention was caught by a pink teddy bear sitting on the countertop next to a canister of sugar. It looked new, and I'd never seen it before. I picked it up and walked back into the living room. "Where did this come from?"

Mom said, "Oh, that. I completely forgot. Weird, isn't it?"

"What do you mean?"

"This morning, I went out to the porch to pick up the morning paper, and it was sitting right on top of it. Not sure if the paperboy is playing a prank or what."

The teddy bear fell from my shaking hands.

"What is it?" Harrison asked.

A message.

Filled with rage, I thought, *If the Bear wants to mess with me, fine. But mess with my family? That is something the Bear will most certainly regret.* Adrenaline coursed through my body. Harrison reached for the bear from his spot on the sofa. I said, "Don't touch it." I needed to preserve the evidence. This had to go to the team immediately. Although the culprit we had dubbed as the Bear had been careful not to leave fingerprints or any DNA at any of the crime scenes, I suspected he may have messed up this time.

"Why? What's wrong?" my mother asked, concern lining her face.

"I think it's a message from the suspect we've been tracking," I replied.

"The one who kept you prisoner?" she said in disbelief.

I glanced over at Harrison, who had turned as white as a sheet. Despite the fact he'd grown up in a household full of women in law enforcement, this wasn't a topic I wanted to discuss in front of my eighteen-year-old. I needed to put the bear in a plastic bag to preserve any trace of evidence. Ignoring her question, I said, "Do you have a plastic bag to put it in?"

My mother nodded and hurried past me into the kitchen. She returned with a plastic bag and a glove. Using the glove, I picked up the pink bear by its ear, slipped it into the bag, sealed it, and set it down on the coffee table. "I need to try to catch Kieran before he leaves town."

Had the Bear *finally* tripped up? Could his little game be what finally revealed his identity?

FIVE

VAL

Even Kieran's assurances couldn't stop me from feeling uneasy. I knew the Bear hadn't gone after his other survivor, but there was always a first time. Serial killers didn't always stick exactly to their pattern, and that was what I was hoping for. An escalation or a minor slip in the Bear's normal routine could offer up a new clue. The only problem was if it was the Bear sending messages to my mother's house, the deviation from his MO could be dangerous for my family, and that alarmed me.

As I sat huddled on the sofa with Harrison and Mom, Mom said to me, "Okay, now that you've bagged the little teddy bear and have the FBI testing it for trace evidence, do you want to tell us what's going on? Why you think the bear is from your suspect?"

I didn't really want to tell them anything, and I didn't want my captivity, my wounds, and the gory details of my work to be a burden on Harrison or my mother. "The man we're hunting, the one that held me captive, is nicknamed the Bear." I couldn't stand saying his name out loud.

"And you think he's sending you a message? He knows who and where you are?" my mother asked, her arms crossed defensively. I hadn't told my family that the Bear definitely knew my identity and that the FBI was looking for him.

"During my time in the barn, he knew my name, and that I'd been looking for him. I'm the one who linked the crimes to one person. I don't know how he knows, but we suspect he found my ID after he knocked me out."

At this, my mother uncrossed her arms and said, "I don't think it's safe for Harrison to be here."

Harrison stood up in protest. "No. I don't want to leave you."

"Your grandmother may be right. If he's coming after me, both Grandma and I are trained. You're not," I said, hoping he understood I only wanted to protect him. Harrison was a bright kid, but definitely not combat-ready.

"Can't we get a patrol car on the house, or somebody from the FBI to come and make sure he doesn't come near us?" he suggested.

It was a sound proposal. "You're right. We'll work something out."

A loud knock on the door reverberated through the room. Who could it be? Kieran had left more than thirty minutes ago. Was he back? "I'll get it," I said.

But my mother intervened. "You're still injured, you stay there. I'll answer the door."

The door creaked open, and I heard my mother say, "Oh, it's you. So good to see you. Come on in."

Relieved, I patted Harrison on the shoulder and let my hand fall back to my side. A man in uniform walked in with my mother—Brady. It had been twenty years since I'd last seen him. Age had added a rugged look to his features, but the graying temples and lines near his eyes suited him.

I said, "What a surprise."

Brady studied our faces. "I'm sorry, did I startle you?"

I shrugged it off, saying, "It's been a long day. It's good to see you." I gave him a light, one-armed hug, then introduced him to Harrison.

Brady said, "How long are you in town for?"

"A week or more." Eyeing Mom, I realized we hadn't discussed me sticking around after Harrison flew back to the East Coast.

Brady smiled and said, "Hopefully we can grab a beer and catch up."

"I'd like that." I could use a normal social interaction.

"Great! I don't know if I have your current number. Let's exchange details."

We entered our numbers in each other's phones, bridging the two-decade-long gap with a digital connection.

Mom adjusted her headband. "So, Brady, to what do we owe the honor? I thought you were on vacation this week, visiting your children."

"I was. But I was called back."

"Oh?" I raised my eyebrow, intrigued.

"Yes, Scarlett Douglas' mother and father came by the station this morning to report her missing. When they woke up, she was already gone. They've searched everywhere, including around the lake, but there's no sign of her."

I glanced at my mother, a silent question in my eyes. Could it be the Bear? The teddy bear he'd left could mean he was setting up shop in Northern California, and Scarlett Douglas was going to be his first victim here. "How long has she been missing?"

"Two days. Her parents weren't aware they didn't have to wait forty-eight hours to file a report. They could've reported her missing immediately, and we would've been out looking for her, especially considering her health condition," Brady explained, frustrated.

It was a fallacy that you had to wait forty-eight hours to report a missing person. A person could be missing for as little as three minutes, and if there was any indication of danger like a child abduction or the sighting of a woman being forcibly thrown into a van, an immediate report would compel the police to respond quickly, significantly increasing the odds of finding the missing person.

"What kind of health condition?" I asked.

"Scarlett has polycystic kidney disease, PKD. It's a genetic disorder that causes cysts to develop in the kidneys. About a year ago her kidneys began to fail and she was put on the kidney transplant list. She isn't doing very well."

The teddy bear and a missing girl? I didn't believe in coincidences. "So, you came by to ask if we've seen Scarlett Douglas or anything suspicious in the area," Mom asked.

He nodded.

"We've been home since Val was discharged from the hospital two days ago and haven't seen anyone other than her supervisor, who stopped by earlier."

I nudged her and she raised her brows. She muttered, "Val, I really don't think it's related."

"What's not related?" Brady asked.

After a brief, watered-down account of my captivity, the teddy bear left on the porch, and its transport to DC for testing, Brady was quite pale. "I'm so sorry."

"Thanks."

Shaking his head, he said, "No, that's not what I meant. The teddy bear. Do you remember Amanda Carter? She was a few years younger than us. Anyhow, since I was supposed to be out of town, I asked her to drop it off. As a welcome home gift."

My body froze at the revelation. "You left the bear? I don't understand."

Brady continued, deflated. "Don't you remember? It was the summer between junior and senior year. We were at the county fair and you bet me that I couldn't win the little pink teddy bear."

As the forgotten memory flooded back, I found myself sitting down, the air leaving my lungs. The teddy bear wasn't a threat; it was a memento.

"Boy, am I glad to hear that," Mom said, a sigh of relief escaping her lips.

Memories from a carefree summer before senior year flashed through my mind. Those were the days we thought we knew everything, and nobody could tell us otherwise. Brady, a few of our other friends, and I were at the county fair, indulging in funnel cakes and deep-fried Oreos. Brady and I were pretty competitive back then, and he swore he could win anything at the fair. I bet him he couldn't win the pink teddy bear. To do so, he needed to knock down all of the bowling pins, and I knew he was a terrible bowler.

It wasn't the Bear, the serial killer, coming after me and my family. It didn't mean he wouldn't, just that he hadn't yet.

"You proved me wrong and won the pink teddy bear," I recalled, feeling quite foolish now. I dreaded having to tell Kieran that the bear was not from a serial killer, but an old friend.

Mom said, "Thank goodness that's settled."

"I'm so sorry. If I had known..." Brady began.

"You didn't know. It's okay, but this is a relief, and I appreciate it," I assured him. Desperately needing to change the subject, I said, "So, what can you tell us about the search for Scarlett?"

Brady hesitated before taking the hint. "The sheriff's department is putting together a volunteer search team. If anybody wants to help out... although probably not you, considering the state of your injuries."

"Give me a day. If she's still not found, I'll join the team," I offered.

My mother shot me a disapproving look. It was one I knew well.

"I don't think you should be doing that," she said. "You should take it easy for at least a few more days."

"I'm sure I'll be feeling a lot better by tomorrow. I already feel a lot better than I did yesterday. If they still need someone to help search, I'll be there," I reiterated to Brady, while looking directly at my mom.

How could I not help look for a missing person in my own hometown?

"You need to work on healing. If you're out walking for six hours, that's a lot of stress on your body. Concussions are not to be taken lightly. For now, we'll stay here and make some snacks for the volunteers, okay?" Mom suggested.

It was something at least.

Brady nodded. "I agree with Elizabeth. You need to rest. But if Scarlett is still missing tomorrow, I'll call, okay?"

"Okay, let's do that. Good luck, Brady. Let us know if there are any developments, or anything else we can do."

"You got it. Talk soon, Val," Brady said as he walked out, leaving me to wonder. Was it a coincidence that there was a missing person the day I returned home? Did the Bear know this was my hometown and wanted to send me a message? Or was this what paranoid delusion looked like?

I had once been chasing serial killers, and now, I was too infirm to help search for a missing girl, relegated to making sandwiches. But one thing I knew for sure: When the Bear and I met again, he was going to regret what he had done to me, and his other victims. He would soon realize he had crossed the wrong person.

SIX

MAY

"May, how are you holding up?" That question had been echoing throughout my day, each syllable a piercing reminder of my loss. My daughter was gone. How did everyone think I was doing? I was shattered, barely managing to pull myself out of bed. Jack insisted that I needed to, arguing I couldn't cry myself to sleep every night. The idea that she was gone, my sweet, sweet baby, was inconceivable to me.

Gazing into the pale brown eyes of Sheriff Costa, I nodded and managed a whispered response. "Not great, Sheriff, but I appreciate your coming out. Also, thanks to the volunteers."

"It's the least we can do. Please, call me Elizabeth. I'm not the sheriff anymore." Her words were comforting, her empathy palpable.

The woman accompanying her had dark hair pulled into a bun, a bandage on her chest, and bruises on her face and arms. I couldn't help but wonder what had happened to her. She looked awful.

Elizabeth must've noticed my gaze. "May, this is my eldest daughter, Valerie. She's visiting. And this is my grandson, Harrison."

I met the eyes of Elizabeth's daughter. There was an intensity there. She said, "Glad to meet you. I wish it was under different circumstances."

"Glad to meet you too," I said, my voice trailing off.

Scarlett was everything to Jack and me. We had never been happier than the day she was born, her little face pink and squishy, smelling like heaven. Surely Elizabeth had felt that way when her daughter was born.

Elizabeth interrupted my thoughts. "Have you eaten, dear?"

"Just had some coffee this morning."

"You need to eat. We brought sandwiches and homemade cookies," Elizabeth said, a motherly concern lining her voice.

Without Scarlett here would I still be a mother?

Absentmindedly, I glanced down at the table where we kept bottles of water for the volunteers. "I have a cooler. We can put the sandwiches in there." The heat was oppressive, though I felt numb to it. I barely registered that it was July and the temperatures were already reaching ninety degrees. It didn't make a difference to me. But Elizabeth's daughter, Valerie, was sweating profusely through her tank top. She looked miserable.

"That's probably a good idea. We don't want anyone getting sick. I can grab it. Is it inside?" Elizabeth offered.

"Yes. Jack's inside, he can help."

Elizabeth turned to her daughter. "Stay here, I'll be right back." Valerie simply nodded.

There was something about her I couldn't shake. I found myself blurting out, "What happened to you?" Normally, I wouldn't be so intrusive, but I didn't really have much left in me for polite conversation.

"Bit of a scrape is all," Valerie answered, evasively.

A scrape? "Like a car accident?"

"Something like that," she replied vaguely.

"Oh," was all I could say, my thoughts drifting back to my daughter.

"I'm sorry to hear your daughter's missing."

"Thank you." The tranquilizers my doctor had prescribed were helping me maintain some composure, suppressing my urge to dissolve into a blubbering mess. Perhaps that was contributing to the numbness that seemed to pervade me.

"Are you in law enforcement too?" I asked Valerie.

"FBI," she replied. "Just home on leave, spending time with Mom and Harrison. We would be out there with the volunteers looking for Scarlett, but doctor's orders."

FBI.

I swallowed, suddenly understanding the sharpness in Valerie's gaze. I'd seen it on TV; the people closest to the victim were always prime suspects until ruled out. She was assessing me, scrutinizing whether I had done something to my daughter. That was the unnerving sensation I couldn't shake. "We've been fortunate with so many people helping. I'm under a doctor's care as well, otherwise I would be out there searching too. I just can't..."

Harrison piped up, "Don't give up hope, ma'am. Everybody's out looking for Scarlett. I'm sticking by my mom's side today, but if she's still missing tomorrow, all three of us will be out there looking for her."

I turned to the FBI agent and asked, "Should you be out walking tomorrow? It's hot as heck out here, and you don't look like you're in great shape."

"It looks worse than it is, trust me. I'm used to working under worse conditions," she asserted.

Not a desk jockey then. "What do you do for the FBI, if you don't mind me asking?"

"I work with the profiling team, mostly on interstate murder, and kidnapping."

She was an expert. If anyone could find Scarlett, I was sure I was staring at that person. "Sounds like you might be able to help us find Scarlett?"

Without emotion, she stated, "That's right. If she isn't found by tomorrow, I will find her."

Could she do that? Could someone from the FBI assist the sheriff's department? My thoughts were interrupted as Elizabeth, Jack, and Henry emerged from the house with the cooler. I shot Jack a look, unsure if he could decipher it.

"You must be Harrison, and you're Valerie?" Jack addressed them, and they nodded in affirmation. "Thank you for coming out and helping with the volunteers. We appreciate it."

Henry stepped closer to Valerie and Harrison, extending his hand. "I'm Henry. I live a few doors down, at the top of the hill."

Valerie looked him up and down. Did she view everyone as a suspect? "Nice to meet you. Were you home when Scarlett went missing?"

Henry's bald head glistened. "No, I was at my other home in Southern California. When I heard about Scarlett's disappearance, I drove up to help find her."

Valerie seemed only semi-satisfied by Henry's explanation. What world did this woman live in where she was suspicious of everyone?

"Henry is a good friend and has been a big help. He owns the insurance office in town." I eyed my husband and Henry, adding, "Valerie's with the FBI. She works on teams to profile murderers and kidnappers."

Recognition sparked in Jack's eyes. "Sounds like we got lucky. Maybe you can help out?"

Elizabeth quickly jumped in. "She's just been through an ordeal. She's supposed to be resting—doctor's orders."

"I'll be up and running in a day or so. If Scarlett still hasn't been found, I'll help find her," Valerie promised.

Jack shrank into himself. "Hopefully we'll find her by tomorrow."

Valerie studied Jack as she had done me. She hadn't cleared

us yet. I was still curious about what had happened to her. Some people had an immeasurable strength inside them—off the charts. I had a feeling Valerie was one of those people, just like her mother. Unfortunately, I wasn't, and I didn't know how long I could go on. Everything seemed so pointless without Scarlett.

SEVEN

VAL

The nightmares continued. And I didn't know how long they'd last. It had been five days since my team had rescued me—why wasn't I over it yet? Using my pajama top, I wiped the sweat from my brow. Throughout my years with the FBI, I had met numerous survivors. I'd been privy to their stories, their experiences of being held captive and ripped away from their families and friends. I learned that every moment was a waking nightmare for them, but I hadn't realized how consuming it could be even once you were safe and sound. I couldn't allow my experience in that barn to take over my life.

The Bear was still out there. And I was trapped in my own mind. Sweating through the bedsheets, I was worrying everyone around me. I was still sleeping with the light on and had to take a pain pill to find any semblance of rest. My physical wounds were healing, but I suspected the mental scars would take a little longer.

I grabbed the bottle of water from my nightstand and took a hearty gulp. I had to keep my energy up and I couldn't let myself wallow in self-pity. To everyone else I acted like I was fine and ready to get back out there, fighting the good fight. But alone in my room, I knew I needed rest. Despite being a trained agent, I was still human. My thoughts returned to the conversation I'd had with Kieran.

Why couldn't I take his advice to rest and not worry about getting back to the team? Maybe if I had been the one to give this advice to another agent, they wouldn't take it either. We were trained to persevere, to fight for justice, to incarcerate the depraved. Not to crumple under pressure. The visible wounds would soon disappear and the pain wasn't even that bad anymore. It was mostly an energy issue, my body using its reserves to heal my body.

My mind was sharp, and I didn't want my mother and son to worry. How long would it take Kieran to call me if they found the Bear? I doubt they would, considering they had packed up the Nevada operation already. With my free hand, I pulled my phone off the charger and texted Kieran.

V: Any updates on the Bear?

He texted back immediately.

K: Not yet. Working on it. Get some rest.

Using one hand, I tapped out my reply.

V: Thanks. Feeling better.

K: Have you called the department therapist?

I set down my water bottle.

V: Not yet. Soon.

It had actually slipped my mind, but it would have to wait

because I didn't feel ready. Despite the fact I knew I should, I wasn't ready to admit to anyone the toll the situation had taken on me. But in a silver lining thought, I was happy to have the opportunity to spend time with Harrison. I wasn't sure how much longer he'd want to hang out with me. Once he was off to college, meeting new friends and girlfriends, he might not have time for me.

Peeling off my sweat-soaked clothes, I headed toward the en-suite bathroom. Mom had remodeled it from my teen years. It was a gray and white scheme with marble tiles and a walk-in shower with a rain feature. Heavenly.

After a hot shower, feeling clean and fresh, I padded down the stairs into the kitchen. Mom was already at the table reading a newspaper and sipping her coffee.

With a smile, I said, "Good morning."

"You're chipper. How are you feeling?" she asked.

"Better," I replied. It was true. My headaches had subsided and the burn of my carving had dulled.

She raised her eyebrows, clearly skeptical.

"I am better. I'm not one hundred percent, and I'll be the first to admit it, but I am improving. A good night's rest did the trick."

"Nightmares?" she said, probing further.

Walking over to the coffee maker, I filled my Rainbow Brite mug with the hot brew, the steam wafting up with a comforting scent. "I'll probably have them for a while. I know I have to take it easy, but that doesn't mean I can't do anything."

She studied me apprehensively as I joined her at the table. "You do look better," she admitted. "Less like..."

"The undead?" I offered, raising an eyebrow.

She chuckled. "Well, I wasn't going to say it, but yes."

"Did you ever get into any scuffles with a perp that put you in the hospital?" I asked. She had been a sheriff for as long as I could remember, but I couldn't recall her ever being injured on the job.

Setting down her mug, she nodded. "When you were little, there was a domestic situation that had gone awry. I got in between the husband and wife. The wife was okay, but I ended up with some cracked ribs. And just like you, I tried to go back to work too soon, tried to do it all."

Domestics were known to be one of the most violent and dangerous situations that law enforcement encountered. My mom was lucky; she'd only had one encounter that had landed her in the hospital.

"Did you take it easy after that?"

She shrugged, feigning innocence. "No. But I had your dad back then to help take care of you and your sister. Maxine was just a baby then."

I vaguely remembered my mother telling me she was on vacation from work, but she had to go to the doctor a lot. I was probably about eight or nine at the time. She hadn't divulged much, which, in retrospect, was probably for the best.

Switching gears, I asked, "Any news on Scarlett Douglas?"

"Not that I know of. I haven't heard from Brady, but the papers still list her as missing." She pushed the paper across the table. Sure enough, there was Scarlett Douglas' photo. Blonde hair, brown eyes, freckles on her nose, but her eyes were tinged with sadness. I wondered if it was due to her ongoing medical treatment or if she simply hadn't been feeling well that day. "And you haven't heard from Brady either?"

"No," I admitted, realizing it was time to remedy that. As I brought the phone up to my ear, my mother said, "Who are you calling?"

"Brady," I said, just as he picked up.

"Hello."

"Hey, it's me, Val."

"What's going on? How are you feeling?"

"Pretty good. I was wondering if there was any news on Scarlett Douglas."

"Not yet. The team searched all night. We don't think she's anywhere near the lake, from where we now believe she disappeared. Her parents told us the lake was one of her favorite places to go. If somebody grabbed her, they've taken her to a secondary location."

The mention of a secondary location sent chills down my spine. It was universally understood that if someone was trying to take you somewhere else, you had to fight like your life depended on it, because it probably did. "Have you expanded the search?"

"Are you trying to work the case with us?"

It would give me something to do. Not that spending time with Mom and Harrison wasn't something. Despite my lowered energy, I could only spend so much time on the couch watching movies. "Would you let me?"

He paused, then asked, "Are you even allowed?"

Ignoring the stern look from my mother, I reassured him, "I would just be a volunteer. There are other volunteers, right? I'm no different."

"And what would your mother and son think about this?"

Harrison wasn't up yet. How would he feel about it? Maybe he'd like to volunteer with me. "I haven't talked to them about it yet, but I have a lot of experience with this, Brady. I could help question friends and family, look for patterns or recent behavior changes."

He laughed, and it sent me back to our younger years. "Sounds like you're trying to take over the investigation and it's not even 9 a.m. Are you even up for it?"

Was I up for it? "Physically, I'm up for the challenge. But I don't want to step on any toes," I said, although I didn't quite mean it. My guess was the sheriff's department wasn't terribly experienced in finding missing persons, and I was. "I'll talk to

Harrison and my mom. They may want to help with the search."

"We're working out where to search next. Like I said, we searched all around the lake. She's not there. We're bringing in search and rescue dogs today, in case we missed something."

"Have you considered calling in the FBI?" It was standard in suspected kidnapping cases.

He chuckled. "Just so happens the FBI called me."

"Fair enough," I conceded. "You owe me a beer anyway. We could meet and talk about the case."

He sighed. "Aren't you supposed to be spending time with your family and focusing on getting better?"

"I'm fine. And I'll talk to them. They'll want to help."

"Okay, give me a call when you've devised your plan."

He still knows me, even after all these years. "Will do."

"What was that about?" my mother asked as soon as I hung up.

"Scarlett's still missing. They need my help. I have experience that the investigators in this town don't."

With that disapproving look of hers, she said, "Do you think that's such a good idea? Valerie, look at you. You look a wreck. Less of a wreck, but a wreck nonetheless. And how are your wounds?"

"I just changed the bandages, put on some fresh Neosporin. That's helping with the pain. Now, I'm drinking coffee. After some breakfast I'll be good to go," I reassured her.

I still needed to talk to Harrison to see how he felt about me helping out with the investigation. As if on cue, Harrison entered the kitchen still in his pajamas, his brown floppy hair pointing in all directions. "Good morning to my favorite ladies," he cheerfully greeted us.

He gave me and then my mother a kiss on the cheek. It was hard to feel down about the world when Harrison existed within it. What an awful feeling for Scarlett's parents to not know where their daughter was. Scarlett's parents... I felt they needed to be looked into a bit more. Their grief seemed real, but there was something else lurking behind their eyes—apprehension, fear. It could have been nothing of course—after all, their daughter was missing—but something gnawed at me.

"What's for breakfast?" Harrison asked.

"That depends on what you're cooking," Mom retorted.

"I am adept at making eggs, even omelets, scrambled, sunny-side up. What can I make you? Your egg wish is my command."

Harrison's father liked to cook and used to have Harrison by his side ever since he'd climbed up on a stool to stand next to him as he prepared dinner. As Harrison pulled out a frying pan, he asked, "Have they found Scarlett yet?"

I knew he'd want to help. "Not yet. I was just talking to Brady about the investigation."

"Oh yeah?"

"They didn't find anything around the lake, but they're bringing in dogs today to see if they can pick up on her scent or find something the volunteers might have missed."

Harrison set the frying pan down on the stove and leaned against the counter. "Are you going to work the case?"

"I offered to help. This is my area of expertise. I could help the locals pinpoint who may have taken Scarlett. I can talk to her friends and family, and look at patterns of behavior."

Harrison appeared to consider this, then asked, "Could I help?"

Eyeing my mom, I said, "I'm sure there are things you could help with. And we should be helping. Scarlett's one of our own. Right, Mom?"

"You're right. We are a community. It's good for us all to work together," my mother agreed, likely knowing I wouldn't drop it.

"We'll all help," Harrison said, a hopeful glint in his eyes.

"I'll talk to Brady and see where he needs us the most."

"A family that investigates together stays together, right?" Harrison quipped.

I walked over to my son and squeezed him. "I love you."

"Love you too, Mom," he said as he turned back to the refrigerator and pulled out a carton of eggs.

It was official—we were going to find out what had happened to Scarlett. In that moment, I wondered if fate had brought me home to find Scarlett Douglas. I didn't usually believe in that kind of stuff, but anything was possible. And I could use the distraction. It was decided; I would find Scarlett. I had lots of questions, and I planned to find *all* the answers.

EIGHT

VAL

The diner was how I remembered it, with its nostalgic white tabletops and red vinyl booths, the scent of pie crust and coffee filling the air. The coffee was delightfully sweet with a hint of chocolate. It had been a while since I'd had a mocha, but I was on "vacation." Sitting across from Brady, I noticed he was eyeing me carefully, not dissimilar to how Kieran had looked at me the other day. The concern in his eyes questioned my capability, but my bruises were healing, as were my cuts. I wished everybody would stop bothering me about it. I was a seasoned FBI agent, not a three-year-old who'd tripped and fallen in the sandbox.

"How long have you been back?" I asked him.

"It's been three years now."

"Is it weird to be back?" Brady was my only high school friend who had returned to our hometown—a small, mostly rural community a few hours north of the San Francisco Bay Area. All of us had sworn we were destined to go on to bigger and better things. Most of us had.

He sipped his coffee and said, "It's a little eerie. But it's nice and quiet—well, up until recently."

"I suppose it's a far cry from the SFPD?" I knew a few folks who had worked at the San Francisco Police Department before joining the Bureau, so I'd heard quite a bit about it.

"That it is. San Francisco has a lot more action."

"What department?"

"Major crimes. Mostly grand theft, burglary, and narcotics."

I hadn't realized how out of touch we had become.

"Quite a jump from major crimes to a small-town deputy sheriff."

"It's a nice change of pace. There's only so much of that you can handle, or at least as much as I could handle, as I found out. Plus, it allows my kids to have a place to go where they don't have to worry about muggings or the influences of a big city."

"Do you have custody?" I asked, without thinking. I'd only learned of his divorce from my mother. "Sorry. Mom told me you were recently divorced."

"I figured. My ex got custody since our split occurred during their high school years. We didn't want them to have to change schools. My daughter, Paige, will be a senior in high school this fall, and my son, Zach, just finished his first year at UCLA."

Decades apart yet we'd lived parallel lives. "No kidding. Harrison starts MIT in the fall."

He glanced down at my ring finger.

I continued, "His dad and I both live in DC, and Harrison goes pretty freely between our two houses."

He nodded as if he understood the arrangement. "He seems like a great kid."

"He is."

Our waiter brought over our lunches. I had ordered grilled cheese with a side of French fries, going all out. The extra fat would help absorb the pain medication. Grabbing a fry, I took a bite of the crunchy, salty goodness. "So, what's going on with the Scarlett Douglas case?"

"Search and rescue is scouring the area around the house and lake with dogs as we speak. I'm just on a break here to meet with you, to see how you can help. I didn't think you'd take no for an answer."

I smiled.

"Same old Val."

"I'm home, and there's a missing person—how could I *not* help?"

"You won't get any argument from me because I know how it'll end. But what do your superiors at the FBI think about you working a case?"

"I'm just a volunteer," I said, rather coyly.

He raised his sandy brows. "You didn't tell them?"

I shrugged and ate another fry. "You know, I like to think that being in law enforcement means we're doing something good. I'm just trying to do something good."

After swallowing a mouthful of burger, Brady said, "I get that. I'm willing to take any advice you have for us. We don't have much experience with a disappearance like this. It's nice to have somebody around who does. Don't get me wrong, the sheriff's department is great, but they're not a profiler with the FBI."

"Happy to help any way I can."

"If this was your case and you weren't just a volunteer, what would you do?" Brady asked.

I sat a little taller, feeling like I was finally back in my element. "First of all, I'd want to interview the parents, then her friends—anybody in her life—to get an idea of what she'd been doing up until her disappearance, her state of mind, and any future plans she may have had. I'd put together a timeline, and I'd want to find out as much as possible about her state of mind."

"She's now been gone seventy-two hours."

With a look of skepticism, I said, "And we believe the parents?"

"You don't trust the parents?"

"Until we find Scarlett, or we can rule them out, everyone is a suspect."

Brady shook his head. "I've only been back three years, but the Douglases—they love their daughter. Her parents have done everything in their power to help her. She's their only child, I just can't see them doing anything to hurt her."

"Could it have been an accident?"

"I doubt it. They are helicopter parents to the nth degree. Because of her health issues, Scarlett lives in a bubble, built by her parents. They watch her like a hawk."

"So how did she go missing?"

"Mrs. Douglas suspects Scarlett snuck out early in the morning before they woke up. The last time May saw her was when she tucked her daughter in the night before. She said Scarlett had a paperback novel in her hands, like she usually did."

Tucked in a sixteen-year-old? "Why would Scarlett sneak out?"

"I guess if we knew that, the case might be a little easier."

"No chance she was kidnapped from the house?"

"No sign of forced entry."

The details were not adding up. "Have you interviewed her friends?"

"No, but Scarlett's mother said she called her friends and nobody's seen her."

Scarlett was a teenager, so interviewing her friends would be my priority. "What about press coverage? Is anybody handing out flyers? Have her parents done a press conference?"

He shook his head.

Something was nagging me about this case. Perhaps I just needed more information.

"I talked to my mom and Harrison, and they both want to help with the case."

"How old is Harrison?"

"He's eighteen and resourceful. We could have him make flyers and post them around town."

"Great."

"And my mom used to be the sheriff..."

"Maybe she can help the Douglases with the press conference. They seemed resistant to it when I mentioned it. We hope to find her quickly, but unless search and rescue come up with something, I think that may be the logical next step."

My mother had always had a way with the locals. It was a good suggestion. She would likely make the Douglases feel at ease as they pleaded for their daughter on the evening news.

"Back to my role as a volunteer—can I talk to the parents?"

He nodded. "I don't see why not. But I'll accompany you, that way whatever they say is on the record. It's a good idea, bearing in mind you're less biased than I am, seeing as you still have them in your suspect pool and I ruled them out immediately."

That's why you're not supposed to work cases in which you know the victims.

"I can live with those terms."

Brady threw a fry across the table at me, and I laughed and said, "You know, despite the years, I don't think you've changed one bit." At least as far as his personality went. He was no longer that scrawny teen from all those years ago. He was well built, and from his tan skin he likely spent a lot of time hiking the local trails.

"Why would I? I've always been pretty awesome."

Same old Brady. He was like the big, goofy brother I'd never had. "No argument from me."

When we'd finished our lunch, I said, "Ready to go over to the parents?"

"Yeah, let's head out. It'll take us about fifteen minutes. They live near the lake."

Geographically, it wasn't far, but the windy roads would

slow us down. The timeline was perfect; the drive time would give me the opportunity to call Mom and Harrison to update them on the game plan. "Let's do it."

As we were getting up to leave, Brady received a phone call. "Deputy Tanner." His eyes widened as he listened. He grabbed his wallet, threw two twenties down on the table, and said, "Okay, I'll be right there."

"What is it?"

"The dogs picked up Scarlett's scent."

NINE

VAL

On the two-lane highway lined with redwoods and pines toward the lake, Brady and I found ourselves reminiscing about our high school days—the dances, the prom, and just how naïve we'd all been. Back in my teens, I thought everything was so significant: what I wore, who kissed who, and which boys liked me. These thoughts led me to wonder what was important to Scarlett. From all accounts, she was a sixteen-year-old young woman, fighting for her life, and in desperate need of a new kidney. I couldn't help but think what life was like for her. It was probably starkly different from mine at her age. From what Brady had said, her parents were smothering her. Maybe she had snuck out that morning, simply trying to get some distance.

We edged near the first turn out that included a few homes, some small and some gigantic. Growing up in the town, I didn't have many friends up by the lake. It was thought of as the wealthy area for residents with second homes, with a few locals scattered about. Brady took a left off the winding path and onto a leveled road. He pulled up in front of a moderately sized home blocked by multiple search and rescue vehicles. The scene was much more chaotic than just the day before, when volunteers were scouring the woods around the lake.

"Not many neighbors," I observed.

Brady responded, "Just a few."

"Have you questioned the neighbors yet?" I asked, thinking back to the day before when I had met the Douglases' helpful neighbor, Henry.

"Just one. The two homes on either side of the Douglas home are empty. According to Mr. and Mrs. Douglas, they are vacation homes, and the owners are likely back at their primary residences. The only neighbor we talked to was Henry Tate, who lives at the top of the hill. He's a semi-local. Shares his time between the lake house and Southern California."

I remembered meeting him yesterday when we dropped off sandwiches. He'd said he hadn't been around when Scarlett had gone missing but had driven up to help with the search. "Mrs. Douglas said he owns the insurance company in Rosedale."

"He does. He doesn't work there; he has a few employees who run the place. Donates to local charities and sponsors a few little league teams. Pretty upstanding guy. He comes up for time away from the big city."

No alarm bells were ringing, but that didn't mean we wouldn't look closer.

I climbed out of the car and followed Brady to a man in a vest, a German Shepherd sitting by him.

Brady waved. "Hey, Porter." Porter glanced over at me before Brady added, "This is FBI Agent Valerie Costa. She's volunteering to help us with our search. Val, this is Porter. He is the head of the search team."

Porter, who looked like he could double as a lumberjack with his thick dark beard, looked surprised. "FBI?"

"I'm on leave. Home, visiting my mother."

"Sheriff Costa," Brady added.

"I thought the name was familiar. Nice to meet you. Looks like you've been in a fight."

The bandage on my chest and the bruising were a dead giveaway. "Just a little scuffle," I said, trying to downplay my captivity.

Porter gave me a skeptical look before turning his attention to Brady. "The dogs picked up on Scarlett's scent. It's a direct line down to the edge of the lake and back to the house, nowhere else."

Brady said, "So, she could have walked out to the lake, had an accident, or was taken."

"Or she came back to the house and was taken on the road or inside the house. Or she met up with someone and didn't tell her parents," I added.

Brady said, "True. Also, we don't know how old the tracks are. Her parents said they take her for walks pretty frequently. It's where they suspected she might've gone that morning when they found her bed empty."

"Did your team find anything interesting out there?" I asked Porter.

He shook his head. "Not really. The area is mostly inhabited by people out fishing or hiking who are staying in the homes around the lake. The trails there are popular. But nothing seemed out of place. We didn't find any torn clothing or any items we believe belong to Scarlett. No sign of foul play."

So, the only thing search and rescue had confirmed was that Scarlett's family owned a home in the area, and they regularly went on hikes or walks. It wasn't much to go on. If they had cadaver dogs scouring the area, they might have told us a different story.

Brady and Porter shook hands. Brady said, "Thanks, Porter, for everything you've done. We'll keep you updated."

"Nice to meet you, ma'am." Porter tipped his hat at me as he headed toward an SUV parked on the street.

Turning to Brady, I said, "Not terribly useful, was it?"

He sighed. "No. If they'd picked up a scent leading to another house, that would've been useful."

With nothing gained, I was itching to speak to Mr. and Mrs. Douglas. "Should we talk to the parents now?"

Brady agreed. We made our way to the front of the house and he knocked on the door. The grief-stricken May Douglas opened it, looking just as distraught as she had the day before at the volunteer check-in station.

"Afternoon, May. How are you holding up?"

She eyed me and said, "The same."

Mrs. Douglas was in her early forties, and with blonde hair and brown eyes it was clear which parent Scarlett took after. May moved slowly and was likely on tranquilizers or some other medication that slowed her movements. It was an apparent sign of intense grief over her daughter's disappearance.

She led us into the living room with a large fireplace and a set of beige sofas. "Please, have a seat."

Mr. Douglas, standing at five foot ten with a bit of a gut and thinning hair, appeared from down the hall, asking, "What's going on?"

May sat down and said, "This is the FBI agent we met yesterday. She's going to help look for Scarlett."

Jack eyed both Brady and me before sitting down next to his wife. "Can I get you anything?"

"No, we're fine, thank you," Brady responded.

With the weather as hot as it was, I was glad to have brought water with me. The forecast was predicting triple digits.

Jack said, "I saw you talking to the search and rescue team. Did they find something?"

Brady said, "Yes, they were able to confirm Scarlett's scent leading to the lake from the house."

Jack nodded. "That's what we suspected. That she had gotten up before we did to go on a walk by herself."

"Was that something she did often?"

May shook her head.

"Is it possible Scarlett was meeting someone, a friend or boyfriend perhaps?" I asked.

The Douglases exchanged glances.

May responded, "I don't think so. She hadn't mentioned any plans, and we didn't hear any cars coming up the drive. We would have heard if there had been. It's pretty remote up here."

I considered their statement. "What can you tell me about your neighbors?"

"Oh, our next-door neighbors aren't here. They haven't been here for a few weeks," May said.

"And your neighbors up the hill?" Brady asked.

"Well, there's the Tates but they hadn't been up for a few weeks either, up until yesterday. Henry is at the office today, but he spent all day yesterday helping us look for Scarlett. Their next-door neighbors, the Carmichaels, haven't been up since the spring," Jack added.

I made a mental note to look up the property owners' primary addresses. Just because May and Jack hadn't seen them didn't mean they hadn't been there. In these types of cases, you had to look under every rock and boulder; sometimes that's where you found the best clues.

"What can you tell me about Scarlett? Does she have a lot of friends? Does she like music or dancing?" I asked.

May looked at Brady. "Didn't we already go over all this?"

"We think it's a good idea to go over it again. Val is a decorated FBI agent, and getting her perspective could be incredibly valuable. We all have the same goal. We want to find Scarlett," Brady tactfully explained.

May folded her hands in her lap. "Before her kidneys started to fail, which was about a year ago, yeah, she had a lot of friends. Went to school like every other teenager. I wouldn't call her boy-crazy, but she did have crushes. She loved to sing." At this, Mrs. Douglas broke down.

Jack put his arm around his wife, looking at us as if we had been the cause of her pain. I couldn't even begin to imagine what it must be like to have a missing child, but I knew it must be extremely difficult, especially if you thought the worst, which they seemed to be doing as they were already referring to Scarlett in the past tense.

"What did you do in the weeks leading up to her disappearance?" I asked.

Jack said, "We didn't go anywhere or do much. With her health declining, the doctors were concerned that travel would be too much for her. And it's summer, so school's out."

"What about her friends? Did they come to visit?"

May wiped her tears. "No. Scarlett wasn't feeling well, and she didn't want her friends to see her like that. She didn't want them to feel sorry for her."

A self-conscious, terminally ill teenager? It was possible. "Have you already provided the names of her closest friends to Deputy Tanner, so we can speak with them?"

"No, we haven't. But they were the first people I called when we couldn't find her. They said they hadn't seen her."

"If you could provide us with that information, we can talk to them again. Sometimes kids don't want to get their friends in trouble. Maybe they'll be able to provide some useful information that will help us find her."

May nodded and lifted herself off the couch, making her way to the kitchen to get a pen and paper.

I stared back at the father and said, "I know this must be difficult and I can only imagine what you're going through. I will do everything in my capacity to find Scarlett," I added, "You have my word." And I meant it. The Douglases were my age with a child close to Harrison's age.

"We appreciate that," he murmured.

May returned, handing me a piece of paper.

"Thank you. How was Scarlett feeling the night before she disappeared?" I asked.

"She seemed okay, just tired. She went to bed early. When I went in to say goodnight, she was reading one of her books like she always does," May recounted.

"And she's sixteen, right?" I confirmed.

The Douglases nodded.

"My son is eighteen, and he's going to college in the fall. I remember when he was sixteen, he was touring colleges and deciding what he wanted to do with his life. Did Scarlett have any plans for the future?"

A terminally ill teen could easily decide that she was tired of the pain, of the doctors' visits, and choose to end her life on her own terms. Suicide couldn't be ruled out, but indications of future planning made it less likely.

"She wanted to go to college. She wanted to go to prom. We even bought a dress," May said.

"Sounds like she had a lot to look forward to," I said. They stared at me blankly. Without their daughter, they had become hollow. I braced myself as I was about to ask some questions that weren't going to make me very popular.

"Why do you think Scarlett would've snuck out to go for a walk by herself?"

May shrugged. "I don't know. She's never done anything like that before. Maybe she just wanted some air. I really don't know. I wish she had told us," she said.

"Is there anyone you can think of who might have wanted to harm Scarlett?"

They shook their heads.

"How about any strange phone calls or anything unusual leading up to her disappearance?"

They shook their heads again.

"Was Scarlett a happy teen?"

Mr. Douglas said, "She was always upbeat, despite not feeling very well."

"Do you know where your daughter is?"

May jolted back. "Of course not. That's why we called the police."

"I apologize. These are standard questions the FBI asks in missing person cases. But I also have to ask, is there any way there could've been an accident and Scarlett was hurt?"

Jack turned beet-red and said, "Look, I don't know what you're insinuating, but we would never hurt our daughter. You can go now."

As I suspected, I wouldn't win any popularity contests. I glanced at Brady and knew it was time to wrap it up. I turned toward the angry parents and said, "Thank you for talking with us. I assure you, we're going to do everything we can to find out what happened to Scarlett. I promise you." Neither of them would look me in the eye.

As Brady and I exited the home, he said, "Did you have to be so hard on them?"

"Yes, I think I did."

"Meet me at the car. I'll go in and try to smooth things over."

While Brady returned to the Douglases residence, I took a stroll along the quiet street up to the neighbor's house and peeked in through the windows of the rather large cabin with wood siding and cream trim. Sure enough, the interior appeared devoid of human activity, and it didn't look like anybody had been there in the past few days. I continued on up to the top of the hill. The homes looked just as deserted with the exception of a silver BMW parked in the driveway of the house at the far end.

Maybe the parents were innocent. They certainly had the outrage of parents who would never hurt their child. If that was the case, what did happen to Scarlett?

TEN

AVA

The heat was stifling, but it wouldn't stop me from looking for Abby. When Mia stopped coming to the center, I figured she had moved on, slipped out of the city, and saddled up to a new group. But when Abby stopped visiting the center too, my instinct told me something wasn't right.

Both Mia and Abby used to visit the Grace Center every night for dinner. A couple of regulars who visited our resource center and kitchen serving the unhoused and those in need of a hot meal. The two were teens, different yet similar in many ways, both with tragic stories of lost youth and innocence.

When I first met Mia, she was fifteen and hadn't been on the streets long. She couldn't believe there was a place that would give her food for free. I was the first person to explain to her there were shelters she could go to, but she refused. Instead, she stuck to a group of teens that looked out for each other, Abby being one of those teens. Abby had been the one to explain what happened if you went to a shelter—you could get ratted out to Child Protective Services and end up in a group home. A fate neither of them wanted, and I didn't blame them.

Over the course of the year Mia confided in me how she had

left home after a terrible fight with her mother. I tried to convince her to resolve things or at least let her know she was okay. Mia had gotten upset and said her mother didn't care about her as her numerous boyfriends were her priority—even after Mia was brave enough to tell her mom one of them had been abusing her. It had shattered Mia's sense of security. My heart broke for her; I knew the pain all too well.

I had left home at fourteen and had no idea of the horrors of the foster system. It only took two placements to realize I was better off on the streets. But I wasn't foolish enough to think I was the average homeless teen. I was lucky, and a woman at the community center—the Grace Center—took an interest in me and told me I could have a better life. Dana showed me the way, and I managed to avoid addiction and reach adulthood in decent shape. After two years studying psychology at a community college, I transferred to Long Beach State and earned my degree. I could have gone on to graduate school, but I knew my time would be best spent helping homeless teens, like Dana had helped me. And I liked to think that in my eight years at the center, I'd helped a few.

Having gotten to know Mia, I was surprised when she suddenly stopped coming to the center a month ago. But I knew the streets were hard and knew there was a strong possibility she'd moved on. Something didn't feel right, but I thought maybe she would come back eventually. That was until last week, when Abby also stopped coming to the center.

Abby, at only seventeen, had been on the street for several years and knew firsthand the darkness of human depravity. Abby had left home when she was thirteen years old, claiming her stepdad was inappropriate with her. She did what she had to in order to survive on the streets, and she struggled to stay sober. I didn't judge; I listened and tried to help. Abby seemed to have been doing well, as the last few weeks before she went missing I hadn't smelled alcohol on her breath and I was sure she was on the right track.

But both of them were now missing.

Over the past month and week, I had been constantly asking people if they had seen either of the girls but nobody recalled seeing them.

I didn't know their last names, but I had some photographs from our last Christmas dinner. Someone had come as Santa, and the girls had had their pictures taken with him. In the photos, there was a glimmer in their eyes of how they must have been before their childhood was stripped away from them. The uneasiness I now felt had me walking the dirty streets of Los Angeles, trying to find them.

Some of these kids didn't realize there were people who cared about them. Maybe not the families they were born into, but there were a lot of people rooting for them. There was a limit to what we could do at the Grace Center, but we could provide them with a hot meal, information about programs, and a place to sleep, for a night, if they chose to accept it.

I approached a group of kids in dirty jeans and T-shirts, surrounded by piles of cardboard and belongings. I didn't know their names but their faces were familiar. From what I'd heard, they were dealers. I showed them Abby's photograph. "Hey, guys, have you seen this girl around?"

The teen with the scruffy beard and dark hair said, "No, haven't seen her in a while, actually."

The other boy said, "That's Abby, yeah? You know, now that I think about it, I haven't seen her in a couple of days. That girl owes me money."

Could Abby be on the run because she didn't have the money to pay? I thanked them and kept going. The roar of the highway above and the hot exhaust fumes were starting to take their toll on me.

A lot of people turn their noses up at the unhoused. They

see the dirty, unwashed faces begging for money and food. But few people stop to think about what must have brought them there. If they had loving homes, would they have ended up on the street? Not usually, but it did happen. A drug habit or another series of bad decisions could drive anyone to a life on the streets.

I pressed on, venturing into one of the roughest neighborhoods in the city, where dealers were on one corner and sex workers on the next. Approaching a group of women I was familiar with, I said, "Hey, ladies."

"Ava, what brings you here? We don't usually see you out," Carla, who frequented the Grace Center, said.

"I'm looking for two girls, Abby and Mia. Have any of you seen them?" I handed her the pictures.

"Can't say I've seen either of them in a while. How about you?" she asked the other women, who all shook their heads.

"I'm beginning to get worried," I admitted.

"It's dangerous out here," she said.

I was all too aware of the dangers, and grateful for the warm bed and food I had at my apartment. The way these people were living was treacherous and unhealthy, and I wished I could do more. "Well, if you see them, let me know. And if you run into them, tell them I'm looking for them and ask them to come by the Grace Center."

Carla said, "Will do, Ava. You take care."

Carla and the other women participated in survival sex work to get by. Like the unhoused, they were looked down upon by the "upstanding citizens" of LA, but they had more heart and compassion than most.

"You too. Stay safe," I said, turning to leave. I wondered whether the police could help, or whether they would assume, because the girls lived on the streets, that they had simply run away or had left of their own accord. I remembered Abby telling me she'd met a guy, a new boyfriend with a car. She was so excited, and although I told her he sounded too good to be true, I didn't have the heart to warn her about how bad the new boyfriend's intentions could really be.

A black-and-white patrol car rolled up next to me.

"Afternoon, officers," I greeted them. I recognized one of them who regularly patrolled the area.

"What are you doing out here, Ava?" he asked.

"Looking for a couple of our girls, two teens, Mia and Abby. Haven't seen them in too long. Have you?" I handed them the photo of the girls posing with Santa Claus.

They glanced at the photo and handed it back. "Haven't seen them," one of them responded, the other shaking his head. "Do you think something's happened to them?"

"Mia, that's the blonde, went missing and I assumed she'd moved on with a new group, but when Abby went missing, I started to worry. We'd just had a conversation about her future, but she had also just met someone. She thought he was a golden ticket, but I wasn't so sure." I hoped the feeling of dread would fall away, but it was strong.

"She's likely holed up with the boyfriend."

"It's possible." But my gut said no.

"Well, if we see them, we'll let you know."

"Thanks."

"Are you heading back to the Grace Center?"

It was getting late and I was exhausted. "Yeah."

"Do you want a ride?"

I agreed, partly to escape the heat and partly in the hope of garnering some sympathy for Mia and Abby from the officers. During the drive back, I broached the subject of formally reporting them as missing.

"Mia has been gone a month, Abby about a week. Nobody's seen them. I've been asking on the streets and in the Grace Center. I'm really getting worried. Can I officially report them missing and you can put them in the database? Have people looking for them?"

"You're not a parent and they don't live with you, so it might not do any good. Abby's likely with the boyfriend. Did she tell you anything about him?" one of the officers said.

"All she said was that he was good-looking and drives a gold Honda Accord," I replied.

"Gold Honda Accord. We'll ask around, keep our eyes open, and let you know if we hear anything," he promised.

As we pulled up to the Grace Center, I thanked the officers, my heart heavy with worry for Mia and Abby. Walking into the Grace Center, blind hope made me think I'd see them sitting at the counter eating crackers like they used to. But the Grace Center was nearly empty at this time of day, as we prepared for the dinner rush.

Society might have turned its back on Mia and Abby, but I wouldn't. I was determined to find them. I only hoped I wasn't too late.

ELEVEN

VAL

Harrison set down the stack of flyers with Scarlett's beaming face prominently displayed, along with a bold "Missing" at the top, onto the granite countertop. "We've plastered them on lampposts and handed them out to all the local shops. Nobody's seen her," he said, his voice reflecting a sense of defeat.

Mom nodded, looking just as disheartened.

"What's your plan for the flyers now?"

"We could post them in the woods around the lake. In case anyone who was in the area and saw something returns there," Mom suggested.

"Not a bad idea," I said. "Have you met with the Douglas family? Are they prepared for a press conference?" I asked, shifting gears.

"I did pay them a visit," Mom said. "And they're not very happy with you. They said they're struggling to cope, and being interrogated by my FBI agent daughter didn't help."

Without hesitation, I retorted, "I treated them like I would treat any other missing person's parents. If they're more sensitive than usual, we might need to ask why."

"They've been through a lot, Val. That could be why," she said, in their defense.

Perhaps they were guilty of something else. It didn't have to be of hurting their daughter. "Well, I have a list of Scarlett's friends. Brady and I are going to head out and talk to them. Maybe they can shed some light on what Scarlett was going through, other than what her parents have told us."

Mom walked over to the coffee maker and began preparing a fresh pot. "That's a good idea. She might have just run off. What do you think, Harrison?"

"If there's anything Mom has taught me, it's that people don't typically vanish without a trace. There has to be a reason. If they couldn't find her near the lake, maybe she ran off. I knew plenty of girls in high school who got tired of their parents' rules and ran away. They came back, of course. Maybe there was an argument they're not telling you about," Harrison theorized.

Despite insisting on a career in computer architecture, I thought he'd make a fine agent. I said, "It's strange how the dogs couldn't pick up any scent of her beyond the lake. She could have been picked up by a friend or boyfriend."

"But she's been so sick. Would she really run off?" Mom asked.

"Maybe. From what I've heard, her parents watched her constantly. Perhaps the pressure got to her," Harrison reasoned. With a hint of annoyance in his voice, he added, "Teens want freedom. Parents tend to smother."

Ouch. "Did I smother you?"

"No, you're the best mom in the world." He paused and glanced at my mother. "And you're the best grandma in the whole world."

A born diplomat. Maybe he'd be better off as a politician, I thought amusedly. "Sure."

"How's Brady getting on?" Mom asked, shifting the focus.

"Says he likes the peace and quiet. Well, up until Scarlett went missing."

My son interjected, "And you came into town. You are a force, Mom."

Feeling encouraged by the faith of my mother and my son, I voiced my determination. "True, and I'm determined to find Scarlett. It might not just be a coincidence that I came home when someone went missing. Maybe there's a reason I'm here, other than to visit with the two of you, the most wonderful people I know. I'm going to help find Scarlett."

Mom turned on the coffee maker and leaned against the counter. "You have a gift, my dear. Perhaps you're right, maybe the Lord or the Universe or something brought you here, kept you safe so you can help Scarlett and her family."

It was a pleasant thought. I liked to believe that good things happened sometimes. This was something I had to remind myself of, having such a dark and dangerous job. We profiled the worst of humanity, people who fell outside the normal ranges of the community. There was always something distinct about them, a "screw loose" in colloquial terms. That might be something in either their upbringing or their brain chemistry that made them view their fellow humans differently, leading them to actions the majority of society found shocking. To them, however, it was normal.

A knock on the door alerted us to the fact Brady had arrived. Since discovering he was the giver of the teddy bear, I was a little less on edge.

"Okay, I'll meet you guys for dinner after Brady and I go talk to Scarlett's friends."

I gave Harrison a hug and my mom a kiss on the cheek before heading out to the front porch to meet Brady.

. . .

Brady sat next to me at the house of Tonya Silva, one of Scarlett's best friends, as I asked when she had last spoken to Scarlett.

"I haven't spoken to her since school got out. When you called to set up an appointment, I called our other friends, and no one has spoken to her since school let out, either."

"But that was almost two months ago, right?"

Tonya nodded. "It's strange, right? I mean, Scarlett was one of the girls in school who was always really friendly, but we weren't that close. I mean, we weren't like Gabby and Scarlett close, you know?"

I thought back to the list of Scarlett's closest friends that Mrs. Douglas had given us. I didn't recall there being a Gabby or a Gabrielle on it. "Gabby?" I said.

"Gabby Peterson. She isn't on your list?"

Strange. If her friends knew about Gabby and her parents didn't, then perhaps Scarlett had a few secrets after all. "I'll have to double-check. What can you tell us about Gabby and Scarlett's friendship?"

"They were thick as thieves, as my grandma says. Gabby was always by her side at school, and I'm pretty sure when they weren't together, they were texting, you know?"

"Do you happen to have her phone number?"

"Yeah, but she lives next door. She might be home."

Next door, and not on the list? "Are you good friends with Gabby?"

"We're not super good friends. We hang out in a different crowd, you know, like when we were younger we were Girl Scouts together and played soccer. But it was kind of hard to get in between Scarlett and Gabby. Gabby was so sad when Scarlett was in the hospital. She went in and out a few times over the last year. But Gabby was so sweet, she rallied all of us to write cards, send flowers, and visit Scarlett in the hospital. She's a really good friend. You should definitely talk to Gabby."

We thanked Tonya and headed next door.

As we knocked on the door and waited, I turned to Brady and said, "Do you think Mr. and Mrs. Douglas deliberately didn't include their daughter's best friend on the friend list?"

"They were so upset, maybe it slipped their mind," Brady suggested, but the look on his face told me he didn't buy it either.

A pale teenager with dark hair pulled into a ponytail opened the door. "Hello, can I help you?"

Brady, wearing his beige deputy's uniform, made it easier to explain. "Are you Gabby?" he asked.

"Yes," she said, hesitantly.

"I'm Deputy Sheriff Tanner, but you can call me Brady. This is Valerie Costa. We're looking into the disappearance of your friend Scarlett."

A tear escaped from Gabby's eye. "Have you found her?" she asked anxiously.

"No, I'm sorry. Can we ask you a few questions about Scarlett?"

She hesitated, then said, "Yeah, come in. My parents aren't home, but it's okay."

I wasn't entirely sure that she should be letting two strangers into her house, even if Brady was in uniform. Nevertheless, we accepted her invitation and she led us into the living room.

Seated, I said, "When was the last time you spoke with Scarlett?"

"It's been two and a half weeks. I'm really, really worried. We've never gone that long without talking."

"How often did you talk to her?"

"Every day..." She seemed to want to say more.

"It's okay, you can tell us," I assured her.

"Well, her parents didn't want her talking to anybody, but

we texted every day, all day long, and called whenever they weren't hovering. Scarlett and I shared everything."

Red flags popped up. "Why didn't her parents want her talking to you?"

"Scarlett didn't tell me exactly, but during one phone conversation when her mom was in the shower, we FaceTimed. The last time I spoke to her, she told me she was going to LA and would be better soon and that she had a surprise, but she couldn't tell me what."

Troubling. "After that conversation, did you text her?"

"Yes, but she never texted or called back. Like one minute she's so happy, and then nothing. And now she's missing. I think something is really wrong."

Scarlett used to text or FaceTime her best friend every single day, and then one day suddenly stopped. Maybe Scarlett had been missing longer than we thought.

"You said she was going to Los Angeles?" I asked.

She nodded. "Scarlett said her family was going to Disneyland. And that when she got back, she would tell me the surprise."

"But she never told you what that surprise was?" Brady asked.

Gabby shook her head and sniffled. "No, I never heard from her again."

Something didn't add up. "May I see the text messages Scarlett sent you?"

Gabby handed me her phone and I opened up the text chain between her and Scarlett. Scrolling through the exchanges made my heart break—silly conversations about boys they thought were cute, about clothes, and complaints of Scarlett's parents smothering her and how parents were the worst. However, there was also a text where Scarlett defended her parents, asserting that she knew they loved her. Intriguingly, there was nothing in the text chain about LA or a surprise. But these messages went back weeks, months.

"Do you mind if I borrow your phone for a few hours to go through the messages?" I asked.

Gabby seemed shocked. "Will you give it back?"

"Of course."

"What if Scarlett calls?"

"If Scarlett calls, I will run back over here and give you your phone so you can talk to her." And I would, I really would. But Scarlett had been officially missing for at least three days, and statistically a happy ending was starting to look increasingly unlikely.

"Okay."

Brady looked at me oddly, as if he wasn't quite sure what I was aiming at.

"Did Scarlett have any boyfriends?"

"No, we just had crushes. We weren't the most popular with boys, but I think that was because Scarlett was sick, and I guess sick isn't hot."

The teenage angst was palpable. "How did Scarlett get along with her parents?"

"She loved her parents. They did everything for her. They were so devastated when her kidneys started to fail. They did everything they could to help find her a donor, but they were running out of time."

"Did Scarlett ever say she was feeling smothered or wanted to get away?"

Gabby shrugged. "She would never say that to her parents, but to me, she admitted she felt claustrophobic. She didn't get a lot of alone time, you know? Her mom was always making sure she had everything she needed, constantly asking her how she felt. She told me she liked talking to me because I never bugged her about it."

Understandable. "Do you think Scarlett may have met up

with someone and went away to have a break from her parents?"

She shook her head, tears now streaming. I pulled tissues from my tote and handed them to her. If Gabby was right, maybe we needed to take this investigation in a different direction. And if what Gabby said was true, Mr. and Mrs. Douglas had lied to us, and that was never a good look.

As we got back in the car, I asked Brady, "What do you make of that?"

"It certainly contradicts what her parents said."

"Yeah, and I've got a hunch. We need to bring the dogs out."

"Search and rescue already had dogs search the area."

Shaking my head, I said, "Cadaver dogs."

Every part of me hoped I was wrong, but it would be the only way to be certain Scarlett was nowhere near the lake or her parents' home.

TWELVE

VAL

Back at the Douglas home, I waited outside as Brady spoke with Mr. and Mrs. Douglas, hoping to warm them to the idea of speaking to me again. They certainly hadn't been fond of me before, but if we discovered their daughter's remains on their property, their disdain would undoubtedly escalate.

The cadaver dogs had been deployed for several hours already, lending their keen noses to our grim task. The stark reality was that it could take weeks for such trained dogs to become available; however, I knew a few handlers who owed me a favor. In this line of work, friends in important places were as good as gold.

Brady emerged from the home, beckoning me inside. As I entered, I received cold stares from both May and Jack Douglas, but I didn't let their silence deter me. With a polite nod, I greeted them. "Good afternoon, Mr. and Mrs. Douglas. Thank you for speaking to us again."

Jack retorted, his voice laced with bitterness, "Brady made it seem like we didn't have much of a choice."

"We appreciate it all the same," I replied evenly. They absolutely did have a choice to engage, or not, with law enforcement.

However, if they were innocent, cooperating seemed the most reasonable route to locating their daughter.

Sitting across from them, the atmosphere was decidedly icy, the air-conditioning set too high and the Douglases offering nothing in terms of comfort—no tea, coffee, or even a simple glass of water. Just frostiness.

I began, "We met with Scarlett's friends yesterday and we wanted to ask you a few things."

"Okay," Jack responded gruffly.

"The list you provided us didn't include Scarlett's best friend, Gabby Peterson." At this, May's eyes widened ever so slightly. "Did you forget to add her name to the list?"

"I must have," she stammered, crossing her arms over her chest defensively.

"We were able to speak with Gabby, and she shared some things we would like to confirm with you."

Now they were clearly worried.

"Did you know that Scarlett texted and talked to Gabby every day?"

May shook her head. "No. We asked her not to use the phone. The doctor didn't think it was good for her to use a cell phone—they emit radiation that could have adverse health effects."

While I was aware that cell phones emitted low levels of radio frequency energy, a non-ionizing radiation, there was no conclusive proof of any adverse biological effects. However, I also knew that some individuals believed cell phones were harmful. Perhaps given Scarlett's health, her parents' restriction was born out of excessive caution. As a parent, I could sympathize. Not that I would have done the same. "Gabby says the texting and calling stopped two and a half weeks ago. Did something happen two and a half weeks ago that would have led Scarlett to cease communication?"

May looked down and said, "No."

"Another thing that Gabby mentioned, which caught us by surprise, was that Scarlett said she was going to Los Angeles, to Disneyland. However, you said she spent all summer at home. Did you take a trip to Disneyland?" I asked.

Silence filled the room. As neither parent spoke, I instinctively glanced at Brady, who looked as puzzled as I was. "Did you go to Disneyland?" I repeated.

Jack slowly shook his head. "No, we had planned to, but she... she wasn't well enough."

"And what about Los Angeles? Did you go there?"

Again, he shook his head. "No, she wasn't feeling up to it," he replied hastily.

We had multiple avenues to confirm whether or not they had left town—airline tickets or hotel reservations. A car journey to Los Angeles would have taken approximately eight hours, and there would have been an abundance of traffic cameras en route. Although sifting through footage could take weeks. But if Scarlett truly wasn't well enough, it could explain the discrepancy between Gabby's account of them having gone to LA and the Douglases' insistence they hadn't.

May said, "Anything else?"

After combing through hundreds of texts on Gabby's phone, we hadn't found any more clues about Scarlett's disappearance. "No. Thank you for your time," I responded.

As we were about to leave, Jack turned to us, an apprehensive look on his face. "Do you think she's still out there? Is that why the search and rescue team is back?"

My eyes darted to Brady, who had clearly not disclosed to Jack the true purpose of the cadaver dogs' visit. Unlike search and rescue dogs, cadaver dogs were trained to detect the scent of human remains.

Brady explained, "I know this will be difficult to hear, but we're trying to rule out all possible scenarios. The team searching your property and around the lake are not search and rescue handlers. They have cadaver dogs trained to detect the scent of human decomposition."

May let out a startled gasp.

"It's just to rule out the possibility she's still here," I quickly added.

A wave of sobs overtook May.

My heart ached for her; she was clearly a mother in deep grief. Yet, our questions remained unanswered. "There's still hope we can find Scarlett alive," I reassured them.

May's sobbing intensified, and Jack looked away, holding his nearly inconsolable wife.

Jack looked at us and said, "Can you give us a few minutes, please?"

Brady nodded, and we quietly excused ourselves from the home.

Outside, Brady broke the silence. "Her reaction seems genuine. She's clearly devastated her daughter is gone."

"Did you ever doubt it?" I asked him. "Still, there are inconsistencies, Brady. What if she went missing well before Saturday? Why else would she have stopped talking to Gabby? I've got a bad feeling they're not telling us everything."

Brady's phone buzzed. "Deputy Tanner," he answered, pausing to listen before looking over at me. "Okay, we'll be right there." He ended the call and turned to me. "Two dogs hit at the same spot."

THIRTEEN

VAL

Wasting no time, Brady and I started the one-mile trek to where the dogs had hit on the scent. Adrenaline propelled me down the dusty, dry trail surrounded by shrubs and a mix of redwood, oak, and pine trees. No houses were visible once on a downward slope. The shimmery lake, one of the largest in Red Rose County, was a stunning sight. Brady and I moved quickly, only stopping once to take a break.

"How are you holding up?" he asked me.

Prior to my injuries, I would have sprinted the mile and we would have already been at the spot. "I'm okay. Let's keep moving."

He nodded, and we quickened the pace until we spotted the team. Two men with two beautiful German Shepherds standing at the edge of the vast lake.

"Finnegan, what do you have?" I asked.

"Champ first alerted, and then Daisy," he replied. Cadaver dogs were incredible, but they were just one tool in finding bodies. Sometimes what they indicated was nothing at all, and the dig team would unearth absolutely nothing. The excitement was often premature. It could easily have been that a dead body had been there but wasn't there anymore. Although it was uncommon for two dogs to be wrong. And considering it looked like the earth had been slightly disturbed, as if somebody had dug a grave and then made a considerable effort to cover it up, it was worth investigating.

"Have you called in the Evidence Response Team Unit?"

"No, I wanted to wait until you got here. How should we handle this? Do you want your local CSI team? Or I could call in the FBI's ERTU. They already know I'm here and said they'd step in if needed."

How many graves had the Red Rose County CSI team unearthed? Probably not many. "Brady, are you okay with bringing in the ERTU? They likely have more experience in this type of situation. And we can have the evidence transferred to the county if necessary."

"I have no issue with it. The ME and lab have their hands full, but it will be useful to have any evidence collected brought to Dr. Edison and her team. The extra help with the dig would be appreciated."

Finnegan's bright green eyes met my stare. He was handsome in a classical, outdoorsman kind of way. Tall, strong, and an easy smile. Finnegan and I had worked a few cases together over the years and I knew he operated mostly on the West Coast these days. He was reliable and I knew if he had a spot in his schedule, he would be happy to help out.

I said, "Well done."

He said, "Well, let's see if we find anything before singing our praises. I'll make the call."

Like all the advancements in technology, we couldn't rely on a single one to find the truth. Often, cadaver dogs would help us figure out where something could be, but until we could definitively prove it, we were digging in the gray, but not completely in the dark.

With Finnegan on the phone to the ERTU, Brady turned to

me and said, "Honestly, I didn't expect for the dogs to hit on anything."

"You never know, it could be something, it could be nothing, or it could be Scarlett."

I watched the dogs receive their treats while they stared dutifully up at their handlers. Brady said, "If it is her, why would the perp bury her out here?"

"Opportunity. Maybe Scarlett was out in the morning hours, alone, and a predator spotted her. Killed her and buried her. Dead bodies are difficult to move on your own."

Brady nodded. "If it is Scarlett and it was an opportunistic crime, we could be looking for a fisherman, as they're out in the early hours. Or a local who regularly hikes the trails first thing in the morning."

"Could be."

At that point, anything was possible.

As we waited for the ERTU, Brady and I discussed theories in the event we found Scarlett buried where the dogs had hit. Suddenly, we heard movement emanating from the trail. I had assumed it was the team, but instead it was Jack, May, and their neighbor Henry storming toward us. Jack was in the lead, looking furious.

"What is going on?" he spat.

"The dogs hit on a spot under the tree."

"What does that mean?" May asked.

"It means the dogs detected something may be buried here," I explained.

May gasped.

Henry placed an arm around May. She had said he was a good friend.

Swiftly, I added, "It doesn't mean she's here. It means she could be. It's not one hundred percent."

Brady eyed me to try to stop me from explaining all this to the parents. After all, I was just a volunteer. But I wasn't exactly one to step back and let somebody else take control.

"We have the FBI's Evidence Response Team Unit coming out to dig to see if Scarlett's been buried here," Brady informed them.

May burst into tears. Jack moved closer to his wife, and Henry took the hint and moved back to allow Jack to comfort her. The Douglases whispered among themselves but stopped at the sight of the approaching ERTU in coveralls carrying equipment.

Brady shook hands with the lead technician, and we all stepped back and watched quietly as the team set up a tent and tables. While we waited, I observed the Douglases' reactions.

They looked broken.

Maybe my instincts were wrong and they had nothing to do with their daughter's disappearance.

The silence was deafening.

While I was working on Scarlett's case, I didn't have to think about what had happened, that *he* was still out there. The Bear could still come after me and my family. The thought hadn't materialized, but it kept replaying in my mind over and over again. The words he'd said to me, his mannerisms, his eyes through the dark ski mask. We had made the assumption he was a white male in his early thirties, and my captivity had confirmed it. I only wished I had a better description, other than dead-blue eyes that haunted my thoughts each time I shut my own eyes.

In need of a distraction, I turned my focus to the Douglases, who were clinging to each other like their lives depended on it, while Henry hung his head as if bracing for the worst.

The team began to dig. I didn't know how long it would take. It could be an hour or more depending on how careful they needed to be and the state of the body, assuming it was a body.

Unable to sit still, I pulled out my phone and called Kieran to see if he had any updates on the case.

"Hey, Val. How are you doing?"

"Doing okay."

"How are your injuries? Are you able to get around okay?"

I rolled my eyes, replying, "Yes, they're healing nicely. I've got bandages, the bruises are still a lovely shade of yellow and green. I'm a real sight for sore eyes."

"How are your mom and Harrison?"

"They're doing well. We've been a little distracted, helping out on a missing persons case in town."

"You're working?" Kieran asked, incredulous. It wasn't exactly a secret, but I hadn't disclosed it either.

"A local girl, sixteen, went missing the day after I arrived. I've been offering my help to the local sheriff's deputy as a volunteer to see if we can find her. Mom and Harrison too, they've put up flyers."

"And any sign of her?"

"Cadaver dogs hit on a spot about a mile from her house. Near the lake. ERTU is here now."

"Did locals call them, or did you?"

"I had a hunch, called in a favor to get the cadaver dogs out quickly."

"You're supposed to be on leave."

"I am. I'm just a volunteer."

"You're supposed to be resting, healing, and spending time with your family."

"I am. As soon as we leave here, I'm going home to have dinner with my mom and Harrison. Mom's teaching Harrison how to make her famous marinara and garlic bread."

"I'm jealous," Kieran teased.

"Any updates on the Bear?"

"No. No need to worry about that right now. The team is on it."

"So, you've captured him, and I don't need to worry about anything? He knows my name. He could know where my mom lives or where I live. He could come after my family." If he knew my name based on the identification I had on me when I was captured, he definitely knew where I lived.

"But he hasn't, has he?"

Frustrated, I shook my head. As far as I knew, Kieran had never been held captive by someone he was investigating, so he couldn't possibly understand what I was going through. "I want to make sure he is behind bars. I got away, but he's killed fifteen people. Don't forget that."

"Nobody's forgetting, Val. The team is still searching for him."

"Any new leads?"

"No. We're still working off the evidence collected from your scene. Searching for other possible locations he could be using or setting up his next take."

Whispers from the dig team caught my attention. They glanced up and looked over at Brady and me. They found something. "Right. I have to go."

"Val, watch yourself."

"I'm just a volunteer, working with an old friend," I assured him.

He sighed. "Stay safe and get some rest."

Before he could say goodbye, I rushed over with Brady. The technicians were down on their knees, brushing dirt off what looked like a body wrapped in linen. Over my shoulder, I saw Mr. and Mrs. Douglas, who hadn't moved from their spot, despite the activity around the grave.

The team worked for a few more minutes, delicately brushing back the dirt as they peeled away the linen, revealing a badly decomposed body with blonde hair—resembling Scarlett Douglas.

I stepped back, and Brady said, "I'll notify the parents."

Following behind, I studied them as he broke the news. They stared out, wide-eyed as if unaware of what was going on right in front of them. Brady said, "We found a body—it could be Scarlett's. We're not certain yet though. Testing will have to confirm it."

Mrs. Douglas hung her head and cried. Jack looked away. Henry shook his head in disbelief.

I was about to say something when Brady pulled me aside by the arm.

"Ow," I yelped under my breath. If my arm wasn't bruised, it wouldn't have hurt that much.

"Sorry. I forgot." He continued, "What are you doing? Are you seriously trying to interrogate the parents?"

"We need to find out if they know something. If it isn't Scarlett, we would still have to question them considering the proximity of the location to their home."

"Not yet. Look at them."

After a quick glance, I said, "They're broken up. But Brady, do you see what they're not?"

He cocked his head and said, "What?"

"Shocked."

He glanced back over at the Douglases, their neighbor, and then back at me. "As I said, let them be for now. I'll have one of the officers drive you home."

"You're kicking me out?"

"I'm not kicking you out. I just think it's best to give the Douglases some space right now."

Considering I was a volunteer, only there because Brady had allowed it, I didn't fight him. But I continued to watch Mr. and Mrs. Douglas, as I wondered what had happened to their daughter.

FOURTEEN

VAL

"How long have you been with the sheriff's department?" I asked Deputy Baker, my chauffeur. He was a kind, younger man who had picked me up at the edge of the trail head after Brady suggested I leave the crime scene.

"Five years now."

"So, you worked with my mom?"

"I did. We were all sad when she retired, but we understood. It's a demanding job, especially for a sheriff."

My mom retired at sixty-seven. I thought she could still work, but she told me she was slowing down and it was time to hand over the reins to somebody younger, someone with more energy. Having grown up with my mom, I had a hard time imagining someone stronger or with more energy—both physically and mentally; she was a rock. She had done it all, raising my sister and me by herself and serving as sheriff of a midsize county.

"She loved her job but wanted to enjoy her golden years, as she put it."

"What's she been up to lately?"

"She's been working on her garden and she comes out to visit Harrison and me several times a year. We're in DC. And she likes to travel with her Red Hat ladies."

"When your mom was the sheriff, I thought she was Superwoman," he said with a chuckle.

"Oh, I'm pretty sure she is." They were big shoes to fill. Both my sister and I tried, every step of the way. Mom was a legend in our town. Everyone knew better than to mess with her or her kids.

As we pulled up in front of my mom's house, Baker said, "Here we are. Tell your mom I said hi."

"Will do. Thanks, Baker."

I entered the house, and it was only then I realized I had never been thrown off a crime scene before. Not that Brady was totally out of line. It was his investigation, and I didn't have the right to question any suspects without his approval. Still, it stung.

Inside, the scent of tomatoes, basil, and garlic filled my senses. *Smells like home*, I thought, as I shut the door behind me and locked it.

In the kitchen, Mom was throwing a handful of pasta into a pot of boiling water.

"Oh, hi, Val."

Harrison stirred the sauce and said, "Hi, Mom."

"Smells incredible in here."

Mom said, "He's a natural. Finally, one of my descendants has the cooking gene."

Mom didn't cook much when we were growing up. We ate a lot of ready-made meals, or when she was feeling particularly ambitious, she'd cook a bunch of ziti and stock it in the freezer. My sister and I fended for ourselves quite a bit, but it certainly didn't extend to homemade Italian cooking. Sandwiches were more our specialty.

"Well, then, you're welcome."

"How did it go at the Douglases? You were gone quite a while."

I set down my purse and said, "Do you have any wine?"

Mom gave me a disapproving look. "Should you be drinking? You know alcohol inhibits healing and you're still looking like you went nine rounds."

"I feel fine," I assured her, adding, "but it was rough."

"Oh?" she asked, completely ignoring my request for wine.

"It's part of an ongoing investigation, so I really shouldn't say," I said, eyeing my son, who didn't need to know the horror of the day.

Mom abandoned the boiling pot and walked toward me. In a low voice, she asked, "Did you find her?"

I whispered back, "We found a body."

"Is it Scarlett?"

"Keep this between us, but maybe. The remains are in an advanced state of decomposition but the size and blonde hair fit Scarlett's description. They found the body wrapped in linen, and buried near the lake under a beautiful old oak tree."

She had been buried with care. Not the actions of an opportunistic predator, as Brady had thought.

Mom shut her eyes and murmured, "How are the Douglases holding up? They must be thinking the worst."

Of course they were. "They are shattered."

"I can only imagine."

"Yes, and when I was about to ask them about the remains, Brady said it was best I went home."

Mom said, "He must understand he has to question them."

"I'm sure he does, especially once they confirm it's Scarlett." I had left the scene before the medical examiner showed up, and so I couldn't ask when they'd be able to tell us more about the body. After we confirmed the identity, we would have to try to figure out how and why she was killed. "Oh, by the way, Baker says hi."

"Oh, I liked Baker. He's good with people and really cares."

"Do you know the Douglases well?"

"Just by reputation. I know they loved their daughter and seemed to be trying to find a donor. Their neighbor helped them organize a drive trying to find a match, with no luck." As I listened to Mom, I wondered if she missed being on the job. "But if the body was wrapped, it's possible whoever buried it likely knew and loved them, right?"

"That was my assessment."

"Do you think her parents are involved?" Mom asked, as if the idea had just come to her.

"It's possible."

"But it only took you three days to find her body. They're both smart and must know she'd be found?"

"You'd think. But not everyone is up to date on the latest in forensic science. Maybe they didn't think she'd be found. I think the bigger question is why would two devoted parents end up burying their daughter and then report her missing?"

Harrison called out, "Grandma, the pasta is boiling over."

"Oh dear!" Mom hurried back to the pot and I took a seat at the table. My body harshly reminded me it was still in the healing stages.

Mom poured the pasta through the colander in the sink and took a seat next to me. Harrison carried the pasta, sauce, and garlic bread over to the table along with plates and silverware before pulling out a chair and sitting across from me. "Maybe they didn't bury her." He gave us a smirk. "If you're trying to keep secrets, you should talk more quietly."

"How much did you hear?" I asked, surprised.

He smiled. "All of it."

Great. Well, the cat was out of the bag. "What did you mean, maybe they didn't bury her?"

"You're assuming because she was buried by someone who cared for her, it was her parents. Surely there were other people who also loved Scarlett. Maybe somebody else took her, killed her, and buried her, thinking nobody would ever find her. Assuming it even is Scarlett."

It was plausible. "When Brady gave the parents the news she'd been found, I focused on their reactions. They were sad, broken, devastated, but they didn't look surprised." However, I supposed they could have suspected she'd be dead, considering how long she had been gone and her medical condition.

Mom crossed her arms and said, "There definitely could be more to this, Val. And I'm not usually one to force advice on people, but you need to push Brady. Scarlett deserves the truth to be found."

Brady had worked robbery and grand theft in San Francisco, but murder and missing persons investigations were a very different animal. The town didn't get many murders or kidnappings, so he didn't have the experience. He had me to help, but if he didn't want it, he should have been calling the local FBI office to get people with real experience to work the case. The autopsy would provide clues as to what had happened, at least to the body, and then we could go from there.

While we'd been talking, our dinner was getting cold. I couldn't wait to enjoy the first Italian meal cooked by my son. I certainly hadn't taught him any of our family recipes, but his father, although not Italian, was a talented chef. It was one of the things that had attracted me to him when we first started dating. He could cook like nobody else. We were young and didn't realize the world could tear us apart; that I would grow and change, and he would too. I only wished I had learned that before we'd had Harrison. I hated that he grew up in a broken home, even though Nathan and I co-parented in a very civil and congenial way.

After we split up, Nathan and I decided we had to be the

best parents we could for Harrison. Fighting or blaming one another would only cause him pain, and that wasn't right. I had swallowed years of heartbreak for my son, but watching him across the table, his homemade marinara dripping from fresh garlic bread, I knew it was worth it. "So, tell me about your trip."

After chewing a large mouthful of garlic bread, he said, "It's going to be awesome. Roger and I plan to start off in London and meet up with Scott and Kyle before heading to France."

"Sounds incredible."

Harrison continued to eat and talk at the same time. "Yeah, and then we have it all mapped out. Originally Kyle thought we should fly by the seat of our pants and make no reservations, but I prefer to know where we're going and ensure we have a roof over our heads. I don't find sleeping on the streets because we can't find a hotel adventurous."

A hardship my son would likely never know. My son grew up privileged, more than I had. Not that I ever went without, but Harrison had gone to private school, the same one his father had attended. He would never know the struggle of living paycheck to paycheck or not being able to afford college. Despite this, he was a good kid with a big heart. Maybe I worried about his lack of life experience too much. It was hard not to.

As Harrison continued talking about his forthcoming adventures and train reservations, my thoughts drifted to the body in the grave.

The next morning over waffles, my phone buzzed. I glanced at it out of habit. "It's Brady," I announced.

Harrison said, "Mom, you have to answer it. He needs your help."

I wasn't sure if Brady saw it that way, but I answered all the same. "Hey, Brady."

"Hi, Val. I wanted to apologize for yesterday. I just wanted to tread lightly with the Douglases, but I didn't need to send you home."

"I understand, it's your investigation. But you do know you need to question them, right?" I asked, trying my best to not sound condescending.

"Of course, I just wanted a chance to get the medical examiner's findings back first to determine how hard to go at them."

"When did the ME say they'd be able to complete the autopsy?"

"Well, as you can imagine, we don't have too many suspicious deaths in this county, so she came out to the site right away and I just got a call from her. She's not done with the autopsy and report, but she has found something kind of strange."

That piqued my attention. "What did she find?"

"She hasn't told me yet. She said she wants to show me. Any chance you could meet me down at the station?"

I glanced over at Mom. "Did I hear you correctly? You want my help on the investigation?" I asked, pointedly.

Brady hesitated. "Yes, Val, I do."

"Does that mean you won't kick me off any more crime scenes?"

"Yes."

"All right," I agreed. "Give me a sec."

Covering the mouthpiece, I said, "Mom, can I borrow your car?"

"Sure, I can use Maxine's if there's an emergency."

"Thanks."

To Brady I said, "I'll be there in fifteen minutes."

"See you when you get here," he replied, before hanging up.

Looking back over at Harrison and my mother, I said, "The medical examiner says she found something strange. She didn't reveal what because she wants to show us."

"Now you're getting somewhere. I'm glad Brady came to his senses and asked you for your help. He needs you, but maybe it's hard for him to admit it," Mom stated.

"Well, they say there's strength in asking for help."

Mom squinted her eyes at me. "Exactly."

FIFTEEN

VAL

Inside the Red Rose County sheriff's office, I ran up to Brady, who was standing in the hallway staring down at his phone. Behind him, uniformed deputies and civilians bustled around in an open office space. Brady glanced up and greeted me with a simple, "Hey."

"Hey."

"Before we see Dr. Edison, I wanted to talk to you about the investigation."

With my experience, he should have been begging for my help. Would he? "I'm listening."

"I spoke with the sheriff a few minutes ago," Brady began. "He's agreed to let you help with the investigation in any capacity you need. For example, if you want to question suspects, you can question suspects. If you want to talk to them by yourself, you can."

I raised an eyebrow. *Carte blanche?* "So, you'll let me run it how I would run it?" I asked.

With a bit of humility, he replied, "The official statement is, we'd be grateful for your help."

This sudden shift intrigued me. Was this coming from

Brady, or had the sheriff pushed him? "What's with the change of heart?"

"I was being cautious earlier because I wasn't sure how the sheriff felt about you helping with the case. But after speaking with him, and knowing his thoughts on the matter, I'm all for it. We could really use your experience. I'm concerned it's not as black and white as it may appear from the outside."

At least he had the good sense to realize that. "I agree. Things aren't as they appear."

"Ready to meet Dr. Edison?"

"I am," I said, suppressing any hint of smugness or delight at having a full-time project to distract me from my own thoughts. Harrison and Mom were a good distraction, but Harrison would be leaving in a few days, and Mom had her own life. Constantly worrying about the case was better than fearing shutting my eyes at night.

Brady led me down the hall to the morgue. Inside, the smell hit me immediately. "I should've changed my clothes," I mumbled, unsure if I'd ever get the smell out. The air was chilled, and in the room were metal tables and a row of freezers along the wall. On one table was a body covered in a white sheet.

"Deputy Tanner, good to see you," said a woman with unnaturally red hair and a white coat.

"Dr. Edison, this is an old friend, FBI Special Agent Valerie Costa. She's helping us with the investigation."

Dr. Edison was about forty with fair skin and pixie-like features. If she'd grown up in the area, I would've recognized her.

"You can call me Sally, or Dr. Edison if you have to, but I think the formal title makes me seem old. It's nice to meet you," she said, before we shook hands. Turning her focus back to Brady, she said, "I'm guessing you want me to take you through what I found."

I said, "Yes, please."

She walked over to the body. "First of all, I'll tell you the biggest news. We were able to compare dental records and can confirm it is Scarlett Douglas."

As I had suspected. Brady and I exchanged glances and I thought he had suspected it as well.

"But that's not why I brought you down here. That could have been a phone call. I had you come down because I wanted to confirm a few details of the case before the announcement. Some of my findings aren't lining up with the case notes."

"Like what?" I asked, realizing I was already taking over the investigation.

"How long ago did Scarlett's parents report her missing?" she asked.

"Five days ago," Brady responded.

Dr. Edison harrumphed. "Based on my initial look at the body and the rate of decomposition, Scarlett's been dead for two to three weeks. Based on the temps in the area and depth of her grave, I'd say closer to three weeks."

The revelation felt like a punch to the gut.

Brady looked at me and asked, "So, they lied?"

Yes, but why? "The parents are definitely hiding something, but the timeline fits. When we interviewed her best friend, Gabby, she told us they texted every single day, but two and a half weeks ago all texts and calls stopped. Radio silence. At the time, I thought it was strange considering she'd only been reported as missing for a few days. We asked the parents if anything had happened during that time that would cause Scarlett to drop communication with Gabby. They said they couldn't think of anything."

Dr. Edison gave me a knowing look.

"Have you determined the cause of death?" I asked.

She slipped on a fresh pair of gloves, then pulled back the sheet, exposing what remained of Scarlett's head and neck.

"Nothing definitive yet. I sent some samples to the lab for a tox screen and a few other tests. I've been reviewing her medical records, and there are some inconsistencies with what I've seen."

"Like?" I pressed.

"Well," she said, as she pulled the sheet down further, revealing Scarlett's abdomen, "you see this here?" She pointed to a spot that looked like a large scar. "I haven't finished the autopsy yet, but there's nothing in her medical records that would point to her having a scar on her abdomen."

My mind started swirling with thoughts. "An amateur or a professional?"

"Based on the neatness of the wound, I would say it was someone with medical training."

"Any signs of foul play?"

She shook her head. "Mind you, I don't get a lot of murders out here, but I still don't see any obvious sign of foul play. I think the results of the toxicology report will be telling. But as you can see, there aren't many signs of trauma beyond decomposition—no skull fractures or broken bones."

No signs of trauma, and she had been dead for up to three weeks. We needed to restart the investigation with the knowledge she'd been missing close to three weeks as opposed to five days. Had the parents deliberately led us on a wild goose chase?

Brady asked, "Is there anything else you can tell us about Scarlett's body, like what may have happened to her?"

"If she were seventy years older, I'd say it looked like she died of natural causes and somewhat peacefully."

"Possible poisoning?" I asked.

Dr. Edison hesitated. "That's one possibility. Once I complete the autopsy and get the lab results back, I'll let you know definitively. But I called you in because I thought the timeline would be important."

"We appreciate that. I'm assuming you've sent the sheet she was wrapped in to the lab for testing?" I inquired.

"Yes, the ERTU was thorough with their evidence collection. Thanks for that. In addition, we also sent out soil samples around the body to be analyzed."

"Great. Sounds like you and the team have it under control." It was refreshing.

"We do. I'll call when I hear anything."

As we prepared to leave, I said, "It was nice meeting you."

"You too."

Brady and I exited the morgue and I let out a breath. Despite the number of visits I'd made to various morgues, I didn't think I'd ever get used to them.

Brady said, "We need to notify the parents."

"And ask them why they lied to us."

Brady nodded. "I'll drive."

SIXTEEN

MAY

I paced the living room, my mind teetering on the precipice of despair, cascading through every worst-case scenario. What were we going to do? Why was Jack maintaining such eerie calmness? It didn't make sense. They found her. What if *they* found us? Would they think we killed her? We had reported her missing to the police—surely they had ways of finding out what had happened to our little girl.

In the days immediately following her death, I took solace in knowing she was close to us. I would hike down to her resting place every single day, kneeling down in the dirt, placing my hands gently on top of her grave. I hoped for a sign, her spirit, her presence, anything to know my little girl was still with us.

A wave of fear swept over me, making me shiver. How would we go on? Would they throw us in jail? It was our fault. No. It was my fault. My insistence. It was a bad idea, and I knew it. High on grief and desperation, I couldn't bear to lose Scarlett.

Jack spoke, breaking the tense silence, "You're going to wear out the rug, May."

I glared at him. This wasn't the time for jokes, but I didn't know what it was time for. Was there any point to anything anymore?

"How can you be so calm?"

"We didn't do anything wrong, May."

"No? It's not wrong we buried her and then reported her missing?"

"No, I don't think so."

That was debatable. I knew it wasn't legal.

After the deputy sheriff and that FBI agent had left, I'd frantically searched the Internet to learn of all the things we could be arrested for. Filing a false police report by reporting Scarlett missing. Secretly burying a body. The fact that we'd handled her with love seemed irrelevant; they could still charge us with desecration of a corpse. "I think we need to hire a lawyer."

"You're overreacting, May. We didn't do anything wrong. She was our daughter. There's nothing wrong with wanting to bury her near us."

That was not how it worked, and I knew he knew this. Why was he in such denial? It was all coming crashing down on us. We were about to lose everything, but maybe we already had. It was my fault. I should confess and let them do what they wanted to me. I didn't care anymore. "If we don't want to spend the rest of our lives in jail, we need to get a lawyer."

"A life sentence? You're talking nonsense, May. At most, we'll get a fine for filing a false police report."

"That's not true."

"They may not even suspect us. We could say it was someone else. Make something up."

I shook my head, raised my fists, and screamed, "Enough with the lies! Enough! I've had enough!"

"Now you're being hysterical, May. You need to calm down. We'll get through this. They can never know the truth. Do you understand me?"

Filled with rage, I stared at the man I had married, the man who seemed like a stranger right now. Or maybe it wasn't him who had changed. Maybe it was me. Maybe he was just the same as he always had been, and losing Scarlett had forever changed me. It felt like there was nothing left to live for, but I wasn't a killer. I would keep our secret, even if I had to take it to my own grave. "We need a lawyer, Jack. We need a lawyer to talk to the cops. We don't want to mess up. We don't want this to get out. You know what will happen."

"We're broke, May. Our savings are drained, we took out a second mortgage on the house. We can barely afford to live as it is. How will we pay for a lawyer?"

He had a point. We'd spent so much on Scarlett's treatments, our search for a donor, a search for a cure, anything to keep Scarlett with us a little longer.

We were broke, and not just financially.

A knock on the door made me jump. Was it the police? If it was, I knew what I had to do.

SEVENTEEN

VAL

The door creaked open and an apprehensive-looking May Douglas peered out. "Deputy Tanner, Agent Costa, please come in," she offered, her voice just above a whisper. She had been expecting us.

As we stepped inside, she gestured toward the dining table. "Please, have a seat."

Jack, unusually quiet, looked at both of us and echoed his wife's invitation. "Yes, please come in."

The air was thick with tension and unease, as if there had been a cosmic shift since our last visit. Was it simply because we had found the body, or was it because they were finally ready to tell us the truth?

Taking a seat next to Brady, I watched as May turned her attention to us. "May I offer you something to drink? Water? Tea?"

It was as if May was a different person, no longer the crumbling mess of tears.

"I'm fine, thank you."

"None for me, thanks," Brady said.

May shrugged and seated herself across from us. Jack

followed suit. There was a moment of silence before Brady said, "We're sorry to have to tell you this, but the medical examiner has confirmed the body we discovered is Scarlett."

May nodded and Jack said, "It was what we feared. Thank you for finding her."

Their calm demeanor was unsettling. I glanced over at Brady and tipped my head, indicating I would take the lead. "We are terribly sorry, and I'm sure this is a very difficult time for you both, but we have to ask you some questions."

Jack nodded. "We figured as much."

"Did you have any idea Scarlett was buried down by the lake?" I asked, my tone steady.

Jack shook his head. "No, we didn't. Whoever took her must have placed her there. Maybe they were full of remorse and wanted to return her to her favorite place. I wish we'd known," he added, his Adam's apple bobbing as he swallowed. Beads of sweat dotted his forehead, despite the overbearing air-conditioning in the home.

"It must've come as quite a surprise," I remarked, barely concealing my skepticism.

"Yes."

His story about somebody killing their daughter and burying her in her favorite spot was, quite frankly, ludicrous. "Do you remember seeing anybody near the lake around the time of her disappearance? Or when you did the search?"

Again, Jack shook his head.

He was lying. Badly. But I continued with the softball questions, really just a means to make them comfortable so that when I went in for the kill, they would be rattled, caught off guard, and they'd slip up and tell us the truth.

"Do you have any idea who could have hurt Scarlett?" I asked.

"No, we didn't have any enemies. Scarlett was a good kid, a great daughter," Jack said.

I turned my attention to May. She was too calm. Had they devised this story together to cover up what they had done? "Mrs. Douglas, can you think of any reason why somebody would want to hurt your daughter?"

May shook her head slowly. "Nobody would ever want to harm her. I don't know... I just don't know."

I allowed a moment of silence to settle, hoping to lure them into talking. Most people find silence uncomfortable and, in an attempt to fill the space, they usually trip themselves up. Just as I had hoped, Jack finally asked, "Any leads on who might have done this?"

Brady responded, "We have a few leads we're looking into."

"Oh, good. Our neighbor, Henry, has kindly offered to put up a reward for anyone who comes forward with information."

"That's good to know."

I cast a quick side-eye to Brady, and I began. "Mr. and Mrs. Douglas, did you bury Scarlett under that old oak tree?"

Jack fidgeted in his seat, while May stared straight ahead, not meeting my gaze.

"Of course not, that's ridiculous. We would never hurt our daughter. Never," Jack said, his voice rising.

I countered, "When was the last time you saw your daughter?"

"Five days ago. She was tired and wanted to go to bed. We said goodnight to her, and that was it. We never saw her again." Jack's voice wavered as he spoke.

Pointing out that their daughter was already dead at that point wouldn't give us the desired effect, so I let his statement hang in the air. "This must be very difficult," I offered, before pressing on. "As you know, we spoke with Gabby, Scarlett's best friend, and she told us she hadn't heard from Scarlett in about two and a half weeks. That was unusual because they texted and FaceTimed every day. Did anything happen about three weeks ago, give or take a day, that would've caused her to stop talking to Gabby? Anything at all? Maybe even something small like she was sad, or tired, or just wasn't feeling well?"

May hadn't moved an inch, and Jack sat frozen. If I had to guess, I'd say they knew we were onto them.

"No, nothing," Jack managed, his voice barely above a whisper.

"That's really odd because we just came from the medical examiner's, and she told us something really interesting." I paused, watching as May bowed her head as if she knew what was coming. "Her preliminary assessment is that Scarlett died nearly three weeks ago."

Brady picked up from there, his voice steady. "You couldn't have seen your daughter five days ago, because she was already gone. Can you explain that?"

Jack opened his mouth to say something, but May placed her hand on his shoulder. "No," she said quietly. "I did it." May's eyes met mine, filled with a raw, resigned determination. "I'll tell you everything. It was me. I killed her. I buried her and then I reported her missing so the doctors would stop asking where she was. She wasn't showing up to her appointments, and I knew her friends would start asking questions. I chose to bury her under her favorite tree and so she could be close to us."

The only part of her statement I believed was that she wanted Scarlett close to her.

Brady pressed further. "How did you kill your daughter?"

May nodded. "I couldn't bear to see her suffer anymore. I gave her too many painkillers so that she would go peacefully."

"Jack, did you help May bury Scarlett?" Brady asked, turning to Jack, who was as white as a sheet.

Maybe he didn't know his wife was going to confess.

May continued, "He didn't help me. It was all me. Jack had nothing to do with this, nothing at all. Leave him alone. It's me you want. I confess. It's all my fault." A single tear fell from the corner of her eye.

The look in her eyes, the vibe I got from her when we walked in, it was defeat. Something felt off about this, but I wasn't sure what. May wasn't telling us the whole truth; I'd bet my career on it. But why?

Brady said, "May, nothing you've said to us today is admissible in court because you weren't under arrest and you weren't read your rights. I'm now going to place you under arrest and read you your rights. It'll be your choice whether you wish to make any additional statements."

She nodded, stood up, and placed her arms behind her back. Brady read her Miranda rights as he cuffed her. I didn't think handcuffs were necessary, but it was almost as if May wanted them, like she wanted to be punished. She reaffirmed, "I did it. I killed her. I buried her. I did all of it."

I shook my head, knowing there was something off about the confession. Did May realize all confessions had to be corroborated with physical evidence? We needed to tread carefully because if we couldn't find evidence to back up her statement, she would be released, at least from the murder charges, and then we might never find out the truth. Whatever May was hiding, I feared she would keep it close to her chest, even if she had to guard it with her life.

EIGHTEEN

VAL

With a sigh, I mumbled, "A gallon of coffee ought to do the trick." Weary from a sleepless night, I trudged down the stairs and into the kitchen. Mom was already at the stove, her morning energy in full swing, while Harrison sat at the table, engrossed in a newspaper. An actual, physical newspaper that he could hold in his hands. It was a quaint touch of nostalgia in our digital age. "Good morning."

"Morning, Val. How'd you sleep?" Mom asked, without turning away from the stove.

I had slept terribly. Whenever I'd closed my eyes, I had been assailed by disturbing visions of Scarlett's face in a grave. Each time I'd awoken from the nightmare, I'd struggled to get back to sleep, only for the image to morph into my own face in that grave. It was as if my mind was locked in a macabre dance between the barn and the grave. Nevertheless, I replied with a subdued, "Fine."

"You're famous, Mom," Harrison announced suddenly, his eyes still glued to the print. "Your name's in the paper."

"What do you mean?"

With a flourish, he held up the *Red Rose County Gazette* to show the front-page headline: "Missing Girl Found, Mother Arrested: A Community Mourns."

I was stunned. How had they gotten a hold of the story so quickly? And why was I mentioned? Trying to keep my voice steady, I said, "Where do they mention me?"

"It says, 'With help from FBI Agent Valerie Costa, the girl was found near Lake Rose late Wednesday.'"

I wished I had not been named in the newspaper. They could have simply mentioned the FBI's involvement, omitting my name altogether. As I wrestled with my thoughts, Mom filled a mug with coffee, perhaps sensing my claim of a "fine" sleep was far from the truth. She handed me the mug, and I joined Harrison at the table.

"Let's hope it doesn't get too much further outside of Red Rose County," I said, taking a cautious sip of the hot java.

"Why?" Harrison asked, genuinely curious.

"Because I don't want any serial killers, like the Bear, knowing my current location. Let's just hope he doesn't read the *Red Rose County Gazette*," I said, trying to sound casual.

More than a week had passed since my team had found me chained to a beam in that abandoned barn. My physical bruises were now fading, and makeup had completely concealed whatever was left. However, the Bear's signature would be etched on me forever.

Nobody spoke.

Breaking the uncomfortable silence, my mother walked over to the table and pulled out the chair across from me. As she sat down, she asked in a soft voice, "Should we put in a security system?"

Maybe I was making something out of nothing. And now I'd freaked out my family. I assured her, "I don't think there's anything to worry about. Trust me, I feel sorry for him if he tries to get into this house. Between you and me, he doesn't stand a chance."

That was, of course, unless he took us by surprise. But this was our territory, our home. We were armed and could be very dangerous. Harrison, on the other hand, not as much. He was a smart kid, but he didn't have weapons or law enforcement training. But Mom and I, we were more than ready.

Mom looked skeptical and Harrison couldn't hide his concern. In an attempt to lighten the mood, I said, "Let's talk about something else, something that has nothing to do with death or serial killers. What should we do this weekend? Now that we've found Scarlett, I only have a few things I need to work on with Brady to make sure we have, in fact, uncovered the truth."

Harrison said, "You don't think Mrs. Douglas killed Scarlett?"

"We'll know more once the medical examiner receives the lab results and we get a chance to interrogate Mrs. Douglas down at the station. Brady thinks a night in jail might get her to talk."

"Did she say why she killed her?" Mom asked.

"She told us she was tired of watching her daughter suffer—a mercy killing."

In some ways, the narrative was a bit believable, but in others, not at all. How could she have possibly buried her daughter on her own? Sure, her daughter wasn't a big girl, probably no more than 110 pounds, but 110 pounds of dead weight was a lot for a woman of May's size to carry. I explained my concerns, "I'm just not sure everything adds up. When we get the lab results back, we'll get a cause of death. We'll see if the evidence corroborates her story. If not, we'll have to keep digging."

"So, the case isn't closed?" Mom asked.

"Not one hundred percent. But I'm feeling better and I was thinking, why don't we go for a hike up on the ridge?" This time

I actually meant it. A hike sounded like a nice way to spend a murder-investigation-free day.

"Are you sure you're up for that?" my mother, ever the skeptic, asked.

"I haven't gotten any exercise in the last week. Look at my face. Makeup covers it up. I've got a few cuts here and there, but those are healing. I'm fine and the trek isn't too bad. It would be nice to get out into nature, don't you think? Harrison's only going to be here for a few more days." And when I said it would be nice to get out into nature, I meant get out into nature and not discover dead bodies. The hike to find Scarlett had been anything but enjoyable.

Mom relented. "All right then. I'll pack us a picnic."

"That sounds great, Mom."

"Are you heading to the station this morning?"

I nodded. "I'm hoping to extract more details from May and figure out what really happened."

"Good luck, dear," she said.

May Douglas, sporting a new set of khaki scrubs, looked pale and shrunken. The room was small with gray walls and a large, darkened, two-way window. I sat across from her, with Brady next to me. We'd agreed that I would start off the interrogation, try to get her to slip up and tell us what really happened. I began with a simple, "How are you, May?"

Her eyes were dull and her hair unbrushed. "I'm fine."

Brady informed me that she'd waived her right to an attorney, claiming she didn't need one. My advice to her, if she'd been a friend, would have been to not say a word until her lawyer advised her to do so. But she wasn't my friend and I would take advantage of her bad decision.

"Did you get any sleep last night?" I asked.

"A little more than I expected," she said. An unusual

response from somebody who had never been imprisoned before.

"We need to confirm some additional details about what happened to Scarlett. Are you ready to talk to us about that?"

May nodded. "Yes, like I said, I did it. I'll tell you everything you need to know."

"When did you decide to kill Scarlett?"

May flinched at the word "kill." "It's been a long year. She was a trooper, never complained. There was nothing else the doctors could do for her, but she never gave up, at least not around us. She was always smiling and endured all the testing and hospital visits, but when she took a turn for the worse, I could see it in her eyes that she... she was tired. Tired of all the poking, the prodding, the pain, the exhaustion, and it seemed like she... she didn't want to fight anymore," she recounted, her voice laden with sorrow.

I wasn't an expert at knowing when somebody was lying, but I recognized the usual signals, and she wasn't displaying any of them. She was sad, and her words showed no hesitation. Perhaps Scarlett had taken her own life or had asked her mother to do it for her. I pressed on, "And when did you realize the time was right?"

"It was three weeks ago. I saw her lying there, she wasn't conscious, she didn't respond when I called her name, and I knew I had to help her. So, I injected her with morphine and it didn't take long for her to die. It was awful... not violent, but just awful knowing my baby was gone."

May bowed her head and sobbed quietly. I had been so sure she was holding back, not telling us the whole truth, but today I saw a genuine sadness and despair in her. I believed she was there when her daughter died, or at least shortly after.

"When did you decide to bury her?" I asked softly.

She lifted her head as Brady passed her a box of tissues. Wiping her eyes, she said, "It was a few hours later. I couldn't let her go, you know? I knew I had to bury her, but the thought of not seeing her face every day... I couldn't bring myself to do it until I knew I had to. She was so beautiful..." Tears formed in her eyes, but she continued. "So, I dragged her from the bed out to the backyard and down to the trail. When she was little, she used to beg me to take her there. She would grab a book and a couple of her favorite teddy bears, stuff them in her backpack and follow me out. At the tree, she'd set out her stuffed friends and read. It was her favorite place on Earth, so I figured that was what made sense. And so, I dragged her down there, dug a grave, and then I rolled her into it and covered her up. That's it."

Brady and I exchanged glances. That couldn't have been how it had gone down. Brady probed, "Did you wrap her in anything?"

May looked confused. "I don't remember."

"How long did it take you to dig the grave?" I asked, ignoring her lapse in memory. She stared at me and I raised my brows. She knew I knew she was lying. Digging a six-foot grave was exhaustive work, and there was no way she could have done it alone.

"A long time," she finally said. "I don't know exactly how long."

I rested my hand on my chin and really looked at May Douglas, trying to figure out what had really happened. It wasn't what she'd said. Maybe she had been present at her daughter's death, but somebody else had to have carried her, wrapped her in the linen sheet, and buried her. Was it Jack? But it didn't make sense why she would cover for him, or why he wouldn't confess. If her story were true, it would be classed as euthanasia, but she had covered up the crime and reported her missing. With a good lawyer May could plead assisted suicide and probably wouldn't get more than three years. Then again, considering the circumstances, with a great lawyer she may not get any jail time. There was no way the district attorney would put May in front of a jury.

But if she really had given her daughter morphine to end her suffering, why had she hidden the body? Was she afraid she could be prosecuted? She didn't seem scared. Had she had enough time to come to grips with it?

My heart beat faster and I sat up straight. "May, where did you get the morphine?" It wasn't standard. The only time they prescribed morphine was under hospice care settings, and Scarlett hadn't been in hospice care.

May froze.

Brady reiterated my question. "You had to have gotten it somewhere, May?"

She quickly said, "I stole it from the hospital during one of Scarlett's visits."

Morphine was kept under lock and key and only accessible by hospital staff. She was lying again, but why? Had someone helped her? If someone had indeed helped her euthanize her daughter, then someone had also helped her steal morphine from a hospital and, possibly, the same person had helped bury Scarlett's body. My gut instinct was telling me otherwise.

"Are you sure about that?" I asked.

"Yes, of course," she said, more resolute.

Brady asked her a few more questions before having her write out a formal statement and sign it. I didn't like it, not one bit. May was a grown woman, and she was confessing to a crime she may not have committed.

Outside the interrogation room, I said, "Do you recall if they found a matching sheet to the one she was buried in, or morphine, at the house?"

"No, but we weren't looking for those."

"We should search the house again. Look for anything to support May's story." Or disprove it.

"That's not a bad idea. Now that we know what we're looking for."

If we were to corroborate May's story, we would need to locate sheets that matched the one Scarlett was wrapped in, plus morphine bottles and syringes. The absence of those items wouldn't confirm her innocence, but if they were found in the home, it would support her statement. "Any word back from Dr. Edison or the lab?"

"I called Dr. Edison this morning. She said it would be sometime this weekend before she had any more news, at the earliest."

"Has she found anything else that seems out of the ordinary?"

"She didn't mention anything specific, but she did say there were some irregularities. She doesn't want to confirm anything before the lab results come back."

Curiosity was getting the better of me, and I wanted to know if there was any evidence that May had killed her daughter. "Can we get a search team over there tonight?"

"Uh. I'm available. I can call and see if we have enough folks on duty, but it might have to wait until tomorrow."

"Let's go. Call the team on the way over."

He gave me an amused look and then conceded, "Yes, ma'am."

That's what I like to hear.

NINETEEN

VAL

Brady and I pulled up to the house; it was pitch black. Jack had been told after May's confession that the home was a crime scene and he needed to find other accommodation. The neighbors' homes were also dark, likely because they weren't home or they were out of town. The only light came from Brady's headlights and the moon. Adrenaline powered my weary bones as we entered the house. Wearing gloves, I flipped on the light switch and said, "Let's check the bedrooms first."

The house wasn't large. It wouldn't take us long, unless we came across something unexpected. We were there for a cursory review of what we could find quickly. A larger team would have to come in next week. I had learned on the drive over that the sheriff's department couldn't support an all-hands-on-deck search of a home. We had a suspect already in custody, and a girl was dead. Brady explained the budget was tight and overtime had to be used wisely. We agreed to wait for the whole team to conduct a thorough search.

I headed to the bathroom, thinking if there was any medication, it would likely be there, and if not, then in Scarlett's room. The medicine cabinet creaked as I pulled it open. There were several medicine bottles, and I examined the label on each of them. Not one of them was labeled as morphine, which was typically stored in a glass bottle and injected through a syringe. It wouldn't likely be in tablet form. We would have to have the team come back and bag all of these items, in the event Scarlett had actually died from an overdose of a different drug.

I shut the medicine cabinet and searched the countertop and the floors. The shower contents were typical: a loofah, shampoo, conditioner, bar of soap, body wash, and a washcloth. I pulled open the drawers on the vanity—neatly folded towels. The Douglases kept a tidy home. I found cotton balls, cotton swabs, cosmetic items, feminine products, and extra toilet paper underneath the sink. There was no morphine, no sign of syringes or even a sharps container in the event they had regularly injected Scarlett with medication.

With a heavy heart, I moved on to Scarlett's bedroom. The first time we'd visited the house, we hadn't known if she was dead or alive. Knowing Scarlett was gone, I felt a sadness in the air, a heaviness. She had been so young and had suffered so much. I only hoped her end had been peaceful.

From the look of her room, I guessed Scarlett loved the color pink as her bedspread and curtains were a light shade of rose. Her bookshelves were filled with mystery and fantasy novels. Teddy bears were lined up on her dresser. It was heartbreakingly normal. I walked over to her closet and opened the door. I frowned at the sight of what must've been her prom dress. It was turquoise with sequins that ran to the floor. She would've looked stunning in it. I flipped through the clothing on the hangers and searched the boxes on the shelves above. There was nothing unusual, no diaries, no medications. I returned to her bed. It was neatly made. Had May and her accomplice moved her to the grave and then returned to make the bed?

With my phone, I took a picture of the sheets to see if they would match what she had been buried in. I lifted the mattress and felt around for a hidden diary, but there was nothing.

Considering the number of texts she'd shared with Gabby, perhaps Gabby had acted as a kind of diary with whom she'd shared her inner thoughts, except for the surprise she'd mentioned, which had never materialized. I continued to search Scarlett's room, but there were no medications or signs of sickness at all. Perhaps that's how Scarlett wanted it.

"Over here," Brady called out. I followed the sound of his voice down the hall and into the second bathroom.

"What did you find?" I asked.

He lifted a syringe in its sterile wrapper.

"Where did you find that?"

"In the drawer."

"Anything else?"

"There's a few sharps in there too."

"We'll have to check her medical records to see if her doctors prescribed anything injectable. I wouldn't think there would be."

"I wouldn't think so either. Did you find anything in Scarlett's room or the other bathroom?"

"Her room is that of a typical teen—no medications or any signs that she was anything but just that."

"She probably wanted to feel normal," he said. "Let's search the parents' room. There's a guest room down the hall too."

After searching her parents' room and finding nothing of interest, I moved on to the kitchen. Opening and closing drawers and cabinets, I found only standard items. I opened the refrigerator: mostly healthy food—vegetables, juice, chicken—which was likely to go bad with May in jail and Jack kicked out until the investigation was complete. No sign of morphine or anything to corroborate May's story, except for the syringe that Brady had found.

Brady met me in the kitchen. "Anything?"

I shook my head. "There's a linen closet down the hall. You look for the matching sheets and I'll head out to the garage to look for a shovel."

He nodded and headed toward the linen closet.

In the garage, I flipped on the light. There were no cars, but there were racks and storage cabinets along the wall. By the looks of it, one or both of them typically parked in the garage. Like their home, it was organized.

I began my search, opening cabinets and drawers, searching the shelves for anything that would indicate what had happened three weeks ago. Next to a cabinet on the wall, I spotted a shovel. I pulled out my phone and took a photo, then a close-up of the top and bottom. We needed to bag it for evidence; the tip of the shovel still had a bit of dirt on it.

The evidence we found couldn't definitively corroborate May's story, but between the sharps, the syringe, and the shovel in the garage, she could have killed her daughter and buried her. It wasn't a smoking gun, but it made it look less likely that somebody else had committed the crime, not that I doubted she'd had help.

In the living room, I met up with Brady. "Well, we got the shovel, photos of all the linens, and the syringe and sharps. Not a bad haul."

"No." He looked disappointed.

It was how I felt too. "Let's run these back to the station, log them into evidence, and call it a night."

"I'm definitely looking forward to my bed."

Weariness filled my soul. "I hear you." Although I was exhausted, my bed didn't feel like a sanctuary, unlike Brady's. Mine was more of a torture chamber. Who knew, maybe today I had exhausted myself enough to sleep without nightmares for once.

A girl could dream.

On the drive back he asked, "You have any plans this weekend?"

"Hiking up the ridge with Mom and Harrison."

He gave me the once-over. "Really?"

I sighed. "Come on, it's a pretty easy hike and I feel fine." I was tired and run-down, but fine. "You?"

"My kids are visiting, so I'll see what they want to do."

"Sounds nice. Harrison's only here until Monday, so I want to get in some quality time before he heads off to Europe."

"Lucky kid."

"No kidding."

With the evidence collected, I was even more baffled by May's confession. It was possible that it was truthful, but I still didn't think there was any way she could have done it alone. She was protecting someone, but who? The most logical person would be Jack. Would he really let his wife take the fall?

TWENTY

MAY

Through the glass, I studied the man I'd married. The feelings we'd had twenty years ago were intense and fast. I'd thought it would never end, and it didn't for a long time. He was so good to me, to Scarlett, but I had failed him. He had always given me everything I wanted, supported all my decisions. There was only one decision he had fought me on, told me to let it go, but I couldn't. I should have listened. I should have been stronger.

He picked up the receiver, and I did the same.

There was never a moment in my life when I envisioned we would be separated by plexiglass.

"Hi," he said, the sadness in his eyes almost more than I could bear. "How are you feeling? Are you okay in there?"

"It's not that bad," I replied, lying through my teeth.

"Is there anything I can do? Give you money for snacks or something?"

"No, I think that's once they sentence me and I go to actual prison." Neither of us had a criminal record and didn't really know how these things worked, but the booking officer had explained it to me.

The moment Scarlett died, Jack had changed. And so had I.

But something had shifted between us. He looked at me differently, like he could never be anything but disappointed in me.

If only I had listened to him.

He'd always been right.

My despair had led me astray and now I was locked up and Jack was alone.

He didn't deserve that.

"Have they decided on your charges? Are they going to make you a deal or something?" he asked, his voice trembling slightly.

"I don't know yet," I replied. "I told them I didn't want a lawyer, but I've been talking to a few people in here and they said I should at least get a public defender. But I signed the confession. It won't go to trial."

Jack absorbed my words and said, "You didn't have to do this, May. There were other ways."

Like before, I should have listened to Jack. But he was stronger than I was. That's really what all this came down to. I was weak, so heartbroken I couldn't see straight or make the right decisions. I'd thought this might be best, but I wasn't sure of anything anymore.

"It's going to be fine now, Jack. This is the only way for it to be fine."

"What did you tell them exactly? Do they believe you?" Jack asked.

I pointed up at the sign on the wall that said conversations were recorded. He glanced at it and then looked back at me. He looked so defeated, but he had to know I was exactly where I belonged.

"There were only a few things I didn't remember. It was a stressful day, so it makes sense I wouldn't remember everything, like wrapping her in something, you know? I just didn't remember, probably the trauma," I said, trying to convince Jack and anybody who was listening.

"Just tell me why you did this, May. We could have talked about it."

"They would've never stopped. It would've never stopped. There's nothing left, Jack."

"We had us, May. We had each other. We could've gotten through this together."

But it was too late. If he was trying to make me feel like the lowest person on Earth, he'd succeeded. But I'd already felt that way. I was done hurting people. It was time for them to lock me up and throw away the key.

At least with me on the inside, I knew Jack would be safe.

"I'll visit you every day, May. I'm going to get you out of here. Work with the public defender, try to get the best deal so you can be free again. Whatever happens, I'll wait for you, May. You know I will. I love you as much as the day we exchanged vows."

I didn't deserve him, his love, or his patience. "I don't expect you to wait. I could be here a long time."

"Nonsense, May. I looked on the Internet—you may only get a few years, or if we can get you a really good lawyer, maybe just probation. We're going to get you out of here, one way or another. We'll figure it out."

Was that true? Probation? That didn't seem right.

"I'm not sure that's such a good idea, Jack."

"I just want what's best for you and for us. For you to be safe."

He was always so protective of me. But there were limits to what he could do. "I think I'm safer in here than out there, don't you?"

The realization must have finally dawned on him. I was safer in jail than out there, and so was he. For once, I wished he would just let it go.

TWENTY-ONE

VAL

I held my breath to keep the pain at bay as I walked to the front porch. The hike had been tougher than I had expected. My legs were sore and burning from the exertion. My head was pounding; the fitful sleep hadn't helped. I was beat but tried not to let on that I was in any kind of discomfort, considering everyone had advised me against the hike. But I had been determined to prove to everyone I was fine. Despite my physical anguish, the moments in nature with Mom and Harrison were exactly what I needed. The clear blue skies with only a smattering of fluffy clouds, giant green-tipped trees, and rolling brown hills was what I imagined heaven would look like.

Looking over my shoulder, I watched as Harrison stretched near my mother's SUV while Mom made her way to the mailbox. Yep, it was one of those towns where there was a mailbox that stood proudly outside the family home. Staring out at the old neighborhood with the large lots and woodland scene, it was as if Mom lived right inside a national forest. The idyllic town had friendly neighbors you'd likely see at the annual Fourth of July parade, and a downtown where you couldn't go without running into someone you knew. It was like going back in time where bad things didn't happen—other than the occasional murder.

I still wasn't sure exactly what had happened to Scarlett Douglas. I wished her mother would tell us the truth. I'd been playing the different scenarios in my mind, wondering what could've happened. The only thing I could think of was that somebody had helped May kill her daughter. If Scarlett was truly suffering, I supposed it made sense, but it just didn't sit right with me. There was something May wasn't telling us.

Mom pounded up the steps. She handed me an envelope and said, "Boy, you didn't waste any time with the change of address." She chuckled while she unlocked the door, and Harrison and I followed her inside. After being informed of my four weeks' leave, I'd finally decided to stay with Mom during that time. As it was, we only saw each other four or five times a year, and with Harrison going to Europe, it was an opportunity to spend more time with Mom.

Glancing down at the envelope, I felt something stir inside of me—a cautionary feeling. Handwritten address and name, no return address, but it was stamped—priority express mail. It could be from work or from Harrison's father. Those were the only two I had notified of my mother's address and where I would be.

I walked into the kitchen and pulled open the utility drawer. Removing my mom's letter opener, I carefully opened the envelope and pulled out the card inside. My heart raced and I felt dizzy. I placed my hand on the counter to steady myself.

My mother approached. "What is it? Are you okay?"

I turned to look at her. "It's from him."

"Him? Who?"

"The Bear."

My mother's eyes grew wide. "Are you sure? What does it say?"

"It says, 'Agent Costa, congratulations on breaking the case. Until we meet again, S.'"

My mother said, "Maybe it's just a prank or a hoax."

My captivity hadn't been in the news and I hadn't told anybody but my mom, Harrison, and Brady. He'd found me. He'd found my family. He knew where they lived. "I have to call Kieran."

My mother went to a drawer and pulled out a large plastic bag. "Place it in here." I dropped the envelope and letter inside. My mom zipped the plastic bag shut. "Call Kieran."

Harrison, from over her shoulder, asked, "What's going on over there?"

My mother turned to explain and the color drained from my son's face.

I wouldn't allow this to happen. I wouldn't allow him to have this effect on my family. I would make him pay. Furious, I called Kieran.

"Hey, Val. What's going on?"

"He sent me a letter," was all I managed to say.

"Who did what?" I explained the situation and Kieran replied, "Okay, so it's bagged. We have two options. Either we have the local FBI team come out and process it for fingerprints, DNA, anything he may have left behind, or you can ship it to DC."

"Time is of the essence, don't you think?" Somehow, I knew the Bear wasn't done with me. There was something about how he'd said my name when I'd been in his grasp.

"Of course. I'll put a call into the local FBI office and get someone out there right away." Kieran added, "Are you okay, Val?"

"No, I'm not okay." I shook my head. This was what I'd feared the most.

"Understandably, Val. Have you called the therapist yet?"

I let out a breath. "No, I haven't had time. I've been

spending time with Harrison, my mom, and working on the Scarlett Douglas case."

"You need to call the therapist. It's a stipulation of you returning to duty. I need you to promise to call on Monday."

"I will. I promise."

"Good. Hang in there. I'll make the call and make sure this is dealt with. Also, we can ask the locals to keep an eye on the house if that makes you feel better."

"He mailed it. He wasn't here. Do you think he would be that bold?" I thought he could be, even as I asked the question. He was a sadistic killer who was probably enjoying taunting me. What would he do next? Take my son? My mother? Me?

"I'll call Brady and see what he thinks. I'll have a security system installed."

"Call me if you need anything."

"Thanks." Ending the call, I turned to my mom.

"What's going on?"

After I explained that the local FBI office would come out to pick up the letter and process it for fingerprints, DNA, anything that could lead us to the identity of the Bear, I said, "Mom, I know I've been against this before, but I think maybe it's time for a security system."

She nodded. "We can do that."

"I'll call Brady to see if he has anyone at the sheriff's department who can do surveillance to make sure nobody's poking around the house until we can get the cameras installed."

"That sounds like a plan."

I walked over to Harrison and wrapped my arms around him. "It'll be okay, Harrison. There's nothing to worry about."

I stepped back, and the look in his blue eyes would forever haunt me. "How can you say that, Mom? A serial killer knows where Grandma lives. He sent you a letter. I'm supposed to be calm about that? I could lose you or Grandma, or he could come after me."

I had the same fears. But what was I supposed to tell my eighteen-year-old son? That he was right? That, even so, I would do everything I could to protect him and my mom? "You're right. It's okay to be afraid. But as long as I'm here, and you're here with Grandma and me, there's no way anybody can get to you, or to any of us."

"But I'm only here for two days and then I'll be on my own."

"It'll be okay. If he's after anyone, it's me. You'll be safe on your trip." Would he? I couldn't make him cancel it. Harrison had been looking forward to this trip all year.

"That doesn't make me feel better. Maybe I should stay with you instead. Europe will still be there after you catch him."

My boy.

"It's up to you. But I'll be fine. I promise."

"I'll think about it."

As I embraced my only child, rage bubbled up inside me. The Bear was going to regret the day he messed with me and my family. I would hunt him down like the monster he was until I caught him. And he would pay dearly.

TWENTY-TWO

VAL

Sweaty and angry, I stood outside my mother's home, waving to Brady as he approached. The FBI team had already picked up the letter and taken my statement. They assured me they'd have full analysis by close of business Monday.

"You didn't have to come out here, Brady. I know you have your kids this weekend."

"No problem. They're ordering pizza and picking out a movie to watch tonight. How are you holding up?"

"I'm so furious I could scream." And I had—into my pillow, that was.

Brady nodded. "That's completely understandable. And I know somebody who owes me a favor if you want to get the security installed tonight or early morning."

I was a trained FBI agent and my mother was a retired sheriff—we shouldn't need security. We both had weapons, but it would be nice to have a warning before somebody entered our home or was near the perimeter. "I'd appreciate that."

"How's Elizabeth? And Harrison?" he asked quietly.

"You know Mom, she's a rock, but Harrison's shaken. Part

of me wants to put him on a plane back to DC so he can be safe with his father before he leaves for his trip. But he's already talking about not wanting to leave me."

I wanted to spend every moment I could with Harrison, but not at the expense of his safety. He was safer away from me.

"I understand, but other than the letter that was mailed, is there any reason to believe he's been near the house?"

"No, but the postmark is from a few towns away, which means he's close."

"You tracked him to Nevada, right? It's a road trip from here; he could have already gone back to wherever he's holed up. He may have never even set foot in this town," Brady reasoned.

It was true, but I wasn't exactly feeling loosey-goosey with a serial killer knowing my mother's address.

"I spoke with some of my old colleagues in the sheriff's department, and we have several volunteers willing to provide twenty-four-hour surveillance. We'll have a car parked outside watching the house until we get the security installed. Would that work?"

It was good to have friends. "Yes, thank you. I appreciate it more than I can say."

"I've got your back, Val. Always have, always will."

The look in his eyes told me it was true, not that I doubted it, but was there something else there? Before I could even contemplate what, he said, "Okay, an officer will be here in about an hour to do surveillance. I'll stay until he gets here."

"Thank you."

My pride would have loved to tell him, no, please go, but it made me feel safer to have another person there, and it would probably make Mom and Harrison feel better too.

"No word from the medical examiner?"

He looked at me with raised brows. "Do you ever stop working?"

If I wasn't working, I'd be obsessing about the Bear and how vulnerable we were. At least if I was working, I'd be thinking about something else. "I can't turn my brain off."

Brady's phone buzzed. "It's Dr. Edison," he said, looking at the screen.

On the inside, I was doing a happy dance. I desperately needed a distraction.

Brady answered. "Hello. Yeah, sure, give me a sec." He lowered the phone and said, "She's done with the autopsy and the labs are back."

It was what I had hoped for, but I was conflicted and didn't want to leave my family. The smart thing to do would be to wait for the patrol to start watching the house, and make sure my mother and son were okay with me leaving to go talk to the medical examiner.

"Can you tell her you'll call her back? I want to go with you, but I want to make sure it's okay for me to leave once the patrol gets here."

"Understood."

An hour later, Mom and Harrison were insisting Brady and I go talk to the medical examiner about Scarlett Douglas. The patrol was already outside watching over my family. I didn't want to leave them, but I needed to work, but only if it was okay with them. "Are you sure? I can stay. Scarlett isn't going to be any less deceased if I wait."

Mom lowered her gaze. "Val, I know you better than anybody in the world, and I know you're itching to go."

"I'm also worried about the two of you."

"Mom, the patrol's outside. I've got Grandma, and she's one tough grandma. So go. But you'll be back later, right?"

"Of course."

We would finally find out if Scarlett's mother was telling

the truth about killing her own daughter, or if she had been lying through her teeth.

TWENTY-THREE

AVA

Standing at the detective's desk, I said, "Any luck finding the gold Honda Accord?"

He sighed. "I've sent out a few feelers, but nothing so far. I'll let you know if we find anything."

I had a sinking feeling the police weren't taking this seriously. I now had three people missing. Yes, they were high risk and had a history of running away from their homes, usually out of necessity due to abuse. Now, they were being forgotten. I had a bad feeling they weren't just running off to bigger and better things.

"There's been no sign of Mia or Abby," I continued, my voice strained. "And now a third person is missing. His name is Ethan. I saw him just three days ago." Ethan had been coming to the center for about six months. He was only fifteen but had been on the streets since he was thirteen and had told his family he was gay. His strict Christian family had refused to accept his declaration and tried to send him to a conversion camp. When he'd run away from the awful camp, his parents had told him they wouldn't tolerate his lifestyle, and if he insisted on being gay, he could leave. He'd told me he wasn't as surprised as he should have been but was heartbroken his family had turned on him. He'd ended up working the streets for food and a place to stay. When one of his clients had become violent, he'd decided living in a tent with other kids was better.

"Only three days? He'll turn up."

I wanted to wring Detective Rogers' neck until he took their disappearances seriously. "Normally, I wouldn't be concerned, but Ethan told me he had spoken with Mia and Abby. He said they were fine and he had some big news coming up and not to worry. But when I pressed him about where Mia and Abby were and what they'd been doing, he couldn't answer. I think he was lying about Mia and Abby." Which made me believe the three people's disappearances were connected. Who was luring away these kids? And how? And more importantly, why?

The look the detective gave me suggested he thought I was out of my mind. Maybe I was, but I knew these kids. They came to the center every single day. I knew better than to think good things could happen to these kids out of the blue. Luck wasn't something that was on their side, and now they were gone. Didn't anyone care?

"But now he's missing. All three were happy about something they couldn't tell me about before they went missing. I think they're being lured into something," I added with a shudder. I knew of the danger that hung around these kids. Pimps posing as friends or boyfriends and then, surprise, they turned out to be the boss, forcing the victims to turn tricks and hand over the cash to the friend and lover they'd thought they could trust.

"Ava, we're doing everything we can. We've been keeping an eye out for a gold Honda Accord like your girl said her boyfriend had. You've given us photos of the three missing people. There's not much else we can do."

"You could ask the people on the streets if they've seen

them. Don't you have informants or something to notify you if something strange is going on with the street kids?"

Detective Rogers shook his head. "This is the LAPD, Ava. We're up to our eyeballs in violent crime. We can't spend every minute looking for your kids who may not even be missing. They live on the street—maybe they moved corners or towns. They might have gone somewhere with more opportunities or somewhere more pleasant, like the beach. Bring concrete evidence, and we'll act accordingly. Like I said, we'll keep our eyes out for the gold Accord and the three kids you think are missing."

I stared at him in disbelief. How could somebody who swore to serve their community have so little concern for some of its most vulnerable citizens? I shook my head and stormed out of the police station. Three missing kids and nobody cared except for me.

As I got back into my car, I rested my forehead on the steering wheel. What if this happened again? There were so many bad things that could befall these kids. They were vulnerable, willing to believe anybody who promised to help them. But it was clear the police weren't going to do anything about it. It was time to take matters into my own hands. If those who wore a badge claiming to serve and protect refused to do so, then I would do something.

I started the car and headed straight to the local FedEx office to make flyers of the missing kids. Their parents, their community, everyone had turned their backs on them. But I knew these kids. They were bright. Yes, they were damaged, but that didn't mean they couldn't be fixed and saved. These were kids with good hearts, who still believed things could get better.

At the copy shop, I approached the counter, laying down the three Polaroid pictures of Mia, Abby, and Ethan.

A man with a terrible mustache behind the counter, said, "What's this, ma'am?"

"These are photographs of three missing kids. I need posters, one for each of them. And one with all of them on it. Is there any way we can do that using these Polaroids?"

"Sure. They won't be the highest quality, but I'll work some magic so they're not too bad. What happened to them?"

"Mia here, she went missing six weeks ago. Abby almost two weeks ago. Ethan three days ago. I saw them every single day, and then they vanished."

"Have you reported it to the police?" he asked.

"They won't do anything."

The man shook his head. "Figures. Don't worry. I've got you."

"Thank you."

Forty minutes later, I walked out with a bundle of flyers tucked under my arm. During the drive back to the Grace Center, I thought up a plan. First was to hand out the flyers to anybody who passed by the center, and then I would move on to different neighborhoods until they were found or someone could give me some information.

These kids will not be forgotten.

TWENTY-FOUR

VAL

Brady drove while I tried to push the Bear to the back of my mind. The FBI lab was processing the letter, and I hoped it would lead us to the Bear's identity so he could be locked up and I could have a few words with him. That was a battle for another day. It was time to direct my focus on Scarlett Douglas' death.

How a mother could kill her own child was beyond me. May's explanation—that it was to end her daughter's suffering—was the only justification I could begin to comprehend. As mothers, we protect and nurture. We raise children; we don't eliminate them. Or, at least, we shouldn't. Yet there had been a long slew of bad mothers, driving their children off bridges or poisoning them. It wasn't unheard of, but it wasn't all that common either.

Upon reaching the station, Brady led me past a few members of the sheriff's department. He waved to one. "Hey, Lucy, how's it going?"

The young woman said, "Good. What has you back here so late?"

"Autopsy results are in for Scarlett Douglas."

"Poor girl." Lucy looked at me, seemingly trying to discern my identity or perhaps wondering if I was the FBI agent working with Brady.

There was a pause before Brady introduced us. "Lucy, have you met Agent Costa?"

Her eyes brightened. "No, I don't believe so."

I offered my hand to the woman with perfectly straight blonde hair and large black spectacles. "It's nice to meet you, and you can call me Val."

"Nice to meet you, Val. I work in the research department, handling records and such."

"I'm sure you're invaluable, as are most research teams. We couldn't do what we do without you."

"That's very kind of you."

The research team, often the unsung heroes of detective work, dealt with the laborious task of sifting through phone records, bank statements, and paperwork, finding security footage and social media accounts, and enduring hours and hours of painstakingly dull work. They were more valuable than big shiny diamonds.

I said, "Hope to see you around," as we headed down the hallway to Dr. Edison's office.

Inside the tiny office were two visitor seats and a desk. The walls were lined with bookshelves stuffed with books and piles of loose papers. Motioning for us to take a seat, Dr. Edison removed her glasses and said, "Well, unfortunately, my suspicions were correct."

"Is it that bad?" Brady asked.

"No, but it might make your jobs a little tougher."

I didn't like the sound of that. "Did you determine the cause of death?"

"I did. Her death was caused by a nasty infection."

"An infection?" Admittedly, I had not seen that coming.

Brady said, "How did she get the infection?"

"That is the right question. Based on her lab work, we found levels of three immunosuppressive drugs: prednisone, tacrolimus, and cyclosporine. These three drugs are usually mixed together and prescribed after surgery."

"What kind of surgery?" Brady asked.

I thought I knew the answer, but it didn't make sense.

"Organ transplant surgery."

"Before or after?"

"After. The drugs are used to help prevent the recipient's body from rejecting the donor organ. And based on the autopsy, there is a kidney inside Scarlett that she wasn't born with."

If Scarlett had died of an infection, why had her mother fabricated the story that she had killed her? It didn't make any sense. "Was there morphine in her system?"

"There was."

"But not enough to kill her?"

She shook her head. "No, but it was a pretty hefty dose, likely to ease her suffering."

Had Scarlett's mother known she was sick and refused to take her to the hospital? Had she actually thought the morphine had killed her? "Have you seen this type of thing before?" I asked.

"It's the first time I've seen something like this, especially after a thorough review of her medical records where there is not a single mention of a transplant," Dr. Edison explained. "It clearly states by the physician at the hospital where she was being treated that she was on the donor list, but they never found a match."

"Where could she have gotten the transplant?" I asked.

"Unfortunately, that's where your job comes in. She could've gone to another country, but the circumstances around her death make me think they were trying to hide the fact that she'd had a transplant."

"Why would they do that?" Brady asked.

"Because it's illegal to buy and sell organs, even if the donors are willing. Possibly they wanted to hide the fact they'd participated in something illegal. Maybe they were ashamed. There are countries that regularly buy and sell organs, and it's a booming industry."

"Which countries allow this?"

"The only country that currently allows the buying and selling of organs is Iran."

It was highly doubtful that the Douglases had flown to Iran for an organ transplant for their daughter. The research team had already looked into the parents' travel records, and there were no flights out of the States. So, wherever they got the organ, they had driven there. Maybe Mexico. It was pretty common for Californians to drive over the border for bargain-priced plastic surgeries and medications.

"Is there anything else you can tell us about Scarlett and what she's been through?" I asked.

"Well, she was in kidney failure, according to her records, and she desperately needed a transplant. Perhaps the parents got desperate, drove her down to Mexico or up to Canada, and paid a hefty sum for a new kidney. Maybe they didn't realize the severity of the infection until it was too late to save her."

Had the Douglases risked everything to save their daughter only to end up killing her instead? That would be difficult to live with. "Thank you, Dr. Edison, this has been very helpful."

"If only it wasn't such grim news. I feel terrible for Scarlett. The last year of her life was rough. I wouldn't wish that on anybody."

My sympathy went out to Scarlett but my mind wandered to the kidney donor. Had they given it willingly or as a means of survival? Or worse? Maybe they hadn't had a choice in the matter at all.

We left and headed down the hall.

Brady said, "We'll need to get the research team to start

investigating different medical tourism locations known for kidney transplants."

"Yes, of course, but first I think we should pay a visit to May Douglas. She might be able to provide us with an explanation. Obviously, they took her somewhere to get a transplant, and then perhaps they were too afraid to take her to a local doctor when she got sick—afraid their secret would be exposed."

"And just let her die?"

I was struggling with the thought too. It seemed like a stretch. Would Scarlett's parents go as far as getting an illegal transplant to save her only to let her die to avoid dirty looks by neighbors or jail time?

"It may be that it was too late."

And that's what I wanted to hear from May Douglas. Had she let her daughter die to save herself and her husband from being prosecuted for organ trafficking? If that were true, why confess to murder?

TWENTY-FIVE

VAL

May Douglas was pale, her skin punctuated by dark circles under her eyes. The look she gave me was one of fear—a fear that resonated with the uncomfortable truth that I knew her secret. But I had to wonder, why was she so afraid? She was already in prison for killing her daughter.

"Good evening, May," I said, trying to soften my tone.

"What do the two of you want?" she asked, her voice a raw whisper.

I took the seat across from her and said, "The truth, for starters."

"I told you the truth."

I shook my head. "Mrs. Douglas, you told us that you killed your daughter with morphine and then buried her. Now, with the autopsy complete and her bloodwork and labs back, we can definitively say that's not true."

Her eyes widened, and worry painted her face.

"We know that your daughter died of an infection, a complication from her kidney transplant." I sat back and studied her reaction.

She shut her eyes as if trying to block out the situation, as though we hadn't just uncovered her secret.

I pressed on. "What we would like to know, Mrs. Douglas, is where she received her transplant, and why, when she started to show signs of rejection and a serious infection, you didn't take her to the emergency room."

Mrs. Douglas began to tremble and she shook her head. "I've said all I can say."

The fear she was exhibiting wasn't from us. She was scared of something else, her husband perhaps? "We need you to tell us the truth, Mrs. Douglas."

Brady added, "We will be doing a full review of your financial records and looking for money transfers that would've paid for the transplant. We know it wasn't done through legal means or in this country."

May cocked her head as if there was something surprising in that statement.

Had we gotten something wrong? "What do you have to say, May? Are you finally ready to tell the truth about what happened to your daughter? Why did you let her die?" It was harsh, but I needed to get the truth out of her.

"Let her die?" She stared off to the corner of the interrogation room and began. "I would've done anything to save Scarlett, and I mean *anything*, but I failed her."

"Why didn't you take her to the emergency room when she first caught a fever?"

If she'd prevented her child from getting the medical attention she needed, that was neglect and child endangerment, and she could be prosecuted on those grounds. If Brady and his team brought her to trial, they needed to understand the charges against her. At this point, her confession couldn't be used considering the lab results proved she hadn't killed her daughter with morphine. We were fairly certain she hadn't buried her daughter by herself either. Her confession wasn't worth the paper it was written on.

"I couldn't. Just let me do my time. I don't have anything left anyhow." She turned away, staring at the drab gray walls.

Brady said, "You see, Mrs. Douglas, the problem is that we've disproven your confession. Your confession doesn't mean anything, which means technically we could release you right now. But since you didn't take her to the emergency room, we could rebook you on child endangerment charges."

She turned and looked at Brady, then at me. "You're a mother, yes?"

"I am."

"How far would you go to save your child? Would you break the law? Would you spend your life savings? How far would you go, Agent Costa?" The desperation in her questions twisted my gut.

Her questions were fair, yet I didn't have an answer for any of them. I had been blessed with a healthy child and had never been pushed to make that decision. But I liked to think I would stay within the confines of the law. Still, one never knows for certain until confronted with the dilemma themselves.

"We don't fault you for trying to save your daughter, Mrs. Douglas," I replied. "We just want to know what happened. You've lied to us this entire time, and that's the part I don't understand. What happened to Scarlett? Why was she not taken to the emergency room when she needed medical care?"

Brady stood up and said, "Both parents are responsible for a child, for not bringing her to the emergency room. I'm going to go pick up Jack Douglas. Perhaps he'll talk since Mrs. Douglas refuses to."

I'd never seen Brady adopt the "bad cop" persona, and I had to admit he was pretty good at it.

"Wait, leave him out of it," May said.

"Why? He was also responsible for your daughter's well-being. Why should you sit here while he's out free?" I challenged.

Her face turned red and she screamed, "You think he's free? He's not free, I'm not free, we'll never be free!"

Her reaction took me by surprise. "What do you mean you'll never be free?" I said, with a sinking feeling.

"They threatened to kill us."

I glanced up at Brady, then back at May. "May, we can protect you, but only if we know what you need protection from."

She slumped in her chair. "Jack didn't want to do it. He said there had to be another way. We fought about it until he finally conceded. He didn't want to do it, it's not Jack's fault. It's mine. That's why I'm sitting here and he isn't." May was sobbing now and barely coherent.

"What did Jack not want to do?" I asked softly.

"We learned of a way to get a kidney for Scarlett. She needed one badly and we were so far down on the donor list. But the way we found wasn't legal."

"You paid somebody for a kidney?"

She nodded. "You have to understand. I was desperate. I just wanted my daughter to be better—she should have had her whole life ahead of her. The thought of losing her at sixteen... I couldn't let that happen. Jack knew it was a bad idea. He said that breaking the law wasn't the way to save our daughter."

"Jack was against the illegal transplant?" I tried to understand her perspective. "Why didn't he want Scarlett to receive a transplant through illegal means?" Apart from the obvious legal implications, there had to be something more.

"He didn't trust the people involved. He said that it wasn't as safe as receiving a transplant the legal way, through Scarlett's doctors."

"How did you learn about the illegal transplant?"

May shook her head. "I can't say."

"Where did she have the transplant?"

"I can't say," she said again, her voice just a ghost of a whisper.

"You can't or you don't want to?"

"Look, the person who told us about the transplant opportunity said we could never talk about it. We can't say where it happened, who the doctor was, how we learned of it. That Scarlett couldn't go to any doctor except theirs."

From the fear in her eyes, I had a feeling she wouldn't tell us anything that would point to who was responsible. "What can you tell us about the transplant? How much did it cost? Was the donor willing and compensated?"

She nodded, almost as if she were relieved to finally voice the words, get it off her chest, off her conscience. "We were told the donor was willing and grateful to earn money. The facility was clean with state-of-the-art equipment. Everyone was so nice. I never imagined it would end like this."

"How much did it cost?"

"It was a hundred and fifty thousand dollars. It drained our savings, and we had to take out a second mortgage on the house. It was a lot of money, but we were assured the donor was a great match and that Scarlett would survive, and everything would be great." Her voice wavered.

"What did you know about the donor?"

"Not much. Just that it was someone who wanted to do it. Said she needed the money."

"You never met her?" At least we knew the donor was a she. Although DNA would also tell us that.

"No."

"When did she have the transplant?"

"A week before she died."

Her words connected the dots to Scarlett's trip to Disneyland, perhaps the code for the transplant. Scarlett must've known she was having a transplant and it was the big surprise she wanted to share with Gabby. That she was going to be okay. It was all tragically ironic.

"When did she start showing signs her body was rejecting the new kidney?"

"A few days after. We knew something was wrong. She was weak, but we were told it was because she'd just had major surgery and her body needed time to heal. But she seemed to be getting weaker instead of stronger. We freaked out when we woke up and she was gone. That part is true."

"So, then what happened?"

"We couldn't find her, and... that's when we contacted the transplant team and they helped us find her."

She hesitated when she spoke, like she was leaving out key details of finding Scarlett.

"What are you not telling us, May?"

"We called them right away; said we were terrified she was missing. They helped us find her and they brought her back up to the house. She was so pale, I thought she was already dead, but she wasn't. They examined her and said she wasn't going to make it through the night. Jack and I, of course, wanted to take her to the emergency room right away, but they threatened to kill us if we tried to move her. They suggested we give her morphine to keep her comfortable, to pass peacefully." Tears were now streaming from May's eyes. "So I... I did. I gave it to her. I wanted her pain to stop. I didn't want her to suffer anymore."

Now inconsolable, Mrs. Douglas could no longer speak. I looked over at Brady. I believed her. She was finally telling us the truth, even though she was omitting key information about the people who had not only threatened her life, but who had also had a hand in her daughter's death.

May calmed herself and said, "You're right, I didn't bury her myself. They helped. I couldn't carry her. I wrapped her up and they took her down to her favorite tree. We said some prayers and went back inside to come up with a plan."

"A plan?"

"The team said we had to report her missing, but not right away. They said her doctors and the community would start asking questions about her whereabouts."

It was a horrible situation. Parents pushed to the brink to save their child, only to lose everything. "The team, as you refer to them, are they the ones who threatened your life?"

"If we ever told anyone, they said they'd kill both Jack and me. That's why I confessed, because if you would just close the case, then he'd be safe, and I would be too because I would be in jail and they would know I wasn't going to tell the authorities what had happened."

Her turmoil was palpable. In her mind, she had nothing left to lose except for Jack's life. She'd sacrificed herself for him.

"Thank you for telling us the truth."

"What's going to happen now?"

Brady said, "We'll have to discuss this. We're going to keep you in here for now. We need to decide how to go forward."

We'd keep May's disclosure quiet until we could get to Jack and see if he'd talk to us now we knew the truth. In return for his cooperation we would provide him and May protection. I wasn't exactly sure how but I suspected a call to the FBI's Organized Crime Task Force could help shed some light on how much of a threat Jack and May were really facing.

"You can't let them get to Jack. Please, make sure he's safe."

"We'll keep him and your secret safe, for now." I wasn't sure if May believed us, but at this point, she had no other option.

We had to find out who was behind Scarlett's transplant because they were not only responsible for Scarlett's death and the threats on her parents' lives, but my gut was telling me they were guilty of far more.

TWENTY-SIX

VAL

Since my release from the hospital, I had watched half the Harry Potter movies, been contacted by a serial killer, and found a missing girl. Talk about a week. Despite the craziness of it all, I felt pretty good, mentally and physically. The challenge of understanding the circumstances behind Scarlett's death propelled me forward. It was the fuel I needed to keep myself from obsessing about the Bear. There was nothing quite like solving such a dark puzzle. But my instinct and experience were telling me that Jack Douglas could be in trouble. If the fear was deep enough for May to confess to murdering her daughter, there was no telling what they'd do to Jack if they started to get nervous.

Brady and I agreed it was imperative we reach Jack before anything happened to him. But I couldn't help wondering what Brady and the sheriff's department had in store for May. On the drive through the pitch-black, two-lane highway toward Jack's motel, I said, "Do you plan to drop all charges against May?"

"I don't see why not. After we talk to Jack I'll call the district attorney and see how quickly we can get her released."

"Good. I don't think any jury is going to prosecute her for

the desecration of a corpse, considering she didn't really... she just buried her under her favorite tree. She's sympathetic and a victim, if what she says is true. I mean, it's so outlandish I don't think she's making it up."

"No, and whoever she is dealing with has her scared— scared enough to make a false confession."

It was good to know we were on the same page.

"This whole situation is nuts and it's strange it happened right when you returned home... You're either bad luck or good luck. I'm still trying to decide which."

I couldn't blame him. Was I bad luck? I didn't think so, but I replied, "I'll call the organized task force on Monday to get some help figuring out where the kidney came from and how we should handle it."

"Have you worked with them before?"

"Not much, but from what I understand about organized crime, they deal in just about anything that will turn a profit, including selling organs to the highest bidder. Preying on the desperate, it's sickening."

"Yeah, and what about the donors? How desperate were they to sell their kidneys to make some money?"

"Anyone selling their body or body parts likely doesn't have many other choices for survival."

I had driven past the motel so many times in my younger years. I admired the charming, two-story wood cabin aesthetic that featured a tree-lined backdrop.

Brady parked in front of the reception office and I followed him inside. Jack hadn't answered his cell phone on the drive over, so we had to find him the old-fashioned way. Behind the desk was a man I'd never met before; he was about sixty, with a terrible comb-over.

"Good evening, Dennis," Brady said.

"Deputy Tanner, what can I help you with?"

"We're looking for Jack Douglas."

At this, the clerk scrunched up his face. "You know I can't just give out motel room numbers unless you have a warrant."

Brady said, "No warrant, but you would be helping us out. Maybe you could point to which room is his?"

"Did you try calling him?"

"No answer."

"Well, do you know what car he's driving?" Dennis prodded.

I stepped forward, and said, "Blue Dodge pickup truck."

Dennis scratched the back of his head. "Then maybe you should look for a blue pickup truck and see which room it's parked in front of."

Sharing a glance with Brady, I asked, "Any idea where I can find a blue pickup truck in the parking lot?"

Dennis shrugged. "I might've seen one out back."

Brady nodded. "Thanks, Dennis."

We were about to turn and head out when Dennis pointed at me. "Do I know you?"

"I don't think so," I responded.

"This is Agent Val Costa, Sheriff Costa's eldest daughter."

Dennis nodded in recognition. "I see the family resemblance. I guess I moved to town after you graduated high school, but I knew your little sister Maxine. How is she doing?"

"She's doing very well," I responded. "She's still in the Army."

"Good for her. She was a good kid."

With approval from the clerk, I was sure Maxine would feel utterly fulfilled. "I'll be sure to tell her you said hi."

We exited the office with the jingle of the bell and headed toward the back of the motel. The parking lot was half full, but we spotted the blue pickup truck straight away. I knocked on the door. Glancing at my phone, I realized it was getting pretty late. It would make sense that Jack was already in bed. When there was no answer, I looked through the window, trying to see between the curtains, but I couldn't. "Try calling him again," I told Brady.

Brady dialed. I put my ear closer to the window, and a ringtone sounded inside the motel room. Four times it rang before silencing. Brady ended the call. "His phone's inside, but he's not answering. Let's go talk to Dennis again."

"What are you thinking?"

"I want to get inside. It doesn't make sense he's not answering. His car's parked out front."

"Are you thinking he may have hurt himself?"

It was possible. His wife was in jail for murder, his daughter was dead, and he had potential organ traffickers after him. Maybe he couldn't take it anymore.

Back at the office, Dennis raised his wiry brows. "Back already?"

"We need you to open Jack's room," Brady said.

"Deputy Tanner, you know I can't do that."

"We think he could be in danger. He's not answering his phone, his truck is parked out front, his cell phone's ringing, but he's not answering. I think something is wrong here, Dennis."

"Are you just saying that to get inside?" Dennis looked skeptical.

I stepped in. "Do we look like we're just saying that? A man could be in danger. He could be hurt. Do you want to be the reason we don't get him the help he needs?"

"Okay, but you're my witnesses. You said you think Jack could be in danger."

Brady stepped forward. "If you don't open it, we're going to break it down. How will your boss like that?"

"Okay. Okay. No need for that." Dennis relented, grabbed the ring of keys off the wall, and led us back to Jack's room.

He unlocked and opened the door and stepped back. "I'm not going in there."

Brady and I nodded, and I headed in. The room had two

queen-size beds, a dresser, a TV, and a small sitting area. Despite growing up in the town, I'd never been inside this motel before. The bed looked like it had been slept in, but it wasn't made. There were clothes on the bed, a suitcase on the ground. I made my way to the bathroom. On the vanity sat a toothbrush and toothpaste. There was no sign of life. I turned back around and spotted his cell phone on the coffee table in the sitting area. There was no Jack, no blood, and no sign of a struggle.

Back outside the room, I said to Dennis, "Have you seen Jack at all today?"

"Can't say that I have, but his room's in the back. We don't have a lot of visibility unless he comes by the office."

"Do you have security cameras?" I asked.

"Yeah," Dennis responded.

"Could we take a look at the footage?"

"Oh, yeah, of course. Come on back to the office with me," Dennis said, as he locked up the motel room door. "You really think something's up with Jack?" he asked.

"We don't know. But it would be useful to confirm when he left the motel."

"Well, it's been filming all day, so it'll take you a while," Dennis warned us.

It was what it was. I couldn't stay up all night looking at the video, but maybe the techs could help.

Back inside the office, Dennis said, "We make copies of all our surveillance and save it to the cloud. I can send you a link." He sat behind his computer and inputted some information.

I watched over his shoulder as he opened up the program and clicked on a camera. However, the screen was black. "Dang it, I think that camera's out again," he grumbled.

"Again?" I asked.

"Yeah, sometimes it goes out. Looks like it's out now," Dennis explained.

"All day?"

He didn't answer my question, and continued to click on the keyboard. A few moments later, he said, "Looks like it's been out all day."

Without another word, I exited the office and headed back toward Jack's room, looking up to see the location of the cameras. They were easy to spot, not exactly covert.

Brady hurried behind me. "What are you thinking?"

I pointed up at the camera. "Look at that, right there. Somebody cut the wire."

"Who would do that?" Brady asked, bewildered.

"Somebody who didn't want to be seen." A chill went down my spine as I voiced an unsettling realization. "Jack may be in real trouble."

"And so could May."

"Any way to get the DA to let her go tonight?"

"Don't you need to get home?"

"Don't you?" I countered.

"My kids are going to be here all week. You only have one more day before Harrison leaves, right?"

True.

Apparently, I was too quiet. Brady said, "I can handle it. The sheriff's department can handle it. Go home. Be with Harrison. We can meet up on Monday after he's safely on his flight back to DC."

Plus, I needed to put in a call to the FBI's Organized Crime Task Force and see what the latest deal was with organ trafficking. "Okay. But keep me updated, yeah?"

"Will do."

Was I being paranoid because of the Bear or was it really possible someone had taken Jack? There was no sign of a struggle, but if it was someone related to the illegal transplant organization that had taken him, maybe Jack had let him in and then was forced, at gunpoint, to leave with him. Would someone really take out Jack to silence him?

TWENTY-SEVEN

MAY

Back in my own clothes, I felt more like myself, and relieved to be out of jail. I never thought I could sink so low, but since the police knew the truth, they'd let me go. I wasn't sure I deserved that, but it was a relief nonetheless. I was looking forward to seeing Jack. It had been the loneliest forty-eight hours of my life. At home, I had Jack to share my grief, my emptiness with. He was all I had left.

The female officer escorted me out to the hallway, where Deputy Tanner stood with the district attorney. When I'd first met Deputy Tanner three years earlier, I'd thought he was kind and easy on the eyes with his rugged, sun-kissed look. But that night, all I could see was the man who had witnessed my downfall. Filled with shame, I said, "So, how do I get home?"

"I can take you, ma'am, but your house is still a crime scene. Where would you like me to take you?"

"I'd like to see Jack, but I need my car. Is my car a crime scene too?"

I was in over my head, and I had no idea how to get out of the situation. What would they think about me being released from prison? Would they think I'd talked, spilled secrets, and then come after me and Jack?

"No, it isn't. I can drive you to your car, and then you can head over to the motel. Get a room if you need to," Deputy Tanner suggested.

I found his statement odd. "Can't I just stay with Jack?"

"I can also escort you through the house to pick up a few things. We're not sure how much longer we'll need to keep your house secured."

It wasn't lost on me he had ignored my question. "I'd appreciate that, Deputy Tanner."

The district attorney with his piercing blue eyes stared at me, and I felt like my skin was crawling. He wanted to know everything, but I couldn't—I wouldn't—say. I needed to talk to Jack.

"Mrs. Douglas," the district attorney implored, "I urge you one more time to tell us what you know. We can put you in protective custody if you give us the details of your daughter's transplant. The who, the when, and how."

"Are you trying to get me killed?" I asked in disbelief.

"No, ma'am, I'm trying to make sure this doesn't happen to any more families."

I couldn't think about those other families until we were safe. All I could think about was getting to Jack. I needed Jack. I'd never missed him so much in my entire life. I had been sure I could cope and move on, but spending the rest of my life in prison would have broken me—and I was pretty close to that point already. "Deputy Tanner, please take me to my car."

"Yes, ma'am," he replied.

We drove in silence. Upon arrival, I studied our home that had once been a dream come true. That dream was gone. Crushed.

After being escorted through my house like a criminal, I sat behind the wheel of my car, with a bag full of clothes and toiletries in the back. I felt like a woman on the run—maybe I would be. My name had been in the newspaper, accused of killing my own daughter. I was sure my job was in jeopardy, and probably Jack's too. Pushing through the thoughts, I drove in silence to the motel, trying to focus on seeing Jack.

As I parked next to Jack's truck, I smiled for the first time in days. I was eager to put my arms around Jack. I knocked on his door, but he didn't answer. "Jack, it's me, May," I yelled through the door, and my heart raced upon hearing movement on the other side.

The door opened slowly, and our eyes met. My smile faded.

"Come in," he said.

I hurried inside, and he shut the door behind me. I put my hand to his face, and he winced. "What happened?"

"The same thing that will happen to you if you talk," he warned.

I turned around, and there he was—the man who had ruined our lives.

"What are you doing here?" I demanded, before looking at Jack again. "Are you okay?"

"I'm fine, May," he said, despite his swollen eye and cut lip.

"We need to sit down and have a serious conversation," the man said.

Jack put his hand on my shoulder, comforting me. "It's okay, May. Come on."

Once we were seated, the man asked, "What did you tell the police?"

"What do you mean? I didn't tell them anything."

"Why did they let you go?" he pressed.

"Because my story—what I told them about what happened to Scarlett—didn't match the physical evidence they said they have. They let me go. They couldn't charge me."

"What did you tell them about her transplant?"

"Nothing, just that she had one, and that's it."

"What did you tell them, May?" he asked again, his eyes boring into mine.

"I told them we paid for a transplant a week before she died, that it wasn't taking, and so she got very sick. The only thing we could do was make her comfortable before she passed, and we buried her under the oak tree. That's everything I told them."

"Did you name names, locations, how you learned about it?"

"Of course not. I won't. I never will. I swear it."

"That's really good to hear," he said, but there was no warmth in his words. "But know this—if I get a whiff that either one of you is talking to the police, remember that I can get to you. And it's not just me. I'm a nice person, right, Jack?"

"Yes, of course," Jack said.

"So nice that you beat up my husband?" I couldn't help myself.

"It wasn't him, May. They have people," Jack explained.

My heart nearly stopped.

Of course, they had people to do their dirty work.

I know one thing for sure—I'll never talk. Never.

TWENTY-EIGHT

VAL

"It's not too late to cancel, Mom." Harrison was still worried the Bear would come after him, or me, or my mother, or anybody else we cared about. But my knowledge of the Bear told me he would not target Harrison outside the US. If the Bear had sent me a letter from a few towns away, then he was in the country. Crossing the United States to DC for my son only to turn around less than a day later and follow him to Europe was improbable. I came to the conclusion that Harrison was safer away from me than near me—an awful realization for a mother. I used to believe he was always safest with me, but that was no longer my reality. And it wouldn't be true again until we knew the Bear's whereabouts, identity, and how to isolate him from the general population.

I feared his taste for taunting me might further fuel his twisted pleasures. So far, there had been only one note and not a peep since. I might have been overreacting, but there was also a chance I wasn't.

Once Harrison was out of the house, the guns wouldn't be locked in the safe anymore. And since we were in my car about to drive my son to safety, if the Bear came for me or my mom, we would do everything necessary to protect ourselves, even if that meant putting a bullet in his head.

Over the years, I had interviewed dozens of serial killers, intrigued by their abnormal thought processes and distorted instincts. But I was done with the Bear. I didn't want a lengthy discussion. I wanted him finished. We didn't need yet more data on another sadistic psychopath, he was free to go to hell.

"No, I think it's going to be fine," I said, trying to put Harrison's mind at ease. "And as we agreed, we'll check in twice a day. You can tell me all about your trip, and we can check on each other. Everything is going to be fine."

"But you can't be sure, can you?"

"No, but I'm relatively confident you'll have a wonderful time, and Grandma and I will be safe."

With that settled, I urged him to put on his seatbelt. I wouldn't see him for two months, the longest I had ever gone without seeing his smile. My boy, eighteen years old, was ready to take on the world with his best friends on a European adventure.

On the way to the airport, Harrison asked about Scarlett's case since her parents were no longer being charged with her death. Brady had called me earlier that day to inform me May was at the motel with Jack. It seemed my instincts were off once again, and Jack was just fine. To Harrison, I said, "Not to worry. I'm going to call the FBI and see if they can help figure out what happened to Scarlett. I'm certain this is a lot bigger than just Scarlett."

Harrison wrinkled his baby face. "Is it because Grandma was sheriff that both you and Aunt Maxine are so fearless?"

"What do you mean?"

"Well, Aunt Maxine is beyond tough, and Grandma's, well... she's Grandma, and you're hunting a serial killer and handling Scarlett's death investigation on your time off when you're supposed to be resting. Don't you ever worry it's all going to catch up with you?"

Not until he'd said it had I considered it.

Scarlett's case was an interesting one, and I was eager to get the task force's perspective. I hadn't worked much with organized crime, and the working theory was the surgery location was in Mexico, which complicated jurisdiction issues. If the theory proved to be correct, the Douglases had broken the law in Mexico, not the US. If anyone paid for the illegal sale of organs, it would be handled in the Mexican courts, so it would be a dance between authorities to try to bring the organ traffickers to justice.

Did Harrison have a point? Should I have been running away from the case instead of toward it? It wasn't like me to leave things unfinished.

About to rebut Harrison, my cell rang. It was Kieran.

With the controls of my steering wheel, I answered the call. "Hey Kieran, you're on speaker. Harrison's here."

"Hi, Kieran," Harrison said cheerfully.

"How's it going?"

I said, "We're on the way to the airport. Harrison is flying back to DC. He has to pack for his trip."

"Have fun, Harrison. Val, please take me off speaker. We need to talk."

"Thanks, Kieran," Harrison replied.

"Sorry, Kieran, I'm driving."

"There's an update on the note that was sent to you."

Glancing at Harrison, I said, "Hold on a second, Kieran. Hon, can you put your earbuds in?"

"Do I have to?"

"Please," I pleaded.

He mumbled, "Fine," and pulled them out of his backpack. I watched as he turned on his music. I gave him a thumbs-up and a smile, but he shrugged and stared out the window.

"Okay, Kieran, it's just us."

"The lab results on the envelope and the card are back," he said. "We got DNA and fingerprints, but neither is in any database."

"It's possible he's never been arrested."

"Maybe, maybe not, but there's more." He continued, "The team thought it was strange, and one of them realized the letter was sent overnight, which means he had to actually go into the post office to mail it."

"Security cameras," I whispered, my heartbeat quickening at the thought he might've finally messed up.

"Exactly. We've taken a look at the security footage, and it's a bit puzzling."

"How so?" I asked, bracing for another scenario where the cameras had been disabled.

"I don't think it's our guy," Kieran stated cryptically.

"Why not?"

"I can send you the video for you to verify, but based on your description of the perpetrator, he's a Caucasian male in his late thirties to early forties, right?"

"That's correct."

"On the security footage, the person who sent the letter is a Black male, late teens to early twenties."

My mind raced. Was it a hoax? Why would that person do this to me? And who? Possibly a friend of Harrison's? That didn't even make sense. Harrison didn't know anybody on the West Coast. He was East Coast born and raised. "Any idea who this guy is?"

"Security footage from the parking lot picked up the tags on his car. Agents are on their way to his house to question him."

"Who is he?"

"Not sure, but it's not the Bear."

As I shook my head trying to process this, I wondered why a person would send me a note like that. Was it possible it was someone who was genuinely happy I'd found Scarlett? Or a member of the organ-trafficking team? Maybe it was an entirely different criminal sending me messages.

"Are you still there, Val?"

"Yeah, I'm just trying to figure out what this means. Why would a teenager send me a note?" I voiced my confusion.

"The team is discussing it and will know more after the interview, which should be any minute now."

"Where does he live?"

"Two towns away from you in Redford. He lives only a few miles from the post office that he sent it from. The team thinks he is either playing a trick on you, or he really was happy you helped solve the Scarlett Douglas missing persons case, or..."

"He is working with the Bear and is therefore an unknowing accomplice."

"Exactly. Like I said, we'll know more pretty soon, but I wanted to give you an update."

"Thanks, Kieran," I said, wrapping up the conversation.

"Get your son to the airport safe, and we'll talk more. I'll call as soon as we're done interviewing the man who mailed you that note."

"Thanks." I ended the call and patted Harrison's arm.

Clearly annoyed at having been excluded from the conversation, he took out his earbuds. "Can I be a big boy and listen now?" he said, a hint of sarcasm in his voice, something I'd become accustomed to during his teenage years.

"Yes, dear. It was an update on the letter that was sent to me. It turns out it wasn't the Bear who sent it."

"So, he's not coming after you?"

That was a positive way of looking at things, although I wasn't convinced. But if it made Harrison feel better, I could go with that. "That's right, so you can go on your trip, happy as a clam, free as a bird, enjoying your youth."

"And with Dad's credit card," he added with a smirk.

"And with your dad's credit card. I was thinking maybe once I finish up the cases, I can join you in Europe if you're okay with it. Maybe just a quick vacation, spend a week, maybe Grandma would want to come out too."

"That'd be super cool, Mom. But you wouldn't, like, stay with us, right?" he asked, trying to be diplomatic.

"I think Grandma and I would get our own hotel room," I reassured him.

"Cool. Yeah, that'd be so cool, Mom. I'd love to vacation with you when you're not working a case."

I smiled at his comment, even if it stung a little. He had a point. Our time off together was often spent with me trying to solve cases, and that wasn't exactly how I'd envisioned our mother–son time. I would definitely have to make the trip a priority. Harrison deserved that. "You've got yourself a deal."

An hour later, I hugged my son in front of the terminal before he hurried off toward security.

With Harrison safe inside the airport, my hunt for those responsible for Scarlett's botched transplant would continue. And I had an appointment with the man who'd sent me the note. From the car, I called Kieran back. "Kieran. I want the address of the person who sent the letter."

"Agents are at the house now."

"I want to talk to him."

Kieran sighed. "Okay, but I'll ask the agents to stay until you get there."

If Kieran thought I needed a babysitter, fine. "Works for me."

TWENTY-NINE

VAL

Sitting across from eighteen-year-old Tyler Walker, I studied the beads of sweat on his forehead and his shaking hands. "Hi, Tyler. My name is Valerie Costa. You can call me Val. There's no reason to be nervous, I just have a few questions."

His brows raised, likely surprised that he was sitting across from the person he had sent the note to. "Okay, but I already told the other agents everything," he stuttered.

I glanced over at my fellow agents and back at Tyler Walker. "I need to understand why you sent me a letter in the mail, Tyler."

"I didn't know it was a federal offense to send a letter," he retorted.

Is that really how this kid wanted to play it? "I didn't say it was, but we're curious why you would send a federal agent an anonymous note."

"I just... I thought it was cool you helped out with the missing persons case, that's all."

"How did you hear about Scarlett's case?"

"I have a friend who lives in Rosedale, and he told me about it."

As he spoke, his eyes darted away, and he fidgeted incessantly. The kid was lying. But why? "What's your friend's name?"

"Mark."

"Mark...?" I questioned.

"Mark Smith."

He was a terrible liar.

"Tyler, I have a son your age. I'm familiar with teenagers *and* I'm an FBI profiler. So, I can assess pretty quickly you're nervous, you don't have any priors so you're probably a good kid, but most importantly, you're lying through your teeth. And unless you start talking to us, I'm afraid your squeaky-clean record is going to have a few marks on it. Is that what you want?"

"No, I don't want that."

"So, when the agents take your laptop—you do have a laptop?" He nodded in affirmation. "That's what I thought. You see, they'll go through your search history, every keystroke that you have made on that computer. Even if you deleted stuff, we can still recover it. Did you know that?"

With eyes the size of saucers, he said, "No, I didn't."

The front door opened and a woman bearing a striking resemblance to Tyler entered, bringing the conversation to a halt.

Shocked at the sight of us, she said, "What is going on here? Who are you and why are you in my house?"

"Is that your mother?" I asked Tyler, to which he nodded. I straightened and introduced myself. "Mrs. Walker, my name is FBI Special Agent Valerie Costa and these two agents are my colleagues. We're here because we need to speak with your son about a letter he sent me." I added a few more details, like the fact I didn't think her son was being honest with us.

Mrs. Walker glared at her son and said, "Tyler, you better

talk to these people and tell them what they need to know. We raised you better than that," she chided.

"Mom, I can't," he mumbled.

I glanced over at the two agents, who were as surprised by the admission as I was. But if it was as I suspected, Tyler wasn't behind the letter. He had been put up to it. But by whom? I had a bad feeling about that.

"Tyler, you need to tell us the truth. Did somebody ask you to send me that letter?" I pressed.

At his mother's stern look, he caved. "Okay, I'll tell you what I know. I saw a Craigslist ad to send a letter to a certain address for five hundred bucks, no questions asked. The only stipulation was once I responded to the ad I wasn't allowed to tell anybody about it. I thought it was my lucky day, but things got weird. Still, I did it."

"I'm going to need to see the Craigslist listing and all communications you had with this person," I said.

"The listing isn't up anymore, but I can show you the emails between us."

Tyler's mother said, "Go get your laptop."

I nodded my approval.

Tyler hurried back into the depths of the home. Mrs. Walker said, "I'm so sorry for whatever this is. But not to worry, he will cooperate."

"I appreciate that."

Back with his laptop, Tyler set it on the coffee table, lifted the lid, and opened up his emails. "Here."

Kneeling in front of the computer, I studied the first communication. Tyler had responded to an ad that read, "Easy $500. Need to have a letter sent overnight, to be completed today. Offer expires in thirty minutes."

After reading it aloud to the other agents, I turned to Tyler. "And you responded within thirty minutes to the posting?"

Tyler nodded. "I thought it was my lucky day, but as I said, things got a little weird. But I still did it."

Nothing in this life comes for free. A lucky break could be just the opposite. "What do you mean, weird?"

"Keep reading. He said he'd kill me if I ever told anyone. I was supposed to delete the emails but I was a little freaked by it, so I kept them."

Returning my focus to the computer screen, I read the poster's responses aloud. "Glad to hear it. There's a few rules. One, you can never speak about this, and after it's done you have to delete your emails pertaining to this job. If you break the rules, I'll find you and slit your throat while you're sleeping."

Tyler said, "I didn't know if he was for real or not, but it was five hundred bucks and I figured, how would he ever know who I was?"

There were definitely ways to learn Tyler's identity if the poster was tech savvy. At least Tyler had the good sense to keep the emails which would allow us to figure out who'd requested the letter be sent to me. "We need to keep your laptop for a little while. We'll try to get it back to you as soon as we can."

"Oh, okay."

"Thank you for your cooperation, Tyler. We'll be in touch."

"But what if he comes after me?" he asked, visibly scared.

I pulled out my business card and handed it to him. "If anything out of the ordinary happens, call me anytime, day or night. I'm just a few towns away. Stay vigilant, lock your doors, don't talk to strangers in real life or on the Internet, and stay off social media until you hear from me again."

"Now you have us worried," Mrs. Walker said, her eyes wide.

"Ma'am, you're smart to be worried. There are a lot of dangerous people out there."

Agent Barnes, a young local agent, said, "Special Agent Costa, can I speak with you for a minute?"

"Excuse me," I replied, turning my attention to Agent Barnes and his eager brown eyes.

"Do you really think it's necessary to freak out the entire family?" he asked in a hushed tone. As if I needed to be mansplained how to do my job.

"I think they need to be on guard. I mean, it seems unlikely the Bear would come after this kid, and it's not consistent with his profile, but he's never contacted a survivor either. If it's the Bear, he's going off-script. And he's already killed fifteen people, that we know of. We should take every precaution. Don't you think?"

Agent Barnes paled. "Do you think they should have surveillance on their house? In case the Bear comes after him?"

"That's not a bad idea. I'll put a call in to Kieran."

"We could have some local agents keep an eye out for the next couple of days."

"Great."

"And we can send the laptop out to our lab. Extract the hard drive, check the IP address of the poster. Find this guy."

"Excellent."

Satisfied with the plan, I stepped back over to the Walkers. "Like I said, we'll be back in a few days to return your laptop. Stay vigilant. A few agents will be watching the house for the next few days, just as a precaution. Thank you for talking to us."

They didn't need to know any more details, and telling them I thought young Tyler had been working with a serial killer wouldn't help matters.

The Walkers simply nodded as we exited their home.

In that moment, I realized this could've been a test by the Bear. How quickly would the FBI respond to threats against one of their agents? What was our reach? If this was a game the Bear wanted to play, I thought, *Game on.*

THIRTY

AVA

Staring at the tiny screen, I studied Mia's face. Her bleached blonde hair showed her dark roots against pale skin. She was smiling, but her eyes were haunted. She hadn't posted anything since she'd stopped coming to the Grace Center more than a month ago. My gut stirred. I believed something was wrong, but her absence and silence on social media almost confirmed it. Having listened to enough true crime podcasts, I knew that when a young person stopped posting on social media and hadn't been seen for a while by anyone, it was a bad sign. Mia used to post almost every day, different artwork she'd found around the city. An aspiring artist herself, she wanted to be the next Banksy, a renowned street artist, although she'd said she didn't want to be anonymous. Mia wanted to show the world she had worth.

I couldn't find Abby's social media. I was certain she had one; most kids did, and they all had smartphones. Perhaps she went under an alias online; maybe she didn't want her family to find her. I didn't blame her, but I wished I could find it to see if there was someone in her life I didn't know about. Like the boyfriend with the gold sedan.

Ethan's social media was similar to Mia's. He had only been gone a week but his last Instagram post was also from a week ago. A selfie of him smiling, standing right in front of the center, throwing up a peace sign. His light brown hair and hazel eyes shone—he had a light about him, an aura of hope. I knew his life on the streets wasn't easy. He did what he had to in order to survive, not because he enjoyed that life. The opportunity that had presented itself before he went missing must have seemed monumental. There were two missing teens that hadn't touched their social media since they'd stopped coming to the Grace Center. Three teens that nobody was looking for. I had a sinking feeling that whoever had them knew nobody would be, and that was almost worse than anything they could possibly do to them.

I decided to make another attempt to get the police to take this seriously. Handing out flyers hadn't brought me any closer to finding out what had happened to them. While I had scoured every possible area, there were some places I preferred not to visit alone.

Most of the street kids knew me from the Grace Center and understood I wasn't trying to hassle anybody. However, not everybody had a kind heart, especially those who preyed on street children, using them to make money or to keep them addicted, helping them evade the pain and reality of their lives.

Shaking off the dreadful thought, I turned to Loretta, or Lori as we all knew her. She was an older woman with a hardened look to her. "Lori, check this out." I showed her Mia's and Ethan's social media profiles and how they hadn't posted anything since their disappearance.

Lori nodded. "I hear you," she said. "Some of our kids do just up and leave, but you're right, this feels different. And those three were a few of the ones I thought could break out of the life, you know?"

I did. If they dabbled in illegal activities, it was out of

survival. If they had been born into a different family that loved them fully, I wouldn't even know them. They'd be in school planning for their future, not missing and forgotten about. "I want to go down to Echo Park, find out if anybody's seen them."

"You're not going by yourself?" Lori said.

"I was hoping maybe you or Danny would come with me."

"How about this," she proposed. "We go between lunch and dinner; James can handle things around here."

"Let's do it," I agreed, ready to take the next step.

On the drive to Echo Park, I called Detective Rogers.

"Detective Rogers here, how can I help you?"

"Hi, Detective Rogers. This is Ava from the Grace Center. I've come to you a couple of times about three missing teens: Mia, Abby, and Ethan."

"Ah, yes. Did you find something new?"

"Maybe. I found two of their social media accounts, and neither one of them has posted since they went missing. That's a pretty good indicator they're missing, right?"

"Or they lost their phones or created new accounts under different aliases."

Seriously? I thought it was a bad sign, but he didn't seem to think so. Why would they create new accounts? They didn't have parents going through their Instagram accounts, inspiring them to create "finstas," or fake Instagram accounts, for their families to see, while the real ones were under usernames only their friends knew about.

"Detective, with all due respect, I think this is a glaring sign that something bad has happened to those kids."

"I suppose. We'll keep an eye out. If we catch any sign of them, we'll let you know."

"Could you add them to the missing persons database? Maybe someone's seen them?"

He sighed and then said, "Sure. If you come into the station, we can file an official report." I couldn't tell if he was patronizing me, knowing that I wouldn't let this go, or if he was starting to realize something was genuinely wrong.

"Okay, a couple of my coworkers from the Grace Center and I are heading to Echo Park to see if anybody's seen them there. We have flyers with their pictures on them. We need to find them, Detective."

"Like I said, after you're done with that, come by the station. We'll write up a missing persons report for all three."

"Thank you, Detective."

I ended the call and turned to Danny, one of the newer employees at the center. "They're finally taking this seriously."

"It's about time," Lori remarked.

I shared the sentiment.

We parked and headed toward the encampment. Tents were everywhere, lined up close by. It was a popular place for the unhoused to set up and build their own community. On the outskirts of the city, they still had views of the lake, the majestic mountains, and the high-rises in the distance.

Echo Park was a bit far from the Grace Center, but it was the one place I hadn't handed out flyers yet. Surely, some of the residents would care and understand our concern.

We began asking around. The first man we met shook his head after glancing at the photos. The process continued like that for thirty minutes. I was becoming discouraged; nobody had seen them. Danny and Lori and I met up.

"Everyone I talked to said they haven't seen them," Danny reported.

"Same here. And I think it's weird," Lori chimed in. "If the kids were really moving on, this is where I would assume they would've gone."

Just then, a woman who looked to be in her early twenties

rushed toward us. "Hi, I heard you were looking for some missing teens?"

My heart rate sped up. "Yes, have you seen them?" I handed her the flyer, showcasing all three faces.

Her eyes scanned it, then she shook her head. "No, I haven't. I'm so sorry. Let me start over. My name is Joanna and my sister, Tina, is missing. She's seventeen, and I've been looking for her too. She's been missing for six weeks. Not a peep on social media, none of her friends have seen or talked to her. All communication just suddenly stopped."

Our eyes met, and she continued, "I was talking to some people who suggested I should talk to you. They thought we could share information, see if there are any similarities between my sister's disappearance and your three missing teens."

"Sure, absolutely," I agreed. "I'm Ava, this is Danny and Lori." Holding up the flyers again, I said, "This is Mia, this is Abby, and this is Ethan. They're all missing. Mia has been gone for five weeks, Abby two weeks, and Ethan a week."

"And my sister, Tina, has been missing for six weeks. A week before Mia. Tina told me she had a big thing coming up that was going to make her a bunch of money. I cautioned her. I told her nothing comes for free and when something sounds too good to be true, it probably is."

My heart sank.

"What is it?" Joanna asked, her dark eyes filling with concern.

"These kids, they used to come to the Grace Center. Each one of them told me about something big too. Then, they were never heard from again, except for when Ethan told me he had talked to Mia and Abby and not to worry. He also told me he had a big opportunity, but then disappeared."

Joanna grew serious. "They're connected... They have to be, right?"

She was right. Somebody was targeting the kids on the street. But was her sister a street kid? "Did your sister have any boyfriends? Did she live at home? Did she live in the encampment?"

"She only came into the encampment periodically. Sometimes she would come home, fight with our mom, then leave again. She didn't have a steady boyfriend, no."

"Okay, well, I just talked to the detective that I've been working with, and he's finally agreed to open missing persons reports for Mia, Abby, and Ethan. Do you have one for Tina?"

"Of course, not that they've done anything with it though."

"Well, now that we have four, they'll have to listen to us."

"You're right. The squeaky wheel gets the oil. We can be that big squeaky wheel," Joanna said with a renewed sense of hope.

"We're heading down to the station now. Let's exchange information, and we'll catch up."

"That's great. Thank you so much. God bless you for being out here looking for these kids. Tina is my sister, but you're just out here looking for strangers."

"They aren't strangers to me. They are kids who, if they'd been given a different life, could be moving on to great things, not disappearing with nobody looking for them."

"They're lucky to have you."

If that were true, would they be missing?

THIRTY-ONE

VAL

The small conference room held a round table, four uncomfortable chairs, and whiteboard paint on the walls. Faint etchings of previous notes hadn't been completely erased. The window on the door was the only view to the rest of the sheriff's department. Seated across from me were Brady and Lucy, a member of the sheriff's department's research team.

I said, "The FBI's Organized Crime Task Force is doing us a huge favor by taking a call with us to discuss Scarlett's transplant case."

Although we had solved Scarlett's missing persons investigation, we still needed to know who was threatening May and Jack, and see if we could hold those criminals responsible for Scarlett's death and keep the Douglases safe. I had an unnerving feeling about the case. From the research that I'd conducted online, it seemed like a lot of puzzle pieces just didn't fit.

"Hopefully, they can help us," I said, voicing my optimism. "This is a strange one."

"I agree," Brady responded. He turned to Lucy. "And Lucy,

were you able to make any headway on the research into the Douglases' financials and any travel?"

"Yeah, I think I might've found some interesting things," Lucy said, her eyes alight with anticipation.

"Awesome." I was excited. The Polycom lit up. "It's them," I said, picking up the call. "Hello, this is Special Agent Valerie Costa."

"Hey, Costa, this is Agent St. Claire," came the voice from the other end. "I hear you guys have an interesting case there in Red Rose County."

"We do. With me is Deputy Brady Tanner and our researcher Lucy Kenyon. All three of us have been working the case."

"Your message contained interesting details. Something doesn't seem right. Do you mind going over the details again?" St. Claire asked.

I wasn't surprised he was baffled by the details. The message I'd left him was lengthy, and the case was as convoluted as it was intriguing. I began to explain. "We discovered Scarlett Douglas, aged sixteen, buried about a mile from her parents' home. She died from an infection related to a rejected organ transplant. We got the parents to talk, and they revealed they had paid for a transplant outside of the normal system. They paid a hundred and fifty thousand dollars, but were told if they breathed a word about any of it, the organ suppliers would come after them and kill them."

After a moment's silence, St. Claire finally spoke. "So, I did get all the details right. That is strange."

"How so?" I asked, although I had my suspicions.

"Well, it's strange the parents would be threatened. It's not illegal in the United States to go to another country for surgery or a transplant. It's highly unusual for these people to threaten the Douglases unless they didn't actually go to another country for the transplant."

I glanced at Lucy, who looked like she was bursting to share something. "That was my suspicion as well," I confessed. "But is that something the task force has seen?"

"Honestly, no," St. Claire confessed. "And I'm surprised by it, which is why I had you recap the details. The vast majority of organ trafficking happens in other countries. These traffickers prey on the less fortunate, maybe giving them around one thousand to five thousand dollars for an organ such as a kidney, but then jack up the price for the recipients. It sounds like that's what happened to Scarlett Douglas' parents, as a hundred and fifty thousand dollars is a high price to pay for a kidney transplant."

"Mrs. Douglas said that the facility was clean and looked state-of-the-art," I said.

"This is very concerning," St. Claire commented.

I nodded, although he couldn't see me. "What are you thinking?"

"If this is happening in the US, it's not on our radar. Maybe it's a new operation or maybe it's been going on for a while. But it's something the FBI Organized Crime Task Force needs to be looking into."

"Absolutely," I responded, before glancing at Lucy. "Lucy, did you find anything interesting in your research that would support the theory that the transplant was conducted inside the United States?"

She nodded and opened her file folder. "Hi, I'm Lucy. So, I was doing research on any travel movements of the Douglases before Scarlett had her transplant. I didn't find any record of them passing through any border checkpoints, not to Mexico, and not to Canada. And there were no flight reservations."

"Scarlett had to have had the transplant in the US then," St. Claire concluded.

I looked at Brady and he added, "Maybe in California. It makes sense. As soon as Scarlett went missing, they said they called the team who did the transplant and they helped look for Scarlett. They'd need to be somewhat local to be able to arrive quickly to search for her."

"Did Mr. and Mrs. Douglas say who told them about the transplant opportunity?" St. Claire asked.

"They won't say," I replied. "They claim the organ team will kill them if they do."

"What about the financial statements, Lucy? Did you look into those?" St. Claire asked.

She nodded, then seemed to remember he couldn't see her and verbally confirmed, "Yes. Mr. and Mrs. Douglas, or I should say Mrs. Douglas, said they had to refinance their home and clean out their savings to pay for it. But what I found in their financials was that, yes, they definitely withdrew a hundred and fifty thousand dollars, but it wasn't all at once. When they had to refinance their home, they put money into multiple accounts. In the weeks before Scarlett had her surgery, they had a total of twenty bank accounts, which is highly unusual."

"A bank allowed them to open twenty accounts in two weeks?" St. Claire sounded as surprised as I felt.

Lucy shook her head. "No, it was five different banks. Each bank had four different accounts: one in May's name and one in Jack's, and both a checking and savings account. All of the accounts are almost empty, with a series of withdrawals averaging seventy-five hundred each, totaling a hundred and fifty grand. Now, the bank accounts are worth approximately five hundred bucks. All twenty of them combined."

St. Claire put into words what I was thinking. "Whoa, that is some sophisticated money laundering."

"It's unusual," I added.

St. Claire continued, "They're working with a sophisticated team. They guided the Douglases through every single step of how to filter the money without having to report the withdrawals to the IRS, staying comfortably under the ten-thousand-dollar limit. And they threatened to kill them if they ever spoke about the transactions."

"So, St. Claire, have we got your attention?" I asked, hoping the bizarre details were enough to pique his interest and help us with the investigation.

"Absolutely. I need to run this by my team. Let's keep in touch. Anything you find, please share. This could be a continuation of a Mexican organ-trafficking ring that's moving into California, or a brand-new, opportunistic, homegrown team. It's big business, and I guess I'm a little surprised it's taken this long to get to the US. Nice work, team. You may have made the discovery of the year."

"Now we just have to find the traffickers," I said, contemplating the magnitude of the task ahead.

"That's the hard part, especially if the Douglases aren't talking. You may want to go at them again now that you have more information," St. Claire advised.

"We're headed to their motel room next," I said.

We agreed to keep in contact with St. Claire throughout the investigation and ended the call.

Turning to Lucy, I said, "Excellent work, Lucy." She was young, in her thirties, but clearly was highly skilled.

"This is crazy, right?" she responded, still looking a bit shocked.

"You don't get this kind of stuff in Red Rose County very often, do you?" I asked.

She shook her head. "No, but I used to work for the NYPD, so this isn't my first rodeo. But it's definitely the first time I've seen something like this in Red Rose County."

"I'm certainly glad you're on the team," I admitted, grateful for her experience. Who knew? I had a feeling Lucy was someone I needed to get to know better.

Brady chimed in, "Agreed. Val, are you ready to go talk to May and Jack?"

"Yes, sir."

Since I hadn't heard from my own team about whether they'd been able to track the IP address for the poster of the Craigslist ad who'd sent me the note, I was grateful for the distraction. It was frustrating waiting, but one thing at a time. I could only control what was in my control, and what I could control was questioning May and Jack about the people who'd likely hastened the death of their daughter and threatened their lives. I only hoped they would finally cooperate with us and help put those people behind bars.

THIRTY-TWO

VAL

On the drive to the motel, Brady said, "We need to figure out a way to make them talk."

"Well, if they have enough information to bring down the organization behind the illegal transplants, the state's attorney could use them as material witnesses and would likely put them into protective custody."

"Like witness protection?"

"If they can help bring down the organization, then probably."

"Maybe we should offer the deal to May and Jack, even though it's not certain yet. At the very least, we could protect them here in our own town, right?" Brady asked.

It was something I had been mulling over. They needed protection. And we had an extra room in Mom's house. Of course, Mom would have to agree. I wasn't sure how she would feel about the Douglas family staying with us, but she was very community-oriented and probably wouldn't bat an eyelid at the suggestion. If the Douglases stayed with us, they would have two armed guards—Mom and me—plus, we'd had surveillance cameras installed at the property. Not that we needed additional threats against us. We already had our hands full with the threat of the Bear; we probably didn't need a bunch of mobsters trying to get at us too.

Not to mention we didn't know anything about the organ transplant team. It could be a vast organization or a small group. Super dangerous or all bark and no bite. But if they were as dangerous as a typical human-trafficking ring, they would eliminate May and Jack without hesitation if they thought the Douglases might talk to law enforcement. Personally, I thought they should already have been in protective custody; right now they were sitting ducks at a motel with a non-functioning surveillance camera pointed directly at their room.

"I could ask my mom and see if she's okay with a few house guests for a while."

"Knowing your mom, she would probably agree."

He wasn't wrong. It was weird that Brady and I had once been so close but now I felt like I barely knew him. Yet he seemed to remember our teen years and my mom with such clarity. For me, it felt like the twenty years had put a huge gap between us. And I thought of him as more of a question mark than a close friend. Maybe we could get back to that.

"How are the kids?"

"They're doing well. They're having a blast going on hikes, watching movies, and indulging in junk food—the fun dad stuff."

"Sounds nice. Harrison's father and I split custody so neither of us is considered all that fun."

"How long ago did you break up?" Brady asked.

I guessed, in some ways, Brady and I had become partners when we'd started working on the Scarlett Douglas missing persons case, and we were hunting an organ-trafficking ring together. It was inevitable that the subject would come up. "Eight years now." Not wanting to get into the details, I shifted the ball to his court. "How about you? How long ago did you split up? Seems like it was recent?"

"It was three years ago."

"Sorry to hear that. It's never easy."

"No, it's not. But on the bright side, I moved back to Rosedale and get to have a better life than I did living in the city. I never thought I'd return, as I'm sure you can imagine. When we were kids we thought it was so boring, and wanted to move on to bigger and more exciting things. I found that I actually like the slower pace and the beautiful scenery. I get to hike every day for exercise—you can't beat that. You'll never see me back in a gym. Plus, I get to share all of it with my kids," he added, happily.

Good for him. "I can only imagine raising kids here. But now I can see how it could be nice to know your neighbors and know there isn't too much trouble for the kids to get into." Not that Harrison had ever really been in trouble.

"I see that. I think that's why Scarlett's case seems so devastating to the community. I can only imagine losing a child like that, and I have to wonder what it's doing to May and Jack's relationship. It's hard enough having healthy kids, let alone losing one. Now that she's gone, May blames herself. Maybe Jack blames her too."

It made sense the way Jack had allowed her to shoulder the blame, but it seemed clear May loved him fiercely and would do anything to protect him. Maybe we could use that against them. It was sort of gross to pit a set of devastated parents against one another, but if it meant those criminals couldn't hurt anyone else, it would be worth it. "Well, hopefully they'll start talking to us because if they don't, we don't have many other options for finding out who's behind this."

Brady parked in front of the Douglases' motel room.

We exited the SUV and made our way to the door. I knocked and took a step back. The sound of movement inside confirmed at least one of them was in. Both May and her husband worked remotely, so technically it was their workday and they should be in. The door opened, and May looked startled.

"Agent Costa, Deputy Tanner, what can we do for you?"

"We've learned some new information and would like to ask you and Jack a few follow-up questions."

"Oh, okay. We'll come out there."

Brady and I exchanged glances. "Is Jack in there with you?"

"Yes, of course." She poked her head back inside the motel room and told Jack to come outside to speak with us.

A few moments later, Jack appeared, sporting a bruised eye, a cut on his eyebrow, and bruising on his arm. Someone had gotten to him. May gently closed the kelly-green door behind her, not engaging the lock.

"What did you want to talk to us about?" she asked as if there was nothing new to report to us—like her husband being beaten up.

I ignored May's question and focused on Jack. "What happened to your face?"

"Tripped and fell. I've been so distracted these days. Just clumsy," he said, avoiding my gaze.

"Did you see the fall, May?"

"No, it was before I got back."

Jack wouldn't look at me.

"We've been in touch with the FBI's Organized Crime Task Force, and we've conducted a thorough review of your financials and your travel records. We believe that Scarlett's transplant happened here in California. Is that correct?"

May balled up her fists and said, "You know I can't tell you that. I can't say anything, and I won't say anything." Her eyes practically bulged out of her head.

"May, we can protect you. Working with the FBI, we can talk about making a deal to put you into protective custody. In the meantime, I can check with my mom and see if you can stay with us. We can protect you, May."

"No, you can't. Cops always say they can protect you. I've seen on TV how witnesses end up dead. All we have left is each other, don't you get that? I won't let anything happen to Jack. Scarlett's gone; there's nothing else we can do for her. I really wish you would just leave us alone so we can grieve in peace and get through this." Her voice and her body shook with emotion.

I turned to Jack. "Do you have anything to say about this?"

"Just leave us be," he echoed.

"Why are you protecting these people? Like you said, the only thing you have left is each other. We may be able to relocate you together, make you safe, change your name. They'll never find you."

"In exchange for our careers, our community, everything? Just gone? And they may still come after us?" May seemed determined to remain silent.

Jack added. "No, it's too big of a risk. We have nothing more to say."

Maybe we could go after Jack. He seemed less insistent.

The faint sound of the bathroom door opening inside the motel room caught my attention. "Is there somebody else in the room with you?"

Jack said, "No."

A quick glance back at Jack revealed his terror. May looked scared too. Somebody was inside the motel room, and they didn't want to tell us who. "May I come inside?"

"No, and you're not allowed to enter unless you have a warrant."

I glanced around the parking lot, looking for any vehicles out of place. We needed to record every single license plate, run them through the system, and find out who was visiting May and Jack Douglas. Perhaps the same person who'd roughed up Jack and given him the bruises on his face.

"May, Jack, I think the two of you are making a huge mistake. If this group of individuals is threatening you now and they're as dangerous as you believe, they may kill you just to keep you quiet. If you come with me now, I promise I will keep you safe." I could ask Mom's forgiveness later.

May stiffened. "No, please leave." She turned around and went back inside. Jack followed, keeping his eyes to the ground as he shut the door behind them.

The top lock engaged.

"Brady, get the license plates of every vehicle in this lot; we'll run them. We need to know who was inside that room."

"I'm on it," he said, hurrying toward the first vehicle.

I stayed by the door, straining to hear anything that may be going on inside, but they were silent. They likely knew I was still there.

Glancing up at the broken surveillance camera, I understood why the wires had been cut. Somebody had come in, threatened Jack, and that same person may be inside the room. I had no jurisdiction, no right to break into the motel room to see who it was. They were allowed visitors, and whoever was inside couldn't be held liable for anything without evidence or proper search and seizure.

We had to identify the visitor, make a plan, and tread carefully. The license plates could be our first lead. We could also surveil the motel to see who went in and out.

THIRTY-THREE

MAY

"Who was that?" the man asked, peeking through the blinds.

"Agent Costa and Deputy Tanner," Jack replied, his voice shaky.

"What did they want?"

"They said they think Scarlett's transplant took place in California. They suggested we should talk to them, said they could put us in protective custody."

He approached me, shaking his head. "I'm telling you, they cannot protect you from these people, do you understand?"

"Are you sure? She seemed convincing." And I couldn't let them get to Jack again. They'd roughed him up as a message. *Well, message received, loud and clear.*

"You have to trust me one more time. This isn't my call, and I'm sorry that I got you all mixed up in this, but they won't hesitate to kill you if they think you're talking to law enforcement. Frankly, at this point, you're lucky to be alive. The best advice I can give you is to run. Or at least make it appear you are on the run until the case goes cold. You both work remotely, so as soon as they release the crime scene, sell the house and find a new place to start over. But as of right now, you need to get out of town, maybe to another state that's not too far. Washington's nice, or Oregon."

Staring at Jack's brutalized face, I had to agree with him. They'd only returned Jack if I promised to keep my mouth shut. We weren't safe staying here, and I didn't think the police could help us.

"Okay, we'll leave."

"Make sure they're not following you," he warned.

"We'll have to pack up. If they ask, we'll say we're just going on vacation or just need to get away from this town. We've always liked Oregon."

"It's not too far north."

I thought about the prospect. We still had some credit left on our credit cards. We could charge our expenses for a while until we received our paychecks. I never thought that in my forties I'd be living paycheck to paycheck, but Scarlett's transplant had drained us, and we didn't even have Scarlett anymore. We didn't have our home. Our community. Why was I fighting to stay here? My intuition told me it was all over. Our only hope of a new life was to flee.

I tried to think back to when all of this went so wrong. It had started when he'd told me he knew of a way to help Scarlett. That help had me and Jack running for our lives, ditching the town we'd raised our daughter in. Would it be temporary? Or was everything we had once cherished fading away?

"For what it's worth, we appreciate your help."

"Look, it was never meant to turn out this way. Just be careful and don't, under any circumstances, talk to the police."

"We won't, I promise."

"We won't," Jack echoed.

He pulled back the curtain to look outside. "They're still out there, so I'll stay here for a bit if that's okay."

"It's fine." I walked over to Jack and sat next to him on the bed. I felt like if somebody breathed too hard or the wind blew too strongly, I would shatter. "I'm so sorry, Jack."

"You couldn't have known this was going to happen. I'm sorry I couldn't protect her, and us."

"We can start over. Scarlett wouldn't want us to be unhappy."

Jack frowned. "No, she wouldn't. She really wouldn't. We can move, keep our jobs, meet new friends. Once we sell the house, we'll have a little bit of money. Not much after that second mortgage, but we can do this, May. Put it all behind us, keep Scarlett in our hearts."

I placed my head on his shoulder, trying not to cry. Everything had gotten so, so messed up.

THIRTY-FOUR

VAL

Brady drove around to the front of the motel. Our plan was twofold: first, make the Douglases think we had left the motel by moving the car, and second, figure out which vehicles did not belong in the parking lot, hence uncovering who had been visiting the couple. We entered the motel office, greeted by the jingle of the bell hanging on the door.

"Deputy Tanner, Agent Costa, what can I help you with?" Dennis, the clerk, asked.

I said, "We'd like to run a list of license plates by you to see which ones belong to hotel guests."

Dennis shook his head. "Sorry, but we don't keep that kind of information for our guests. They literally just sign in, give us a credit card, and that's it. They don't have to register their cars. There's plenty of parking, so it's not necessary."

Well, that was a dead end.

"Thanks, anyway," Brady said, his voice carrying a hint of disappointment. He then asked, "Any idea when you'll get your security camera fixed?"

"Oh, I'll have to call the owner and let them know it's broken," the clerk responded with a shrug. His response made me think this guy had no intention of fixing the security camera or telling his boss about it.

Disheartened but not deterred, I said, "All right, thanks again."

We exited the office and headed back to Brady's SUV.

"So, do we run every plate?" Brady asked, his eyebrows furrowed in contemplation.

"Or do we monitor the motel room until someone leaves?" I suggested. Stakeouts were the pits—they could last five minutes or ten hours. As I was about to propose the stakeout, I heard a car approaching from the back of the motel.

"That could be our visitor."

Hurrying to the driver's side, Brady said, "Let's go."

Inside the vehicle, Brady wasted no time following the silver sedan, which I recognized as the one that had been parked next to Jack's truck.

"Can you see what the driver looks like?" Brady asked, his eyes never leaving the road.

"There's just one person in the car. He's wearing a baseball cap. It's difficult to see his face." It wasn't Jack Douglas. It was likely our visitor, or another motel guest. Time would tell.

Brady was skilled at tailing the car, managing to stay three cars back while keeping the silver sedan in sight. The driver didn't seem concerned about being followed. But soon we'd be off the main road, where the only light would be emitted from the car's headlights. As we trailed behind, Brady suggested, "Call Lucy and have her run the license plate."

"Good thinking," I said, pulling out my phone and dialing Lucy at the sheriff's department.

"Hello?" she answered cautiously, likely because she didn't recognize my number. She'd know it by heart if this case lingered much longer.

"Hi, Lucy, this is Val. Brady and I are in pursuit of a potential suspect. Could you run a license plate for us?"

"Sure. What's the plate number?"

I rattled off the details before lowering the phone, telling Brady that Lucy was on it. "Lucy's good. She understands what's urgent and what's not."

That reminded me she had told me she'd worked for the NYPD. I made a mental note to get to know her better. I would be in town for a few more weeks, and it would be nice to have a female friend around.

"Okay, the license plate comes back as registered to a Henry Tate, but this guy lives in Los Angeles?" Lucy's voice rang through the phone, her surprise clear at the information.

Henry Tate also had a home up the hill from the Douglases and owned an insurance office in town. He had helped the Douglases run a drive for potential kidney donors for Scarlett. May had said he was a good friend. Good enough to suggest an illegal organ transplant? "It's likely the same Henry Tate who has a home and insurance business in town. Can you run it and verify it for us?"

"No problem. Give me a few minutes."

I lowered the phone as I explained to Brady who it was we were following.

"What are you thinking?" Brady asked, his brow furrowed.

"May said he was a good friend. He could simply be visiting them in the motel. But if it was an innocent visit, why keep it a secret? Why not let us inside? He could definitely be involved."

If that were the case, it fit perfectly, considering we were still following who we presumed to be Henry Tate, heading toward May and Jack's home near the lake. Each turn the silver sedan made was leading us closer to the Douglas house. His car and ours were the only two vehicles on the dark road.

Lucy came back on the line, breaking my train of thought.

"Okay, good call, Val. You're right. He's got two homes. One in Los Angeles and one right here in Rosedale. And he has a lease for a business in town."

I turned to Brady and said, "It's the neighbor."

"Whose neighbor?" Lucy questioned.

"Scarlett Douglas' neighbor. He said he was out of town when Scarlett went missing but came back as soon as he heard the news," I explained.

"Sounds like you've got some questioning to do," Lucy said, a note of excitement in her voice.

"Thanks, Lucy, we'll call you if we need you."

Henry Tate drove his silver BMW onto his driveway. Brady gunned it and stopped his SUV abruptly behind it. Brady and I hopped out and hurried toward Henry as he climbed out of his car.

"Mr. Tate?" Brady called out, approaching the man with the baseball cap and piercing blue eyes.

"Yes?" he responded, his eyes shifting between Brady and me.

"Do you mind if we ask you a few questions?"

He glanced at his wristwatch and said, "I'm in a pretty big hurry. Is this going to take long?"

"We have a few questions about your neighbors. Have you seen May or Jack recently?" Brady cut to the chase.

Mr. Tate hesitated before answering. If he was smart, he'd answer truthfully, considering we had followed him from the motel. Something inside me told me he knew that.

"Yes, I was just at their motel room checking on them. They're devastated by Scarlett's passing. My heart goes out to them. I was asking if there's anything they needed before I head home to LA."

"That's awfully nice of you."

"I do what I can. They're going through a lot right now."

Yes, they are. How much does he know?

"Do you recall seeing anything out of the ordinary in the neighborhood over the last few days?"

He shook his head. "No. I'm sorry, I really am in a hurry. I need to get going." Without another word, he hurried toward his front door, unlocking it quickly and disappearing inside, shutting the door behind him.

With all my senses on high alert, I stared at the closed door.

"What do you make of that?" Brady asked.

"I think we need to learn absolutely everything we can about Henry Tate."

THIRTY-FIVE

VAL

The phone buzzing on my nightstand woke me from a familiar nightmare. They were not as bad as they had been just a week ago, but still, my sleep was fitful. I was glad for the alarm. Picking up my cell phone, I saw it was Kieran.

"Hey, Kieran. What's up?" I mumbled, still groggy.

"Did I wake you?"

"Yeah, but it's okay."

"It's eight o'clock."

I used to be an early riser, but with my new sleep medication, I slept longer than usual. My body needed it, and so did my brain. "I'm still taking medication to help me sleep."

"So, you're getting some sleep, then?"

"I am." It was the only way I could keep going and continue working on Scarlett's case.

"I just spoke with the lab tech guys. They've tracked the IP address to a library in Nevada."

Well, that woke me up. I pushed myself into a seated position. "Is it the Bear?"

"Not necessarily. When the team called the library to ask about the computer usage, they said they don't monitor it. But they did have a log of who logged in and what library card number was used."

Would the Bear have messed up and used his real name? Not likely. "Were they able to match up the login and the time-stamp for posting the Craigslist ad?"

"They did. There was only one person logged in at that time."

My hopes weren't high it was the Bear. "Who was it?"

"It was a kid, fifteen years old."

"Do you think the Bear hired this one too?" Preying on the young and vulnerable. Sounded like the Bear to me.

"It's possible, but not likely because—"

I cut him off. "Are there security cameras?"

"No, not inside the library."

"What about outside the library?"

"No, there's nothing."

"To log on to a library computer, you have to be registered for the library in that particular county. I'm guessing the person who logged in lives in the county?"

"The team already made a call."

"And?"

"The kid said he hadn't been to the library in at least two years and didn't know where his library card was."

A dead end. "Do we believe him?"

"Yes, plus he was on vacation with his parents when the post on Craigslist was created."

"So, we got nothing from that?"

"The only thing we have left is to ask the library workers if they recall who was there and what they looked like. It's unlikely they'll remember."

"But it's worth a shot, right?"

The Bear had been elusive, smart, and calculating, and he was messing with me. My gut told me it was the Bear sending the message. It wasn't about finding out who had logged on to the computer during that time and posted to the Internet. It was about revealing the true poster. Considering the kid's library card had been missing for Lord only knew how long showed that it was somebody who didn't want their identity to be known.

"You know resources are tight, Val."

"They can make a phone call, though? If not, I'll call. Where is the branch?"

"I'll have an agent call them back and see if they can recall what the person looked like. Ask if they have blue eyes. Caucasian."

It was better than nothing. Every agent had that one case that haunted them throughout their career, and their life afterward. Would the Bear be mine? "Let me know," I said half-heartedly.

"Of course. How's your case going? Not that you're supposed to be working on it."

Ignoring the jab, I said, "Well, it might be bigger than we thought. We got a new lead. We think we have a suspect: the Douglases' next-door neighbor. He seems suspicious. We've got a research team doing a background check on him now."

"But nothing concrete?"

"Not yet. I'm meeting Brady down at the station in a little while to have a follow-up call with the Organized Crime Task Force and talk to the research team about the neighbor."

"If the FBI's Organized Crime team think there's organized crime involved, you can hand it over to them and walk away. Heal up. Spend time with your mom."

It had been almost two weeks since the Bear had held me captive. I felt almost back to my old self, except for the fact that I relied on sleeping pills to get through the night. My bruises had mostly healed, my ego was on its way too. "I'll let you know what they say."

"Or you can let me know when you hand it over to them and walk away from the case."

"Sure thing, Kieran."

He sighed, and I said, "I'll talk to you later. Bye." I hung up before he could question me further. I swung my legs off the bed and stood up. Fully awake, I was frustrated. We knew the Bear was intelligent and would be difficult to catch. That's why I had left the hotel room that night by myself. I'd had a hunch, a big one. I hadn't wanted him to get away. That plan had failed, and now he might be out there, preoccupied with someone else, carving them up. The thought made me sick. He needed to be stopped.

THIRTY-SIX

VAL

Back inside the tiny conference room at the sheriff's department, I shook my head in disbelief as Lucy gave us an update on Henry Tate. His background revealed he was a businessman who owned an insurance franchise, and he was a practicing real estate agent with no criminal record, and no financial problems. Nothing that would indicate he had anything to do with the illegal organ transplant.

"Any known associates? Any dealings with medical professionals or ties to any organized crime?" I asked.

Lucy said, "No, in fact, he's squeaky clean. As clean as they get. Not even a parking ticket."

Not even a parking ticket. The guy we'd spoken to wasn't someone who never got a parking ticket. The air I got about him was entitled, confident. He parked where he wanted to.

"Should we try to get him in a room and question him about Scarlett?" Brady asked.

"Wouldn't hurt. Just because he has a clean record doesn't mean he's not involved."

"True. We should bring him in and see what he knows about Scarlett's disappearance, her collapse at the lake, and then her subsequent death and burial. He might've been there, maybe even helped. Maybe he's somehow connected, and we don't know how yet, but he is."

"It is a bit of a coincidence, with him living in Los Angeles, and we suspect that the Douglases were going to LA, based on Scarlett telling her best friend Gabby she was going to Disneyland."

"That's a good point."

I glanced up at the clock on the wall. "All right, Agent St. Claire should be calling in any minute. Hopefully, he has something for us."

Lucy pushed her glasses up the bridge of her nose. "What if he doesn't?"

"We'll have to take this in a different direction."

"Like what?"

"We'll need to think outside the box." I glanced back at Lucy. "You said he is secure financially. Is he wealthy? Does he have a lot of money?"

"He is pretty well off. He's got a home here in Rosedale and one in LA, fancy cars, a hefty investment account. His bank accounts are full. He does well."

Perhaps he was just greedy and wanted more. Maybe that was why he was wealthy. But as a real estate agent in LA, he could be pulling in seven figures a year just from that. It would be difficult to determine exactly where his income was coming from without pulling all of his records and sifting through them one by one.

The Polycom lit up and I answered the call. "Hey, St. Claire. You've got Brady, Lucy, and myself."

"Hey, gang. I'm here with Agent Grindle."

Excellent. "Thanks for joining us, Agent Grindle."

"Glad to be of help. How's it going?"

"It's going, but not far."

St. Claire said, "I can imagine. I've briefed Grindle. I'll let him take over. He's head of the human trafficking task force—which includes organ trafficking."

The things criminals did to their fellow humans for cash was endless and appalling.

In a low, gravelly voice, Grindle said, "Based on what St. Claire has told me, I've got an inkling there's an organ-trafficking ring right here in California. Do you have any names? Any suspects? A location?"

"We have May and Jack Douglas. Their daughter was a recipient of an illegal kidney transplant. They told us it was a state-of-the-art facility, clean, and everyone seemed really nice. We went to question them yesterday. Jack was roughed up. Someone from this organ transplant group was likely the culprit. Jack says he fell, but my gut says it was a message for them to keep quiet. As far as suspects go, when we were questioning the Douglases, we heard someone in their room, and although they said there was no one there, they insisted we talk outside. We stuck around and waited for the secret visitor to leave. Long story short, we learned it was their neighbor, Henry Tate, who spends most of his time in Los Angeles."

Agent Grindle said, "That sounds like organized crime to me. We'll look into Henry Tate."

"We did a background check. No criminal record."

"We'll look into him even deeper."

Be my guest. "Let us know if you find anything interesting. What do we do next? I spoke with Kieran Fox, my boss at the Bureau. He'd prefer we handed it over to you if you can take it."

Brady shot me a look. I hadn't told him yet. I wasn't one to turn my back on a case, but I was okay with capable professionals taking on the brunt of the work.

"We could if we knew where to start. If we knew where the operation is located, we could have our confidential informants and current undercovers put feelers out to see if there is a hint of organ trafficking in the US. Without a location it's a bit of a shot in the dark. The girl's parents still aren't talking?"

"No, they're pretty adamant they've said all they plan to. We even offered to help protect them, but they're not budging. May says the only thing she has left is her husband and she won't put his life at risk. I think whoever beat him up really put the fear of God in them."

"She may not understand how dangerous these people are. Traffickers don't mess around. And to be honest, if it's connected to a cartel or a large organization, they're lucky they're still alive, considering she was in your custody and then released. That's usually a death sentence."

We needed to protect May and Jack whether they wanted our help or not. Maybe the sheriff's office could provide surveillance until we knew they were out of harm's way. "So, they're in danger."

"I'd say so."

Lucy said, "Could we get DNA from the kidney? Run it through the system and find out where the donor is from? It might give us the location of the transplant, or at least a place to start looking."

I was impressed. "That's a great idea, Lucy."

Agent Grindle said, "Smart. Let us know when it's done."

Brady said, "We'll do that."

Agent Grindle said, "I may have to change my opinion of small-town law enforcement."

With a smile I said, "Lucy used to work with the NYPD."

"Ah. Well, ma'am, Red Rose County is lucky to have you."

Lucy's cheeks turned pink. "Thanks."

Brady said, "We'll talk to Dr. Edison and get the DNA testing started."

"We'll wait to hear from you."

"Thank you, Agent Grindle. You too, St. Claire."

Agent St. Claire said, "Talk soon."

I ended the call.

Eyeing Lucy, I thought, *We'll definitely be friends.*

"DNA from the kidney. That's a smart move. I'll call Dr. Edison," Brady said.

"Very smart. After that, let's swing by the motel and check on Jack and May. They're in danger. We can't let the people threatening them come after them again. It's obvious by Jack's battered face they know where to find them. We might actually want to put a surveillance team on Jack and May. Otherwise, we may be investigating two homicides."

"That's a lot of resources."

"It's two lives."

Brady nodded. "I'll talk to the sheriff."

He had better. What else were the sheriff's department staff doing if not protecting their citizens?

THIRTY-SEVEN

VAL

Thankfully, the Red Rose County crime lab wasn't overly busy with DNA requests. They promised to get back to us within two to three days, at most. Our case had managed to receive top priority, and the sheriff had agreed to put Jack and May under surveillance. Now, all we had to do was inform them, irrespective of whether they wanted our protection or not.

On the drive to the motel, Brady said, "Has Harrison left for his big European adventure yet?"

"He texted me earlier," I replied. "He's packing right now. They're leaving for the airport in about an hour."

"Lucky kid."

"No kidding. How are your kids doing?"

"They left this morning. They've gone home to visit some friends."

Memories of a similar time flooded back to me. I remembered the days when I'd thought my friends were my whole world. The first time I'd come home from college, I barely said anything to my mom, except in passing, as I was constantly in and out, visiting my pals. There were parties, hookups... *Oh, to be young again.*

Brady pulled up in front of the motel room. A cursory glance around the parking lot revealed that two vehicles we'd expected to see were missing. "Their cars aren't here," I noted, feeling a sudden unease.

"That's strange."

We had assumed they'd be working in the motel, as their home was still off limits.

With my hand instinctively on the weapon in my holster, I approached the door and knocked three times. There was no apparent forced entry into the motel room, nor were there any sounds coming from inside. My gaze shifted to the security camera, its wires still cut. The silence made me fear we might have been too late.

Brady, equally uneasy, said, "Anything?"

"No. I'll try again." Knocking once more, I stepped back, scanning for any signs of movement inside. The place felt deserted, not a single sign of life. "Let's go talk to the clerk," I suggested.

"I don't think he'll let us in without a warrant."

"If they're in danger, and I think they could be, he needs to let us in or I'll kick down the door myself." Hadn't we already gone through this? One way or another, I would get inside.

Brady nodded, knowing better than to raise any objection, and we rushed over to the motel clerk, Dennis.

"We need you to open the door to the Douglases' motel room."

He cocked his head, giving us a puzzled look. "Sure. But they checked out last night."

I hadn't expected that. But it did tell us they were alive as of last night's checkout. "Were they alone?" I pressed.

"Yeah, both of them came in to thank me for my hospitality."

Gotta love that small-town charm. "Did they appear

nervous or under duress?" I continued, trying to grasp any possible leads.

He shook his head. "They seemed happy, said they were taking a little time off."

"Did they mention where they were headed?"

"Nope. They just wished me a good night and signed out."

"Can you let us into the room?"

"Sure." The clerk leaned back, grabbed the key from the wall, then used the desk to leverage himself out of his chair. As he ambled toward the door, we followed closely behind. When we finally reached the room, he unlocked the door. I instructed him to stand back as I peered in from the doorway.

There was no obvious sign of a struggle, nor any evidence of a crime scene. Even the beds were neatly made. Turning to the clerk, I asked, "Has housekeeping been in since they left?"

"No, not yet. They should be here in about an hour."

"Can you have them skip this room for now?"

"Sure."

Careful not to disturb anything, I stepped inside. The room was strikingly clean. Looking in the trash bins, I found them empty. I moved on to the bathroom, studying the floors and walls for any signs of blood splatter, droplets—anything that might indicate the Douglases hadn't left voluntarily. Finding nothing, I returned to the sink.

The air was thick with the scent of Lysol wipes or another cleaning product. They had thoroughly cleaned the motel room before they'd left, an action that set off alarm bells in my mind.

I turned around and headed back toward Brady and the clerk. "You can lock it up for now," I instructed the clerk, "and don't let anyone in here until you hear from us, okay?"

"Yes, ma'am."

I stepped out of the room and, lowering my voice, said to Brady, "They cleaned up really well before they left."

"Trying to conceal a crime scene?" he proposed.

"Or any trace of who had been there, or what transpired. Someone might have advised them to do this."

"Maybe someone also advised them to leave town," Brady suggested.

"The neighbor?"

"Maybe."

After the clerk locked the room, we thanked him for his time and headed back to Brady's vehicle. As we set off again, I said, "Let's go pay the neighbor another visit. If he's somehow connected to all of this, maybe he warned them, or lured them to their deaths."

We still didn't have an in-depth background on Henry Tate, considering we'd only spoken with Agent Grindle a few hours earlier. I wasn't sure how deep the Bureau would dig, but I hoped they would find something. We were in desperate need of a lead that would shed some light on what was truly happening.

"Hey," I broke the silence in the car, "after we talk to Henry Tate, want to go out for a drink?" I was more than ready and preferred to avoid Mom's disapproving looks at home.

"Sure," Brady replied.

"We can invite Lucy too. I feel she has some interesting stories. Do you know her well?"

"Not terribly," Brady admitted, "but like I said, she's competent and smart. I'm sure you've picked up on that."

It was good to have another ally at the sheriff's department. I had no idea how deep this rabbit hole would go or whether we'd hand the case over to the FBI. The idea of stepping back and letting them take it didn't sit well with me. It was rare for me to hand off a case and not see it through to its conclusion, and I didn't want to start now.

As we pulled up in front of Henry Tate's residence, the scene mirrored the one at the motel: no car in the driveway, no lights on in the house. Brady and I exchanged knowing glances as we got out and headed toward the house.

I knocked on the front door, only to be met with silence. No movement inside the house, no flickering lights, and no one peeking through the blinds. If I were to hazard a guess, I'd say Henry had gone back home to Southern California. My only question was whether he had taken Jack and May with him.

"He's not here," Brady said, stating the obvious.

"No," I concurred. "We need to find out what happened to May and Jack Douglas."

"Do you think they're in danger?"

"They could be, or they're on the run. But we could use their testimony if this all links back to a major organization. And we don't want the criminals to get to them before we do. Could Lucy check traffic cams to see if she can find their cars or track where they went?"

"That could take some serious time," Brady warned.

"I understand." Waiting for the DNA results from the kidney, finding out where May and Jack Douglas had gone, *and* figuring out whether it really was the Bear who'd posted the job to send me an ominous note had me on edge. I wanted answers, and the lack of progress was terribly frustrating. A nice, full-bodied cabernet with a dark berry finish was calling my name.

THIRTY-EIGHT

VAL

Frustrated by the latest news from Kieran, I chucked my phone onto the bed. I had thought we were making progress, and believed the Bear reaching out to me would put us one step closer to finally catching him. But we had nothing. My mind drifted to my therapy session and the methods I had learned to handle my anger, frustration, and anxiety. I was to initiate a body scan, focus on my senses—what could I hear, feel, see, taste? Gradually, I focused on each part of my body, my head, my neck, my shoulders, my abdomen, my thighs, down to my feet. I let out a sigh, grabbed my phone, and made my way downstairs.

Mom was sitting at the table, reading her old-fashioned newspaper, black readers perched on the tip of her nose. "Good morning," she began, but stopped when she saw the look on my face. "What's wrong?"

"I just got off the phone with Kieran," I explained. "The library workers who were on shift the day the person posted the Craigslist ad have no recollection of who was there that day. All they could say was that it wasn't anybody who seemed out of the ordinary."

"I'm sorry, honey. Unless there's something really distinguishing about him, it probably was a long shot," she said, attempting to console me.

The fact my mother was right didn't make me any less angry. Sure, I had done my centering exercise and wasn't going to break anything, but I didn't have to like it.

She asked, "Do you think the Bear is still in Nevada?"

"Maybe. His pattern has been four victims per state, and then he moves on. He only killed three in Nevada before he captured me, so, technically, he has one more. My guess is he's hunting for his fourth." *Or he's on his way to California to finish me off.*

"That means he's not in California, right?" Mom always had a way of finding the silver lining on a rainy day.

Maybe. "That's true."

If it was true, it meant he wasn't going after my son in Europe or my mother in California. I doubted the Bear would change his pattern and not finish what he'd started, although we didn't have a lot of data points for his behavior toward survivors. For all we knew, capturing me may have thrown off his entire pattern, and he could be right here in California, coming for me. Even though he hadn't finished off the other survivor who had gotten away. It was hard to say. I had suspected he had stalked his victims and planned their abductions with precision. I had been a victim of opportunity, which could have knocked out his previous MO and morphed it into something new.

"How's Scarlett's case going?" she asked.

"It's a waiting game. They're still sifting through surveillance footage, trying to find out where Jack and May went. So far, nothing. And we're still waiting on the DNA results from the donor kidney."

Mom nodded in her sage-like way and said, "Waiting can be frustrating."

"True," I agreed. I eyed the coffee maker and saw a

freshly brewed pot. I poured myself a mug and joined my mother at the table. I took a sip of the hot, mellow brew and set it down.

"How do you like working with the folks at the sheriff's department?"

"It's been pretty good." I nodded. "You know Lucy, the researcher? She used to work for the NYPD. She's sharp as a tack—a real asset. And Brady is good too; he's got good instincts."

"What do you think of the new sheriff?"

"Haven't met him yet."

"He's all right. I think you'll get along."

It didn't really matter. I wouldn't be around Rosedale much longer. I only had a few more weeks until I could get back to my team and continue to actively search for the Bear. "So far, every time I've asked Brady for additional resources for the case, the sheriff comes through. The DNA results are being rushed. They should be back any moment now." That scored brownie points with me.

"It's amazing what technology can do these days. I just can't help but think about the person who gave up their kidney for Scarlett. Not only did it kill Scarlett, but who knows what happened to that donor? Was she willing? Is she feeling a little lighter with some extra cash in her pocket?"

If this organization was threatening recipient families, I doubted they treated their donors very well, which was part of what fueled me to keep working the case and put a stop to them. "Me too. I have a feeling the person who gave up their kidney isn't walking around feeling great about the decision. I get a vibe, Mom, that these are really bad folks."

"You're probably right."

Mom looked a little pale, and I wondered if she was worried about me working so soon. "You feeling okay, Mom?"

"Yes, I'm fine. Just a little tired."

"Is it the stress of me being here, the threat of the Bear, the surveillance cameras? I'm sorry, Mom."

"No, honey, it's not that. I just—you know, I guess I do worry. And Maxine said she doesn't think she'll be able to make it out like she had hoped. I guess I'm just missing my girls. It's so nice to have you home."

Mom wasn't usually one to get sentimental, so she had me a little worried.

"I can visit more. I'm sorry, I haven't been a very good daughter, have I?"

"Oh, you're a wonderful daughter. Both you and Maxine are the greatest joys in my life. But I do miss you. I have my friends and our travels, but I don't know, I guess when you're about to hit seventy, you look back at your life and think about what it looked like before and what it looks like now. Friends pass on, your dad... I have my girls living so far away from me now, Harrison off on a European adventure. Time's going by so fast."

Guilt was beginning to creep inside me. I wasn't sure what was making my mom feel this way. I knew I should visit more. Mom had her friends, but we were the only family she had left. I bet she'd thought when she'd married my dad that they would be spending their golden years together. Instead, she was alone in the house that she'd raised us in.

"I hear you, and I haven't been great about visiting. That's going to change, Mom."

"Oh, don't be silly. I'm just being emotional. I'm so proud of you, and your sister, and of Harrison. What a wonderful young man. Not that I'm biased in any way," she said with a smile.

"I tend to agree with you about Harrison."

"You raised a good one there."

My phone buzzed. I was almost afraid to look, but it was Brady. I said to Mom, "It's Brady," as I answered.

"Just got a call from Dr. Edison. The DNA's back."

"Okay, I'll meet you down at the station." I hung up, took a giant gulp of my coffee, and said, "The DNA's back. I have to go, Mom. Dinner tonight?"

"Sounds great."

I waved goodbye and rushed out of the house, hopeful we had a lead. I was tired of dead ends.

Huddled in Dr. Edison's small office, Brady and I listened as Jonathan, a member of the forensic testing lab with long hair and a relaxed surfer vibe, explained to Brady, myself, Lucy, and Dr. Edison the results of the DNA analysis.

"The DNA is complete. The donor kidney is most likely from a female in her late teens. I ran her DNA through CODIS, no hits."

We had already assumed it was a female in her teen years, based on Dr. Edison's autopsy results. This was completely unhelpful. "Well, thanks for getting this done so quickly."

With a gleam in his eye, he said, "There's more."

He had my attention. "Oh?"

"Her DNA is not in CODIS, but I found someone related to her who is. A familial match. Not just a familial match—the donor's father."

I couldn't believe he hadn't led with that. This was fantastic news. "What do you know about the father?"

Lucy raised her hand. "That's where I come in. I did a full background on the father. The father of our donor is named Edward Martinez and is currently serving a life sentence at Folsom State Prison for rape and attempted murder and a whole slew of other offenses. He's not a good guy. That's why his DNA's in the system."

"Is he from California?"

"Records state at the time of his arrest he was living in Los Angeles, which is where he committed most of his crimes."

"So, it's likely our donor's from LA too?" That was too much of a coincidence to dismiss. Scarlett had told her best friend Gabby she was going to Disneyland. The neighbor lived in LA and most likely so did the kidney donor.

Lucy nodded. "We did a search of all known offspring—children of Edward Martinez—and he has two children, a daughter aged eighteen and a son aged nineteen. Neither has been reported missing."

"That doesn't mean they aren't. Or that they didn't sell one of their kidneys."

"True."

"How long has he been in prison?"

"Fifteen years."

"So even if his daughter was missing or desperate enough to sell her body parts, he might not know?"

"Possibly not."

"Does he have any relatives? Wives, ex-wives?"

"He has an ex-wife. She lives in Los Angeles. Name's Deirdre Martinez, the mother of the two children. I have her contact info."

"I will give her a call and ask her if she knows where her children are."

My heart was racing. Finally, a lead. We were so close to learning the donor's identity, I could taste it.

THIRTY-NINE

VAL

Back in our favorite conference room, we waited as the ring tone emanated from the speaker on the Polycom. A woman's voice answered, "Hello?"

"Hi, this is FBI Special Agent Valerie Costa. I'm looking for Deirdre Martinez."

"FBI?" she asked.

"Yes, is this Deirdre Martinez?"

"Yes, what is this about? And what did he do now? Is Eddie dead?" she rushed out.

I glanced at Lucy and Brady. "I'm not calling about Eddie. I'm actually looking for Eddie's children. You're the mother of his two children, correct?"

"My babies did nothing wrong," she said hastily.

My working theory was that the organs may not have been coming from willing victims, so I said, "I'm sorry, I should have explained. We don't believe either did anything wrong. We're looking for a missing person, one of your children."

"My kids aren't missing," she said, calmer now.

"When was the last time you saw them?"

"About two minutes ago, they're in my living room watching TV."

The second theory was that the donor provided the kidney willingly in exchange for money. "Has either of your children donated a kidney in the past month?"

"Kidney? No."

"Are you sure? Has your daughter been feeling unwell after being gone for a day or two?"

"No. I would've known if she'd had an operation. *Trust me.*"

Another dead end? It couldn't be. "Do you know if Eddie has children from any previous relationships?" An illegitimate child might explain our situation. But also might be more difficult to track down.

"Probably. He messed around on me enough. He's probably got a load of kids out there," she said bitterly.

Trying to sound sympathetic, I said, "I'm sorry to hear that, but do you know of any women in particular that he messed around with that might have had his child? It would have been at least sixteen or seventeen years ago."

"Well, now that I think about it, there was one girl he cheated on me with right before I filed for divorce. She came around saying she was pregnant with his baby."

"Do you know if the baby was Eddie's?"

"I don't know. He lied so much I have no idea what's true," she said dismissively.

Feeling hopeful, I said, "Do you remember her name?"

"It sounded like Annie... Anita! That was it, Anita. She was kinda young, but Eddie got around and didn't exactly check IDs," she said.

"How long ago did Anita say she had Eddie's child?" I asked.

"She came round, visibly pregnant, about seventeen and a half years ago, the day before I filed for divorce."

"I'm so sorry you had to go through that."

"I swear, when we got married, I thought that boy would stop messing around. I was wrong and stupid. I was a lot younger back then. You say one of his kids is missing?" she asked.

"Maybe. We're looking for the donor of a kidney. The kidney is from one of his female children. Is there anything else you can tell us about that time, about Anita and her baby?"

"Oh, wow. Well, that's about all I know. She came round the house, I threw her off the porch. I felt sorry for her, to be honest, but I was angry and hurt and I couldn't see straight. But for what it's worth, I hope this girl is okay. It's not often someone looks for missing kids from our neighborhood, you know?" she said, her voice softening a bit.

I didn't know. "Which part of LA are you in?" I asked.

"Downtown. Right next door to Little Tokyo."

We would have to look up the area. "Understood. Do you know if Anita lived in the neighborhood?"

"Probably. Eddie was too lazy to venture very far."

That, at least, narrowed our search to downtown Los Angeles. "Does Eddie keep in touch with your kids?"

"Nope. Not a single birthday card since he moved out. He's three hundred shades of bad."

It wasn't likely Eddie was in contact with any of his illegitimate children either. "Have you kept in contact with Eddie since he's been incarcerated?"

"No way. I stayed clear of him the second I filed for divorce. Was thrilled when they put him away. I wished I'd seen the evil in him when I met him. Maybe I would've known to run faster."

Hindsight was twenty-twenty. "Ms. Martinez, you've been very helpful," I said, genuinely grateful.

"I hope you find her," she said, her voice filled with a weary kind of hope.

"Thank you," I said.

Ending the call, I turned to Brady and Lucy. "Now we have

to find somebody named Anita who had a child seventeen years ago most likely in or around downtown Los Angeles."

Lucy chimed in, "Sounds like a road trip."

"Let's give Special Agent Grindle a call, let him know what we found. Maybe he's got some agents down south who can help out." I wondered if I could fly down and meet them. There was no reason to sit around on my rear while they got to solve the case we were handing them on a silver platter.

With Grindle on the line, I provided him the update about the DNA, familial match, and the woman named Anita and her seventeen-year-old child.

"Sounds like you're on to something up there," he said.

"Yeah, my thought is we go down to Los Angeles, start knocking on doors, looking for somebody named Anita. She could still be in the same neighborhood she was all those years ago." Or someone else would remember her.

"Not a bad idea. Might be useful to work with local law enforcement. The area is drug-infested, gang-infested, and they aren't shy about shooting a cop," he said.

A bullet hole isn't on my list of must-haves. "Do you have agents in the local office who could help canvass the area?" I asked.

"Yeah, I do. I'll make a few calls. I'll get someone to meet up with you down here."

"I'll fly down. What about you, Brady?"

"I'll need to check with the sheriff."

"Understood. Grindle, let us know when you've assigned an agent."

"Will do. We finished the background on Henry Tate, and we didn't find anything new. But because you now have reason to believe this operation is happening in Southern California, maybe we should put somebody on Henry Tate. Watch him, follow him, see where he goes, who his friends are, who he hangs out with," Grindle suggested.

"That's a great idea. There's no way it's a coincidence that both the donor kidney and the Douglases' neighbor—who was hiding out in their motel room and has now vanished—are from Los Angeles."

"I agree. That's too many coincidences for one case," Grindle said.

"Okay, let's keep in touch," I said, and hung up.

Brady turned to me. "I'll talk to the sheriff and see if he'll approve the travel, if you want some company."

"Sure," I replied.

"I can be on call," Lucy added.

"That'd be great," I said, nodding.

Thinking about my mom, I felt a pang of guilt considering I had just told her I would visit more, and now I would be jumping on a flight to Los Angeles to work a case. But she had been in law enforcement, and she'd understand, I hoped. The look in her eyes that morning had scared me. I'd never seen it before, but I wouldn't be away for long. I could feel we were going to solve this one—I only hoped it would be soon.

FORTY

AVA

Once hopeful the authorities would actually do their jobs, my faith in the police was once again tarnished like old silverware at a garage sale. When the detective finally agreed to take missing persons reports for Mia, Abby, and Ethan, I had a spark of hope. I thought they would look for them, but it had been five days and they had provided zero updates. No sightings of the gold Honda, and no sightings of any of the missing people, including Tina Torres. What about all-points bulletins and lookouts like they talked about on *Law & Order: SVU*? When I questioned the detective, he told me missing persons who may simply be runaways didn't warrant that type of attention. Needless to say, I left the police station in a tizzy.

Speaking with Joanna Torres, Tina's sister, I knew that the four disappearances were connected. Why weren't the police taking this more seriously? There could be a serial killer on the loose and they were just shrugging their shoulders, saying they were doing everything they could. This was a travesty of our justice system. Our most vulnerable needed their help, and they turned their backs on them.

I knew not all cops were bad, but I had only met a few that

weren't. That didn't stop me from continuing to post flyers of the four missing teens around different neighborhoods in Los Angeles, along with Joanna. The two of us had become a force, both resolved to find all of them.

Joanna was currently working on trying to get press attention, to get it on the news, to make the police take action, and hopefully warn the kids on the streets that a predator was out there promising them the world but delivering... I didn't even know what—possibly their deaths?

It was hot and muggy and the exhaust from the cars passing by on the busy street was giving me a headache. With the last flyer handed to an uninterested passerby, I was rounding the corner on my way back to the Grace Center when someone stopped me. A man. He was white, with blue eyes, wearing a baseball cap.

"Are you the woman looking for those missing teens?" he asked.

My pulse quickened. "Yes, have you seen them?" I pulled out my phone to show him the pictures and scrolled through the four images. "Have you seen any of them?"

"Yeah, I know where they are," he replied.

"Really?" I gasped. "Where?"

"It's okay. They're totally fine. They actually wanted me to talk to you, to let you know to stop looking, that you're wasting your time. Everything's fine," he said.

"But where are they then, if they're fine?" I questioned as a prickle, a warning, on the back of my neck told me the man wasn't to be trusted.

But before the man could answer, I heard the squeal of tires on concrete and a gloved hand covered my mouth. My muffled screams made zero impact to garner attention as I was thrown into the back of a van. I kicked and punched until my body grew limp and everything went dark.

FORTY-ONE

VAL

Jogging up the concrete steps to the Los Angeles FBI field office, I felt like my old self again. I hadn't even woken up in a cold sweat that morning. Mom and Kieran had insisted I should be resting and taking it easy in order to get back to normal. I had never taken it easy. It wasn't in my DNA, and Mom knew that.

The Bear, the phantom that had been haunting my dreams for the last few weeks, no longer dominated my thoughts. Sure, he'd sent me that eerie letter, and yes, as soon as I was officially back on the job, no longer hunting down organ traffickers in LA, I'd find him. He'd pay for what he had done to me and his other victims.

On my short flight into LAX, I found clarity.

A team of excellent special agents were back-tracking every possible location where the Bear could be within Nevada and the surrounding states. There was surveillance at my mom's house. She was an armed former sheriff; she could handle herself. But I could tell she didn't want me to go and she didn't like that I was working a case so soon.

It had been almost three weeks since the Bear had taken me

by surprise. What that had taught me was, *Don't let it happen again*. And I wouldn't. Next time I would take extra precautions. I had even started running again and was once again in near peak fitness for a woman my age.

The Bear had had one shot at me, and he'd wasted it. That was on him. It was a regret he would live with for all his remaining days.

Perhaps my therapist was also helping with the nightmares. She had helped me accept what he had done, the Bear, and that I wasn't completely unbreakable. We all had a point where we crossed a line and were no longer our former selves. But the Bear hadn't managed to push me over that line. I was still me, but that didn't mean I didn't want to catch him and teach him a lesson. As soon as the team got credible information of his whereabouts and I was back on active duty, I'd find him.

After checking in at reception, Special Agent Peters met me in the lobby.

"Special Agent Costa, nice to meet you. I've heard good things about you," he said warmly.

"Likewise. Grindle says you're one of the best in LA," I responded.

"Just LA?" he said with a smirk.

He was cute. No, strike that. He was handsome, with salt-and-pepper hair and shiny, ocean-blue eyes that matched the shiny gold ring on his finger. *No, thank you.* We shook hands and he led me to a conference room.

"Speaking with the rest of the human trafficking team, we've agreed we'll put a tail on Henry Tate," he shared. "And we think working with the LAPD to check for any missing persons in the area, or a group of missing persons, and checking hospital records for people coming in with any infections related to the donation of organs is a good place to start."

"How far has the team gotten?" I asked. We had called them only two days earlier to notify them of the DNA results and the connection to Edward Martinez and possibly a woman named Anita. So I wasn't expecting too much.

"Not far. It's Monday morning, so they've just been debriefed," he explained.

"Understood. We also have a researcher up north, in Red Rose County. A former NYPD researcher, she's good."

"Hey, if you have extra hands, by all means, let's use them," he said.

I made a note to call Lucy and have her start checking hospital records for anybody coming in with infections related to transplants who had no medical record of said transplant. "I'm guessing we haven't checked the missing persons database yet?" I asked.

"Not yet," Peters confessed. "It's kind of hard to find somebody with just a parent's first name. It's not how the database is set up. I think reaching out to local law enforcement may be our best bet."

"Who's the contact?"

"We've got a detective downtown who's closest to where we think the organ donor resided. We can talk to him about any missing persons cases that have come across his desk. Sound like a plan?"

"Let's do it."

Peters drove us to the LAPD downtown station, where we were greeted with stares and whispers from the staff before being escorted to a cubicle and introduced to Detective Rogers.

As fit as my new friend Peters was, Rogers was the opposite: he had a bit of a beer gut and a mustache that seemed about forty years too late to be in fashion. My guess was this guy's heyday was in fact the seventies, maybe early eighties. He likely didn't spend much time chasing suspects or pounding the pavement. Perhaps visiting local donut shops was more accurate.

"Pleasure to meet you both," Detective Rogers began. "I hear you wanted to talk to me about a missing person?"

Seated next to the detective's desk, I said, "That's right. We're looking for a young woman, maybe seventeen. We don't have a name, but we have her mother's first name."

"The mother's first name? That's all you have?" he asked, sounding puzzled.

Peters chimed in, "It's unusual, but it's related to a case up north, a big one."

Rogers nodded. "What else can you tell me about the missing person?"

"The young woman would've gone missing approximately two months ago, give or take a week or two," I replied.

Detective Rogers looked at both of us as if he was trying to work out if we were for real. "Just one missing person?"

His question grabbed my attention. "Do you have multiple missing persons during that timeframe matching the description?"

"Maybe," he answered. "We've got a couple of street kids who are supposedly missing. One of the workers at a local recreation center and food kitchen that caters for homeless kids reported a few that she thinks are missing. She filed a report just last week, but there's not a lot to go on."

"Can we see the files?" I asked.

"Sure," he said, rummaging through a stack of files on his desk before pulling out a very thin file and handing it to Peters. Was Detective Rogers a misogynist from the old boys club?

Peters accepted the file and said, "This is kind of light. When did you say the report was taken?"

"Last week."

Peters opened the file and moved his chair closer to mine so we could read the notes together. They were from the woman who'd filed the report, Ava Woods. "All you have is the missing teenagers' first names?"

"Yeah," Rogers shrugged. "They're street kids."

Missing street kids and illegal organs? Could it be connected? It wouldn't be completely surprising if it was, but it was heartbreaking. "So, their parents weren't looking for them, or anybody related to them? A woman at a soup kitchen filed the reports?" I asked, incredulous.

Both of us read each of the individual files filled out by Ava Woods. Chances were she was the person we needed to be talking to, considering this detective seemed to have done absolutely nothing. His only notes on the report were from Ava Woods and all the times Ava had called to ask for updates. No evidence of any detective work.

When I began to read Ava's statement about the third person, my adrenaline spiked. The statement for the missing person, Abby, said she had a new boyfriend who drove a gold Honda Accord. It wasn't a common color. I pointed out the detail on the paper, and Peters nodded as if he agreed it was probably our best clue to find out what had happened to at least one of the missing teens.

"So, in this missing persons report," I said, "it says Abby was dating somebody who owned a gold Accord. Did you run a check to see how many gold Accords are registered in the Los Angeles area?"

Detective Rogers responded, "No, but we have a note among patrolmen to look out for the gold Accord. If anybody sees it, they'll call me."

I nearly had to pick up my jaw from the floor. My gut had been right about this guy. He was lazy and likely counting down to his pension. He hadn't even investigated these missing persons. Peters and I exchanged a knowing look and raised brows at the shoddy detective work, if you could even call it work.

"These are the only three missing persons around this time-frame? This one looks like it was about six weeks ago, this was about three weeks ago, and the last just a week and a half ago?" I asked, trying to keep my actual shock in check.

His eyes lit up as he replied, "Actually, no. There's one more."

Did I have to ask for every single potential piece of evidence he might have on his desk? He was about to hand the folder to Peters when I grabbed it first.

The report had been filled out by the missing woman's sister. She'd reported that the teen had mentioned something big coming up but wouldn't say what. The only follow-up notes were that the sister had also been checking in with the detective, daily.

"Can we get a copy of these, please?"

"Sure, of course. Anything for the FBI."

I handed him back the files and he hurried off, presumably to the copy room.

Leaning back in my chair, I turned to Peters. "So, there are four missing persons within a two-month timeframe, all young teens. Zero detective work done—he didn't even look up the gold Accord. How many could be registered in the Los Angeles area?"

"My guess is not very many. That is the first thing we'll look into."

"And did you see that three out of four mentioned a big opportunity before they went missing?"

"I did. These four could have been the victims of the organ traffickers."

My thoughts exactly.

As we conversed among ourselves, a young woman approached the desk. She looked angry and worried, her eyes wide.

"Can I help you with something?" I asked.

"Is Detective Rogers here?"

"He's just making some copies of files for us. He should be right back."

She appeared distressed. "Oh, I can wait, I guess."

Taking a shot in the dark, I asked, "Are you here to speak to Detective Rogers about a missing person?"

"My sister's case. She went missing, and now I fear that a friend of mine is missing too."

"What's your sister's name?"

"Tina Torres."

One of the missing teens. "And you say your friend may be missing too?"

"Yes, she's been helping me find my sister, posting flyers, asking around." She glanced down at us, suddenly aware we were law enforcement. She could probably see our weapon holsters under our jackets.

Before we could say another word, Detective Rogers returned and looked over at the woman. "I don't have any updates for you," he said bluntly.

"I *figured*. But I'm here because I think Ava is missing," she countered.

Peters and I exchanged glances.

As far as I was concerned, Detective Rogers was off the case. If the four, now five, missing persons were connected to our case, they were in grave danger. I stood and faced the young woman. "Ma'am, I'm FBI Special Agent Costa, and this is Special Agent Peters. We're investigating missing persons. We think you might be able to help. Do you have a few minutes to talk with us?"

She nodded, apprehensively.

Detective Rogers handed Peters the file copies and I said, "Detective Rogers, do you have a conference room Special Agent Peters and this young woman... I'm sorry, I didn't catch your name."

"It's Joanna."

"Where Special Agent Peters, Joanna, and I can talk privately?"

Rogers hesitated before he said, "Of course. Come with me."

With an encouraging nod at Joanna, her demeanor seemed to change from desperation to hope.

FORTY-TWO

VAL

The conference room door shut behind me and I invited Joanna to take a seat. Special Agent Peters was already making himself comfortable. I looked at him and he seemed to understand what I was thinking.

"Joanna," he began. "Like we mentioned earlier, we're with the FBI and I'm with the local LA office. I typically investigate human trafficking organizations, and it's recently come to our attention there may be something going on here in LA. Something new."

Joanna's eyes grew large. "Does that mean that Tina could have been sold into slavery?"

I stepped in. "That's not what we think happened. There are multiple facets to human trafficking. One of them is organ trafficking. I'm sure you understand that it's illegal to buy and sell organs in the United States. Actually, in most of the world. I'm going to tell you something, but it has to stay in this room. Can we trust you?"

"Yes," she said earnestly. "I just hope it helps me find my sister."

"We hope so too."

"I'm from Northern California, where I'm working on a case in which a young woman was the recipient of a kidney transplant. We're now trying to find, through DNA, the person who donated that kidney."

"And you think it's maybe one of the missing teens?"

"It's possible," I answered. "I wanted to explain so you understand the seriousness of this. We won't stop looking for these kids because my gut is telling me..." I paused and Peters nodded in encouragement. "These cases are connected. Time is of the essence. So, tell us as much as you can about these missing people. You mentioned your friend, Ava? She's the one who made the initial missing persons report on the other three teens?"

Joanna nodded. "Yes, I'll tell you everything I know. Tina, my sister, she's seventeen. She told me something big was happening, and she was going to get some serious money and she was going to help us out at home. We have four other siblings. We all chip in to make sure everybody gets to eat and we have electricity. I was nervous when Tina told me about this opportunity because I know good things don't happen to people like us. A few days later, she was gone. She never came back. It's been almost two months. And—"

"And you haven't heard from her? And nobody you know has heard from her?" I interrupted.

She shook her head. "I made a missing persons report two days after she went missing. I don't think they've done anything. You met Detective Rogers. I don't think he's even tried to look for my sister or the other three."

"How did you learn about the other three missing people?"

"From Ava. She was down at Echo Park handing out flyers. I asked her about them and I told her about my sister. All four went missing under similar circumstances. All kids who needed money desperately and would do anything for it. Now, your organ-selling scheme seems to fit."

It does, it really does. "And you say Ava has gone missing?"

"Yeah, we usually talk every single day. We text throughout the day. I've been spending most of my time out there, handing out flyers, seeing if anyone has seen my sister or any of the others. I'm trying to get the news media to run a story but I can't even get in the door. I haven't heard from Ava since yesterday."

"What time did you last speak to Ava?" I asked.

"It was about four o'clock. I went by the Grace Center where she works, where all the missing teens used to go. That's how she knows them. Her coworkers said she hadn't shown up, which is super unlike her."

"Do you know where Ava lives?"

"No, I've never been to her house, but I know she lives alone with her cat."

It should be easy enough to find Ava Woods' address. "It does sound concerning."

"What would they do with Ava, these organ buyers and sellers?"

"We're not sure," I responded. We weren't sure, but I had a pretty good idea. If they had found out she was causing a ruckus over some of their victims, they would want to silence her. "So, you don't know much about the other missing teens?"

She shook her head. "Sorry, I wish I did, but I didn't know them. I was looking for my sister when I met up with Ava, and we joined forces."

"Do you and your sister have the same father?"

She looked puzzled, but said, "Most of my siblings and I have different dads. None of the biological fathers are in the picture."

Joanna's mother was raising six kids on her own? That was rough. No wonder all the kids tried to help out. "Was Tina in contact with her biological father?"

"Do you think her dad did this to her?" she asked.

"No, we're just asking questions, trying to learn as much as we can about Tina."

"She never met him. Mom never talks about him. She said he was no good, like the worst of the worst. She said he was evil and she regretted knowing him, except for the fact that she got Tina from him. Tina is one of the sweetest, most trusting kids."

Where had we heard about a man described like that before? I gave Peters a look like I was about to ask the question that could break this case wide open. "Joanna, what's your mother's name?"

"Anita Torres. Why?" she asked.

I sat silently, thinking of the best way to handle this situation. It could be that Tina was the donor of that kidney, Scarlett's kidney, the one that had failed and ultimately killed her. I didn't think it was the time to tell her because if she hadn't seen her sister in two months, yet part of her body was in a dead girl, there wasn't much hope Tina was still alive. "Do you have a hairbrush or a toothbrush of Tina's we can use to get a DNA sample from?"

Joanna's face melted. She must have understood the implication. "Yeah, I definitely have a hairbrush and toothbrush. She didn't take anything with her."

"That's great. We'll be able to run the DNA and see if it matches any of the missing persons we know about."

"You think Tina may have donated her kidney? But if that's true, why hasn't she come home? She would've come home. She said she would."

Normally, I had no problem speaking to family members in a cold, detached manner; you had to in this line of work. But something about this moment was hitting closer to home. Peters must've sensed it because he took the lead. "We think it's possible these teens were promised money in exchange for their organs. But sometimes, these types of criminals choose not to pay, and if they think nobody will look for the bodies, they may harm them or keep them to harvest additional organs."

The color drained from Joanna's face. "You think she might be dead?"

"We don't know, but if we can get a DNA sample, that will help us find her."

"Okay, I took the bus here. I'll go home and come back?" Joanna asked.

"We can give you a ride."

Peters added, "We have an unmarked car. Don't worry."

She nodded, and we exited the LAPD station, waving to a puzzled Detective Rogers as we left.

Once we'd retrieved the evidence from Joanna's home, we reminded her not to say a word to anyone about what we had told her—we didn't want the traffickers to run for cover. A surprise attack was always preferred.

She agreed, and I hoped we could trust her. At that point, all we had were theories, but my intuition was telling me we were right on track. But even if Tina was the kidney donor, we still had no idea who had bought it... or who had taken it from her.

FORTY-THREE

VAL

After depositing the hairbrush at the FBI lab, I called Brady. Brady was disappointed he couldn't join me on the trip, but the sheriff felt he needed to stay in town and monitor any sightings of Jack and May Douglas. It made sense for us to divide our efforts—him up there, and me down in LA acting as the conduit between our two locations.

"Hey, how's it going down there?" he asked.

"We think we might've found her, the organ donor. A missing person, seventeen-year-old Tina Torres, went missing two months ago," I said. "Her sister told us their mother's name is Anita, and Tina never knew her father. But their mother said he's an evil man."

"That certainly matches Edward Martinez's description," Brady noted.

"That was my thought too. When the scientists compare the two DNA samples, we'll be able to determine whether or not Tina was Scarlett's kidney donor."

"Did you find anything else interesting?"

"Yeah," I said. "I have a feeling, Brady. It's all happening down here in LA. We found that in the last two months four teens have gone missing. They all hinted at something big coming up and then they were gone—three homeless and the other is Tina, who sometimes hung out near the encampments."

"Wow, that's big."

"We'll see. Just because we can find out who the kidney donor is doesn't mean we'll be able to figure out who's behind it," I warned him.

"Any news on Henry Tate?"

"Not yet, but as of this morning the FBI is tailing him to see where he goes and who he hangs out with."

"That's good to hear. Anything we can do up here for you?"

"Any sign of Jack or May Douglas?"

"Nope. Nothing. We've been checking traffic cams. They've either changed cars or they're staying off roads with cameras."

The only solace in that was if we couldn't find the Douglases, then maybe the traffickers couldn't find them either. "If Lucy has any time, there's something else we're thinking might be good to track down."

"What's that?"

"The task force thinks we should check hospital admissions, people coming in with infections from undocumented transplants."

"I'll let Lucy know. I'm sure she'll get right on it."

"Good."

"Oh, by the way, I checked on your mom. She's doing all right."

"I appreciate that." My mom's unusual behavior had me on edge, and I was grateful for Brady's offer to check on her once a day to make sure she was all right.

"What do you have planned next?"

"We think the person who connected all the missing teens is now missing herself. We'll go by her place of work and get her address. She was a no-show for work today."

"That's not a good sign."

"No, it's not."

"I won't keep you. I'll let you know what Lucy finds."

"Thanks. Talk to you later," I said, ending the call. I hopped into Peters' car. "All right, let's go find Ava Woods."

We walked into the Grace Center. There were half a dozen teens, and a few adults wearing T-shirts with the center's blue globe logo on them. They walked right up to us.

"Hi, my name is Special Agent Costa. This is my colleague, Special Agent Peters. We're here to ask you a few questions about your coworker, Ava Woods."

"Have you found her?" one of them asked.

"No, sir. And what's your name?" I asked.

"Danny."

"When was the last time you saw Ava, Danny?"

"She went out for another session of handing out flyers around three o'clock yesterday. She didn't come back after that. I thought maybe she went home."

"Was she supposed to come back?"

"She was, but we're not super strict around here."

That was not a good sign. Everything inside of me said we needed to find Ava and fast. "Has she ever done something like this before, just not shown up?"

"No, and I'm worried."

That made two of us. "Have you tried calling?"

"Texted and left messages. Nothing back."

"Have you gone by her apartment?"

He gasped. "No. Oh dear. If she's missing, there's nobody taking care of Mr. Flowers. Her cat."

"Do you have her address? We'll check her apartment to see if she's home."

Danny nodded. He didn't have to give us the information

without a warrant, but he was obviously as worried as we were. We could easily get a warrant if we needed, but it was easier if he just handed it over to save time and paper. He led us to a back room, sat down behind a desk, and wrote out the information. "I hope you find her. She's one of the good ones, you know."

"We'll do everything we can to find her."

"Thank you," he said.

I gave him my card and said, "Call me if Ava shows up or if you think of anything that might help us find her."

He nodded and we hurried out.

FORTY-FOUR

VAL

We convinced Ava's apartment manager to let us in without a warrant, explaining the seriousness of the situation. He didn't hesitate. After he unlocked the door, I told him to wait outside while Peters and I went to look around. I called out her name several times. The silence was deafening until I heard a faint meow. Movement under a comforter in the bedroom alerted me to what was most likely Mr. Flowers. I pulled up the covers and, sure enough, an orange tabby was looking at me with big eyes. "Are you hungry, kitty? Need some water?" It meowed at me.

Peters met up with me in the small kitchen and said, "She's not here."

"No, she's not."

"And I just received a text from Ron, one of the team doing research, to say her cell phone is either off or the battery's dead."

All signs pointed to the fact Ava was officially missing.

I searched through Ava's kitchen to find food for the cat, filled up its dish, and made sure it had plenty of water before leaving. I made a mental note to ensure we found someone to take care of the cat if we couldn't find Ava in the next twenty-four hours.

We thanked the apartment manager and told him to lock it up and not let anyone else into the apartment. I gave him my business card and told him to call me if he saw or heard from Ava. He agreed. Out on the street, Peters and I stopped to take a breath.

"Now we have five missing persons. Sound like a trafficking organization to you?" I said.

"Unfortunately, yes. At this point, I'd bet a hefty sum that organ trafficking has come to Southern California."

"Do you have the resources to get to the bottom of this, like, now?"

"I'll have to make a few calls, but I think if we can nip it in the bud before it gets too big, we could save a lot of people a lot of heartbreak. I think I can get the station chief to agree."

I certainly hoped so. I had a feeling these kids weren't getting any money for their organs, but somebody was getting rich from them. *Who, though?*

FORTY-FIVE

AVA

My eyelids flickered open, and I was nearly blinded by the bright lights. As I looked around, I noticed an IV pole. I followed the line leading from the machine into my arm. Was I in hospital? Everything was so blurry and I had no idea what had happened or how I had got here.

It was quiet—maybe I was in an intensive care unit or a not very busy hospital. The sound of approaching footsteps filled me with hope that whoever was coming would explain what had happened and where I was.

A man wearing a surgical mask and matching blue scrubs approached. "You're awake."

"Where am I?" I asked, my voice hoarse.

"You're safe, not to worry," he replied in an even tone.

"How did I get here? What happened?" I asked, my mind a swirl of questions.

The man, presumably a doctor or nurse, cocked his head and asked, "You don't remember anything?"

I shook my head from side to side, my confusion deepening.

"We found you passed out on the sidewalk. We brought you

here to make sure you were okay. The nurses have been taking care of you."

I hadn't heard any nurses or any other staff at all. The silence was unnerving. "What day is it?" I asked, my voice barely a whisper. My head pounded.

"That might be enough for today," the doctor said, his voice gentle.

The headache was wicked. Where had I fallen, and when?

The man approached my IV and injected something into the line with a syringe. His words were slow as he said, "Everything will be fine. You just need your rest now."

Something in my gut stirred, an intuition warning me that something wasn't right. But my eyelids grew heavy, and I was too tired to speak or argue. I let sleep take me, hoping for some clarity upon awakening.

FORTY-SIX

VAL

Running on nothing but adrenaline, I studied the faces of the half-dozen agents sitting around the table inside the LA County FBI headquarters. "It's nice to meet you all. I'm confident we'll get to the bottom of this. We will find Ava Woods and the missing kids." It felt good to be working with a team again, and I felt it was preparing me for my return to DC.

Peters said, "Thank you, Val. I think only a trained agent could've figured out what you had going on in Red Rose County. Thank you for bringing it to our attention. The director is very pleased, as you can tell by the six other agents sitting in this room."

Peters had just briefed the station chief on what we believed was a very serious, and potentially new, operation in Los Angeles—organ trafficking. If our theory was correct, they were plucking teens off the streets and selling their organs. Part of me wondered if the folks in charge were acting fast in an effort to keep their reputation intact, considering the human trafficking task force hadn't picked up on any of it until I'd made the call. Or the organ transplant traffickers were good at hiding their tracks, or it was a relatively small operation.

"I appreciate that. Let's get right to it. The clock is ticking. Ava Woods, the woman who has been canvassing neighborhoods looking for four missing teens, is now missing herself. If we're right about the traffickers, she likely was taken by one of them to keep her quiet. She's been missing less than," I paused and glanced at my watch, "just about twenty-four hours. This is good news. If we can find her, it's likely going to lead to the center of the operation."

"Do you think we should put out an APB. Get her face on the news?" one of the younger agents asked.

Peters said, "I think we'll want to search for her right away. But an all-points bulletin or news coverage could spook the folks who took her and force them to do something drastic. Not only that but it could drive them further underground and make it more difficult for us to find them."

"Unless the traffickers don't have her," the young agent rebutted.

Nodding, I said, "It's a fair point. But as of now we'll assume it's the organ traffickers. If we find there is no connection, we can go full force with news and an APB for her." Ava was one of the good ones; she deserved every resource law enforcement could spare to bring her home safely.

Thinking back to my conversation with Ava's coworker, I said, "We'll go under the assumption she was taken near the Grace Center, downtown, when she was handing out flyers with the missing teens' pictures. Her coworker said she left at three and had planned to return around four, but never showed up. We should pull traffic cam footage and see where she was taken. There should be quite a few cameras in the area."

With any luck, Ava would lead us right into their den. Her goal of finding the missing teens may be met—because of her. I only hoped we got to her in time.

Agent Dansen, an older man with a gray buzz cut, said, "I'll take that task."

"Great, thank you."

Peters eyed me. "Based on the missing person report for Abby, she was dating someone who drove a gold Honda Accord. Ava, in her statement, thought that man could be the one who had promised Abby a good opportunity. Let's go with Ava's instincts here. We need to run a search of all registered owners of gold Honda Accords in the area."

I added, "My guess is the owner of the gold Accord may be the one luring the victims into the scheme. Not likely the actual organ specialist, but he could lead us to the people who are."

The young, red-haired agent, Ron, said, "I'll take that one. I'll run a search for the gold Accord."

"Excellent. Do we have any news on Henry Tate? What has he been up to?" I asked.

Agent Lotus, a woman in her early thirties, responded, "The team is still tailing him. So far, he's been to his real estate office and has shown a few high-end homes. He hasn't returned home today."

"Are they recording plates and descriptions of Tate's clients?"

"Yes, ma'am."

"Good," I replied. "I think we need to keep an eye on him. The fact that he lives in Los Angeles is too big of a coincidence, as we also suspect this is where the transplants are occurring."

Heads nodded.

My phone buzzed, and I glanced down at the number, one I was beginning to recognize as coming from the sheriff's department. "Give me a sec, I've got a call from Red Rose County."

Peters nodded, and I stepped away to take the call. "Hello?"

"Hey, Val, it's Lucy," came the familiar voice.

"Hey, Lucy, what's up?"

"Brady wanted me to call you and give you an update. I've called all the local hospitals in Los Angeles, asking about anyone coming in with injuries or infections relating to transplants that weren't in the individual's medical records."

"And what did you find?"

"There weren't any. Not good news if there's an organ-trafficking ring in the area."

"So, what are we thinking? They had a transplant, had a great team, and there are no infections? Or the donors never left the surgery suite?" I thought aloud.

That was the worst-case scenario. Not that we would give up hope of finding the donors alive, but to be missing two months was a long time in any kidnapping situation. Add in the idea that organized crime was involved, it wasn't looking good. If my thoughts on the perpetrators were correct, they were criminals hiding in plain sight.

"Thanks, Lucy. Any word on the Douglases' whereabouts?"

"Nope, they're in the wind."

"How about a BOLO on their license plate tags?"

"It's out there. We're hoping somebody spots their vehicles. I sent the BOLO out to Oregon, Nevada, Washington, Utah, Arizona—all the surrounding states."

"Thanks, Lucy." I ended the call and returned to the group. Everyone was talking. I said, "What did I miss?"

Ron said, "We found something."

I'd been on the phone for what, five minutes? "What did you find?"

"I did a quick search of registered vehicles in LA. Gold Honda Accords—guess how many there are?"

"I don't know, a dozen?"

"Fourteen."

That was lucky. With a team of six, we could probably hunt down the fourteen that night. "Is there more?"

"Yep. One of them is registered to—wait for it," he said, looking up from his screen, a twinkle in his eyes, "Sean Tate."

You've got to be kidding. "Any relation to Henry?"

Ron nodded. "It's his son."

The room fell silent. "It's him. It's both of them. They're involved. We need to find Sean and keep eyes on him. How old is he?"

"The background check we did earlier shows that Henry Tate has two kids—Sean, who's nineteen, and Delilah, who's twenty-three. Sean is a student at UCLA, no work history."

What? Why would Henry Tate have his college kid involved in a criminal organization? Was it possible Sean didn't know that the kids he was luring into his father's side business were giving up a heck of a lot more than a body organ? "We need to know everything about this kid. Check his social media —everything."

"I'm on it," Ron said.

"You thinking what I'm thinking?" Peters asked.

"That Henry is using Sean, his nineteen-year-old son, to lure victims into his organ-trafficking scheme?"

"That's exactly it. But it can't be just the two of them. Besides, the Douglases said that where they had the operation was a clean, state-of-the-art facility. They must be connected to some doctors, nurses... We need to find every single person who talks to or shakes Henry Tate's hand. They could be involved."

"We're going to need more agents."

"I'll call the station chief."

We had to nail these jerks to the wall. We just had to find them and, of course, prove what they'd been up to. We weren't fully sure of all the details yet, but we were close—I could feel it.

FORTY-SEVEN

Pacing the halls of the FBI headquarters, I felt stuck. At that point, it was a waiting game and I hated waiting. Patience wasn't a trait I had in abundance. Especially when I was fixated on finding Ava Woods and the other missing teens.

It was nearing one in the morning and the team had been working nonstop. Thankfully, since the station chief was tight with the director, all kinds of strings were being pulled to get us the resources we needed. Which was a lot. We had to have eyes on anyone who may be even remotely connected. I wanted to be out in the field looking, but we had people for that and I was supposed to be on leave. It was frustrating sitting around knowing Ava and the others needed our help ASAP.

After poring over video footage, we were able to pinpoint the exact location where Ava had been abducted. A man wearing a baseball cap and hoodie had approached her. No distinguishing marks were visible, other than the fact he was Caucasian. With a swift, cruel motion, he had clamped a hand over her mouth and hurled her into the back of a white panel van. There were cheers, hoots, and hollers echoing in the room when we ran the van's plates, only to find that it had been reported stolen a week prior. The van itself had yet to be found.

Our only solace was the knowledge of Sean and Henry's location. They were safe and sound at home, four agents guarding the house unbeknownst to them. Additional agents were deployed, tailing three of Henry Tate's clients. Each of them held a medical degree.

No stone unturned.

The night dragged on, a quiet lull hanging in the air. Peters met me in the hall.

"Why don't you head back to your hotel room and get some rest?" he asked.

I raised a brow and replied, "There's no way I would get a wink of sleep. All I need is caffeine and something to keep my mind occupied." There was no way I could sleep, especially without a sleeping pill. And I didn't want to take one and miss a critical piece of information that could come in.

"Well, you could go grab the team some snacks. They've been working all night and they're not stopping until we find them."

"Not a bad idea," I conceded.

While fetching food wasn't part of my typical FBI agent duties, I felt a bit superfluous at the moment. We had an agent scouring Sean's social media for any connection to our missing persons. So far, he had found none, but he was also tracking Sean's friends, looking for friends of friends, any connection. Henry, on the other hand, had no social media presence outside of his real estate business profile. However, we were sifting through all of his known associates and clients, everyone he'd had contact with over the last three years. At that point, there wasn't much I could do other than to feed the troops.

"What are they into?"

"In-N-Out Burger?" he suggested, a spark of weary humor in his eyes.

Burgers, fries, shakes—they had good taste.

Just as I was about to head back into the war room to get orders, the sound of a call coming in stopped me in my tracks. Without hesitation, I answered it. "Hey, Brady, what's up?"

"We found Jack's and May's cars."

"Who found them? Where? Are they okay?"

"Patrol spotted their cars parked at a small motel. It's on the coast of Oregon, near Cannon Beach."

"And Jack and May, are they okay?"

"Unclear. We haven't gotten a visual confirmation, but I told the patrol to stay put if possible and watch the parking lot."

It was possible the cars had been dumped there. "So, no confirmation they're actually there?"

"They spoke to the clerk, and he said the owners of the vehicles checked in a few days ago. Motel registration lists them as Trudy and Tom Wilson."

That was a big win. "So they're hiding," I concluded. From the law or the traffickers?

"I told patrol to ensure their safety and to keep watching until they get visual confirmation of the two."

"Did the motel clerk tell the officers which room is theirs?"

"Yep."

"Okay, hold on."

Turning to Peters, I said, "They found the Douglases on the Oregon coast."

"Good news," he acknowledged.

"Should we hold them there or pick them up? If we explain what we found, the Douglases may have a change of heart and tell us the location of the medical facility where Scarlett had her operation."

Peters said, "We should pick them up and have them transported down here."

"What if they won't come willingly?"

"Arrest them."

"On what charges?"

Peters nodded with slight smile. "Obstruction of justice."

I could live with that. The Douglases had the opportunity to save lives, not just their own. "Let's do it."

"I'll call the FBI's Portland office," he said, stepping away to make the call.

The adrenaline racing through me made up for the fact I hadn't slept or taken a break since the day before. "Did you hear that, Brady?"

"Yeah, I'll put in a call to patrol to let them know the Feds are coming."

"Thanks. How's my mom?"

"She's doing all right. She seems tired, though. She says she's just worried about you."

"I'm fine." And I was. Not that I couldn't use a little sleep and maybe a burger. But was that really why Mom looked tired?

"That's what I told her."

"Thanks again, Brady."

I ended the call and waited for Peters to finish his conversation with the Portland FBI office. He hung up, stuffed the phone into his jacket pocket, and said, "They will have an agent pick them up within the hour."

"They'll transport them down here?"

"Yeah, but you know it's an eighteen-hour drive."

"Air is much faster."

Peters smirked. "Understood. I'll call them back."

I didn't think Ava had eighteen hours.

Leaning against the wall, I waited for the approval for a plane to transport the Douglases.

Once Peters was off the phone, he said, "It's done. They'll touch down in about five hours. Want some company picking up the late-night snacks?"

"Sure."

Getting Jack and May Douglas into custody was a win.

Assuming that we could protect them, they might be willing to talk to us, tell us what they knew about Henry and Sean's involvement. All signs were pointing to the fact Henry was the one who'd clued them in about the possibility of a transplant for their daughter. All the pieces were starting to fall into place.

But I was still worried about Ava Woods and the missing teens. Knowing what was going on in this particular section of organized crime was one thing. But what was most important was ensuring we found those missing persons alive, if possible. And then ensure these guys never took another teen or another unwilling participant again.

FORTY-EIGHT

VAL

It was six in the morning, when Special Agent Peters stepped back into the war room and said, "They're here."

Fueled with a burger, fries, and caffeine, I practically jumped out of my seat. I was more than ready to interview May and Jack Douglas. Trying to contain my excitement, I forced myself to walk to the interrogation room at a normal pace. I entered the anteroom and stared through the two-way mirror. May and Jack looked frazzled as they kept asking why they were there, asserting they hadn't done anything wrong. It was by design; we hadn't wanted them saying anything to any local agents or local police in case the locals had connections to the organ traffickers. We didn't know much about the organization or how far its tentacles reached. I tapped on the glass, and an agent inside the room nodded, stood up, and left the Douglases alone.

Door shut, the agent extended his hand. "You must be Special Agent Costa?"

"Yes, sir."

"I'm Special Agent Dale, Portland office."

"Thanks for bringing them down."

"Must be important," he remarked.

"It is," I confirmed.

Peters stepped closer. "Hey, Dale. How's it going?"

"All good. The restroom is down the hall, right?"

"Down the hall," he confirmed.

I opened the door and stepped into the interrogation room.

Both May and Jack looked like two deer in the middle of a dark highway staring blindly into my headlights. May's hair was mussed, and Jack's shirt was wrinkled. They'd had a rough morning.

May stuttered, "Agent Costa, you're behind this? We didn't do anything. We told you, we can't talk."

Ignoring May's rhetoric, I said, "May Douglas, Jack Douglas, this here is Special Agent Peters of the LA County FBI office. He's the head of the FBI's human trafficking task force in Southern California."

"Human trafficking?" May said with a crack in her voice.

They had no idea what they had gotten involved in. They just knew they had trusted very dangerous people with their daughter's life. It was a gamble and they lost. I took a seat while Peters took the one next to me.

"First off, how are you both doing?" I asked.

May responded, "We're *not* okay. We were arrested, not told anything, put on a plane, and now we're here, and you're saying we're human traffickers."

Peters clarified, "Nobody is saying you're human traffickers."

I looked at Jack, who had been very quiet and had a look I was familiar with. The man was tired and done. Defeated.

"We brought you down here because we have an update on the case. When we learned about Scarlett's illegal kidney transplant, it raised red flags at the FBI because, as you know, it's illegal to buy and sell organs almost everywhere in the world, including the United States. Based on your movements, we know you had the transplant done here in the United States. This is a major concern for our country and our citizens. Based on what we've learned, we believe there's a human trafficking organization located here in Los Angeles, and we suspect the donors for the organs are not willing participants. We believe they are lured in with promises of cash in exchange for one of their non-vital organs. But then, the traffickers don't pay up, and instead they mostly likely eliminate the donors. *They kill them.*"

Jack lowered his head.

"We have identified some missing persons, teenagers, just like Scarlett. They were young and desperate for cash. These criminals preyed on them. Stole their body parts and likely killed them. We brought you here because we need your help before anyone else gets hurt." We weren't entirely sure what had happened to the missing teens, but it was one of the working theories.

May swallowed hard. "They said they'd kill us."

"How long did it take us to find you? Less than a week."

Jack shook his head slowly while May sat quietly.

I continued, "If we could find you, so can they. We're offering you protection and immunity for your role, but you need to talk to us. We've already uncovered some information and are pretty sure we know what happened with you and Scarlett. If you don't help us, you will be facing felony charges."

Jack raised his head and looked at us with the saddest eyes I'd ever seen.

"We believe your neighbor, Henry Tate, told you about the illegal transplant operation, and he's been your guide for the transplant process. He showed you how to pay the traffickers in cash so as not to alert the IRS. We believe he told you how to clean out your hotel room to not leave a trace behind. We think he is the conduit to the organized crime syndicate that is stealing organs from young people, killing them, and then using those organs to help save wealthy recipients."

Peters chimed in, "How are we doing so far?"

May shook her head. "I didn't... They told us the donors were willing and they were grateful for the opportunity."

"And when you say 'they,' do you mean Henry Tate and his son Sean?"

Jack's eyes widened.

I took that as a yes. "We can provide protection and immunity, if you cooperate. We feel like we're close, and time is really important right now. There is a woman who works at a local community center that helps and feeds homeless teens. She found a pattern of missing teens who said they had this 'great opportunity' and then were never seen again. She is now missing, and if the others have been killed, we can't save them. But this woman, Ava, who went out on her own to report these kids missing, her life is in danger and we need your help to save her."

"I don't know," May said with uncertainty.

Watching Jack's movements, I felt we were close to breaking him. He looked at his wife, shook his head, and said, "That's enough, May. We will cooperate."

"Jack, you can't!" May cried.

"Enough, May. Why do you think our lives are more important than these young people? We have a choice to help. They don't have a choice and are losing their lives." With tears in his eyes, Jack continued, "I'll tell you everything. I remember it all. I wished I didn't but I do."

With relief, and my pulse racing, I asked, "Is our assumption about Henry and Sean Tate, correct?"

Jack nodded. "Henry's our neighbor and was our friend. He knew how desperate we were to help Scarlett. He told us about a doctor in LA. It wasn't exactly legal, but he told us nobody would get hurt. He told us how much it cost and we nearly fainted; we didn't have the money. He suggested different ways to get the money like refinancing the house, draining our savings. So, we did. He told us, just like you said, how to get around the IRS. We opened multiple accounts, we paid them, and then we came here to Los Angeles. We thought it was just going to be a consultation, but the doctor said he had a donor ready to go and she would be so grateful for the money. Said that the donor's family needed the money and she wanted to help them."

"Did you ever meet the donor?" I asked.

Jack shook his head. "No. I thought that was strange. I would think that if I were donating a kidney, I would want to meet the person who was getting it. We asked about her because Scarlett wanted to meet the person who was going to give her her life back, but the doctor and Henry said it was impossible, that she wanted to remain anonymous."

May gasped. "Is the girl dead?"

"We're not sure yet. We haven't located the facility. The only people we know so far that are involved are Henry and Sean Tate, and that's why we need you. These are dangerous people."

Jack continued, "So we went through with the operation. Henry let us stay at his house in Los Angeles so we didn't have to pay for a hotel. He knew we were pretty tapped out. The doctor was really nice. He told us he believed Scarlett was going to do really well, that she was young and she would heal quickly." He shrugged and waved his hands. "Well, you know how that turned out. When we couldn't find Scarlett that morning, we called Henry. He and his son, Sean, helped us check around the lake for her. Henry found her and said she had collapsed. They carried her back home, and he called the doctor and described what had happened. The doctor said it was too late for her and since she was so far down on the donor list, she had zero chance for survival. Henry provided us with morphine so that she would pass peacefully. They helped us bury her before the Tates went back to LA."

Both the Douglases were in tears. All I could think was that their story about what had happened to Scarlett finally made sense—because they were finally telling the whole truth.

"Do you know the address of the facility where the transplant took place?"

"No. Henry drove us there. But it was in an office park."

Peters interjected, "If we brought you there, would you be able to recognize it?"

"Yes."

"Do you have any idea how Henry knew the doctor or the team that did the transplant?"

"He didn't tell us. We didn't ask."

"Did the doctor tell you his name?" I asked.

Jack shook his head.

"Do you know what he looks like?"

"He was white, bald. Fit. He wore a mask, which, now that I think about it, is a little strange. We never met him in his office, it was just in the surgery suite."

"Did you meet anybody else while you were down here for the transplant?"

"Only Henry and Sean, who we already knew, and the doctor. But like I said, he wore a mask. We definitely heard some others but we couldn't see them."

"When you went to the surgery suite, did you walk through an office? Can you walk me through what that looked like?"

"Sure. Henry drove us there. As I explained, it was in an office park, looked like any other medical building. There weren't any names on the walls. You know how when you go to a medical office there's a glass case that has the different practices and the numbers? There wasn't any of that, it was blank. We thought that was strange, but we also knew it was illegal, so we didn't question it. We walked into what seemed like a medical office. It was empty. There was a reception desk but no receptionist, just some chairs. It looked like it was built in the 1970s or '80s and hadn't been refurbished since. But they led us down a hallway into the surgery suite, which was immaculate. Beds, monitors, really clean. It was a stark contrast to the waiting area, which is why it stood out. We felt good about it, knowing that although it was illegal, it seemed like they took a lot of care with the actual procedure."

My mind was racing. It was likely an abandoned medical practice. "Can you remember how long it took to drive from the Tates' house to the surgery center?"

Jack said, "Fifteen, maybe twenty minutes, at most."

Good. "Anything else you can tell us?"

He shook his head.

"What about when she was having the surgery? Where were you?"

"Henry took us back to his house. We didn't want to leave, but he said it was best. So, we went back to his house and waited. They said they'd let us know when Scarlett was awake."

I turned to Peters. "Is it enough to start looking for a location?"

"I think so. It sounds like an abandoned medical practice they were using, or maybe they rented it out but didn't have any business associated with it. I'll tell the team. We'll get a location."

"Thank you, again. Now, sit tight. Can I get you anything? Are you hungry? It's pretty early. Have you had breakfast? Coffee?"

Jack said, "I'd love a coffee, or anything you've got."

I nodded and got up.

May stopped me. "Agent Costa, I'm so sorry. We should've trusted you. We had no idea people were getting hurt."

Of course not. But what most people didn't realize was that most criminal activity, like organ trafficking or something as seemingly benign as buying counterfeit goods, fed into organized crime that funded more violent crimes like sex trafficking and other atrocities against our fellow humans. There were very few victimless crimes.

I said, "I'll be back."

Outside the interrogation room, I sighed. "That information sure would have been helpful before."

"No kidding."

At least we had the information, and now all we had left to do was find the location and Ava and the missing teens and we could call it a job well done. My phone buzzed and I checked the screen. It was Kieran. My boss whom I hadn't told that I was in LA working a trafficking case.

Well, as they say, no good deed goes unpunished.

FORTY-NINE

VAL

A part of me didn't want to answer, but I knew I had to. "I need to take this," I said, stepping aside so Peters wouldn't overhear my boss chewing me out. "Hey, Kieran, what's up?"

"What are you doing?" he said sternly.

"Helping the task force."

"I told you to hand it over to the task force and let it be."

"I'm not going out in the field. I'm just here in an advisory role, like a volunteer. It's more efficient than endless conference calls." When I'd hopped on the plane, I'd known Kieran wouldn't be pleased, but I hadn't considered disciplinary action. He'd always let me work in the gray area when I needed. Why was this different?

"Val, you know I know you better than that. You want to be on the case, so you're on the case. But you also know that's not how it works at the Bureau."

"I had a hunch and it was right. Now I'm helping the team find these guys. We're close, really close. We found May and Jack Douglas. We have them here in LA. We just got out of the room questioning them. They gave us details about the location where Scarlett had her surgery, not to mention confirming that their neighbors, Henry and Sean Tate, were involved in the organ-trafficking operation." I braced myself for a lecture on following the chain of command. After twenty years with the FBI, it was the only thing I still struggled to adhere to.

"Sounds like you and the team did great work. Now it's time to pack up your things, go home, and continue with your leave. You still have two weeks before you're supposed to be on active duty," he said, his tone firm and unyielding.

"Give me one more day in an advisory role. I promise I won't go in the field. Plus, they don't even need me out there. I'll be safe and sound right here at the LA office."

Silence from Kieran was never a good thing.

"Val, put yourself in my position. How would you feel if you got a call from a station chief, thanking you for your agent's great help, which you knew nothing about?"

Ouch. He was right, and I knew it. "Kieran, I'm sorry. It all just happened so fast. One minute I was talking to them on the Polycom, the next I was on a plane to LA. I'm sorry. I know I messed up." It hadn't occurred to me Kieran would be fielding calls from the station chief in LA. Was I slipping?

"Val, I'm starting to see a pattern. You need to watch yourself and start following orders. You already disobeyed one when you left your motel room to go after the Bear on your own. How did that turn out?"

I bit my tongue, knowing it was a rhetorical question. I knew we weren't supposed to pursue the suspect alone. But I couldn't help myself.

"And now you've disobeyed another order. I told you after your conversation with the human trafficking task force that you would hand off the case and end it there, job well done. And we both know you didn't follow that order. Is this something we need to put into a disciplinary plan? Or perhaps we should extend your leave until you relearn that you must follow orders."

Is he threatening to suspend me? "I'm sorry. I'll book the next flight home."

"Will you really?"

"Give me twenty-four hours, Kieran. And I promise I won't go out in the field. I'll stay here in the war room in an advisory capacity, like I've been doing. Twenty-four hours. That's all I'm asking. Please."

After a pause followed by a heavy sigh, Kieran said, "Twenty-four hours, Val, and if you're not home drinking tea with your mother, your leave will be indefinite."

I didn't drink tea, but saying I preferred coffee wouldn't help the situation. "That's fair. Thank you, Kieran."

"Don't make me regret this," he warned before ending the call.

I stepped back over to Peters, who could tell it hadn't been a pleasant conversation.

"Everything okay?"

"It's fine, but the boss is a little miffed I came down here without letting him know. He says I've got twenty-four hours before I must fly home. So, let's go get these monsters."

We needed to find Ava before it was too late. And before I was fired from the Bureau.

FIFTY

VAL

Back inside the war room, where the agents on the task force were busy, I provided the update from the Douglases and they dove right into the task at hand. Their objective was to find potential locations of where the organ transplant surgeries were taking place, where we would find the participants in the organization, and most importantly where they were keeping Ava Woods and the others, if they were still alive.

I felt that we were close to unearthing the truth, but after speaking with Agents Grindle and Peters, I knew we wouldn't take down the entire organization in a day. It could take months, even years, of fieldwork, undercover agents, the whole shebang, to identify every single person involved in the organization. Because of that, I knew at some point I would have to let it go, let them do their jobs, and return to mine.

However, until Henry Tate, his son, and everyone who'd worked on Scarlett's surgery was arrested, and Ava Woods and the four missing teens were found, I was on the case. Ava was a good Samaritan looking out for kids not even related to her. She didn't deserve to die at the hands of greedy criminals.

A text came through on my phone, and a smile appeared on

my face. Harrison had just arrived in Barcelona. He sent a silly photo of him and a few of his friends in front of Park Güell, pretending that the iguana statue was their own personal pet.

My son was in his prime, living a mostly carefree existence. His only responsibilities were to stay alive and go to school. That was how it should have been for these kids, not having to sell their body parts just to have food to eat and a place to stay. What was happening to those kids wasn't right.

Would we recover them all? Was it only four that had gone missing? How long had this whole scheme been going on?

We didn't know. Peters had set my expectations: one, we might never know, and two, it could take a long time, as was often the case with these types of organizations. But, he'd said, it was possible it was a small operation that was just starting out. If that was the case, we had a chance at eliminating it before more people were hurt.

Sending a text back, I told him I was also having fun, and that I missed him.

Suddenly, Ron shouted, "I think I found something."

Peters and I hurried over. "What is it?"

"Here's a medical office that had been vacant but was recently leased by Dr. Bernard Davis."

"Why do we think this could be the place?"

The group was now forming around Ron and his computer.

"Because the building was leased a year ago, but no occupancy permits have been filed, and there are no business licenses for this address. And you want to know the most compelling reason?"

"I do."

With a cocky smile, he said, "His real estate agent is Henry Tate."

"Has he bought homes from him?"

"Yep, and he's one of the doctors we're currently following. You want to know where he is right now?" Ron asked.

"Yes."

Ron tapped his screen. "He's parked at this address."

Ron, with his wild red hair, was becoming one of my favorite members of the team.

"Well done," Peters said. "I'll get the Douglases. We'll put them in a car and see if we can confirm it. I'll have a tactical team come along. If it's the location, we'll go in."

Every part of my being wanted to rush off and go into that building to find out if Ava was being held inside, or if it was the location of the illegal transplants. But I had made a promise to Kieran. "I'll stay back and work with some of the team to see if we can uncover any more information."

Peters knew I was technically on leave, but the others didn't. "Good idea. And once we have a green light on the location, we'll have the team pick up Henry and Sean Tate at their house and search it. Ava could be there too. But this needs to be a coordinated effort."

"Understood." We had the Douglases' testimony, but we didn't want to pick up the Tates without solid evidence of the surgery location.

"I'll call and let you know. We'll have the Tate surveillance team go in once backup arrives."

"Got it. Now go get them."

Peters rushed out of the war room and my jealousy bubbled up. I could feel my cheeks growing red. Trying to distract myself, I turned to Ron. "Not too shabby."

"I've got skills."

"Yes, you do."

And I hoped those skills would help us find Ava Woods alive, along with Mia, Abby, Tina, and Ethan.

FIFTY-ONE

AVA

Lying in the hospital bed, I was awake but didn't dare open my eyes. I had a feeling they had cameras, or some way of knowing when I was awake, so I kept them shut. It was a tactical decision, to listen, to hear what was going on. Each sound, each whisper, might give me a clue as to where I was. Fragmented memories surfaced, warning me of the danger I was in. The recollection had struck me like lightning—the man on the street. He had questioned me about the missing teens before throwing me in the back of a van. The horrifying realization was crystal-clear.

I had to get out of here. I knew I needed to make a run for it —somehow. I had to fight. There was no negotiating with these people. If I didn't, my fate would mirror that of Tina, Mia, Abby, and Ethan—vanished, never to be heard of again.

I suddenly had a sinking feeling. Had anyone realized I was missing? Surely they must've noticed my absence when I didn't show up for work. Truth be told, I wasn't sure how long I'd been here, but my last memory was of returning from handing out flyers and the man throwing me in the van. So they must have known I was missing. I found myself praying they had informed the police, that someone, anyone, would be looking for me. A glimmer of hope sparked at the thought. It was a sharp contrast to the bleak outlook for the missing teens.

Suddenly, a flurry of conversations filled the air, commotion ensued, and voices were raised. I strained my ears, but I couldn't quite make out what was being said. It sounded like there was someone who wasn't supposed to be there, someone claiming they would "take care of it." Did they mean me? Someone would take care of me?

The voices were preoccupied, trying to figure out what to do, whether this unexpected development was bad for them or not. *They can't be talking about me*, I thought. Was someone here to rescue me? And what about the four missing teenagers, were they here too?

Eyes still closed, I thought, *This is my shot.*

Without giving it another thought, I climbed out of the bed and felt the cold floor beneath my bare feet. Carefully, I slipped off the bed, eyes snapping open. To my surprise, I was in a hospital gown, white with little blue flowers. The stark contrast of the cheerful print and my grim situation was almost laughable. I yanked the needle from my arm and beeping sounded. *Dang.* I saw the plug in the outlet and pulled. The monitor silenced.

I stayed low as I made my way in the opposite direction of the voices. Something told me there were cameras everywhere, especially since they had seen someone outside. Every step was calculated, my heart pounding. I had to be careful. My life depended on finding an exit.

Crawling on my hands and knees, I was careful not to draw attention to myself. I turned right, keeping my gaze low, and scanned the area.

Other hospital beds dotted the space, curtains separating

them in an almost clinical sterility. It was only then I realized the vastness of the room I had been confined in. There were four hospital beds, five including mine.

Were there more patients?

Victims?

A fleeting thought crossed my mind, suggesting I might be in a genuine hospital. Maybe I had been rescued and was receiving medical care, but something felt amiss.

With the disquieting thought, I crawled to the next bed, my senses heightened for any suspicious noise. None drew near. I took a chance, standing up for a better look. As I slowly raised myself up, my breath hitched in my throat. "Ethan," I gasped.

Frantically, I shook him, trying to rouse him, to get him out of here. It didn't make sense. He wouldn't stir. I glanced at the monitors, but as I was no medical professional, I had no idea what they signified. However, one thing was clear: Ethan was unconscious, and there was no way I could carry him. A hopeful thought popped into my head—were the others here too?

I needed to escape, but if there was anything I could do to help, I had to try. Slinking back onto my hands and knees, I made my way to the next bed. As I lifted myself up, my heart skipped a beat. The sight was horrifying.

Sweet Abby lay there, one of her eyes covered with white gauze. "Oh no," I breathed, my mind reeling. I touched her arm, tried to stir her, but she, too, was unconscious. My stomach churned violently, threatening to revolt at the terrifying scene.

Leaving Abby behind, I forced myself to move to the next bed, bracing myself for the horror that awaited.

The sight of Mia was enough to bring tears to my eyes.

Once young and vibrant, she was now pale, both eyes covered with white gauze and her arms wrapped in bandages. I tried to wake her, but she was immovable. I pulled back the sheet to look for other signs of injury, but the sight sent me reeling. I quickly covered her again, my stomach lurching.

What had they done to her?

Seized by a sudden urgency, I raced to the last bed. There was no more time for slow and steady. I needed to be quick. A glance confirmed my worst fear. There lay Tina Torres, Joanna's sister. Her eyes weren't covered—rather, she seemed to be in a restful sleep, bandages swathing her arms. I didn't have the stomach to look closer. I knew now, more than ever, I had to escape.

My eyes darted around the room, committing as many details to memory as I could. I hoped to provide useful information to the police once I escaped. If they cared.

The sound of heavy boots broke the silence. Were they chasing me? Had they seen me? Panic set in, and I searched for a hiding spot. No supply closet in sight, but there were two doors with windows offering views to the hallway. Were they running to something or from someone?

Without wasting another moment, I made a beeline for the doors, peeking out cautiously. They must be in another part of the building, maybe another suite. Slowly, I turned the knob, slipped out, and sprinted right. I wasn't sure where the exit was, but I knew I had to keep moving. The sight of a door marked "Exit" filled me with relief.

Pushing it open, an alarm blared, accelerating my heartbeat. I hurried down the stairs, gripping the railing to keep me steady, turned a corner, descended another flight, and finally burst into the parking lot.

Sunlight nearly blinded me. Frantically, I looked in all directions, trying to get my bearings. A vehicle caught my eye, with two men in the front and a middle-aged couple in the backseat. Maybe they could help, or perhaps they were in on it. I had to try. As I hurried toward the car, my gaze met the passenger's. He looked shocked as the door swung open. The vest he wore read "FBI."

Tears welled up in my eyes. "You have to help," I managed to croak out.

"Are you Ava Woods?" he asked, his tone filled with urgency.

I nodded. "They're up there. You have to help them. They're up there."

The driver-side door swung open, and another man in an FBI vest hurried over.

"You're safe now," he assured me, his voice firm yet kind. He made some sort of motion, and almost instantly, a dozen agents in FBI jackets, guns drawn, ran toward the building.

"Second floor," I wheezed. "I think they know you're here."

The man signaled the team, who continued their mission toward the building. "What else can you tell us about the inside?"

"There's... there's people, staff... and four other patients. They're missing teens. You... you won't believe what they did to them."

The man introduced himself as Special Agent Peters. "We know who you're referring to. The four missing teens: Tina, Mia, Abby, and Ethan. We're here to find you, them, and to put a stop to this operation. What else can you tell us about what's inside?"

"I don't know much. But I know they took me, drugged me. I pretended to be asleep and took my chance to get away. I think there are cameras everywhere. I heard commotion, they must've seen someone in the lot. They were worried about visitors. I think they've seen your people."

Special Agent Peters said, "You did really well, Ava. Really well." He gestured to the other man. "This is Agent Calderwood. He's going to take care of you. I need to make a call."

As Agent Calderwood guided me toward the car, I could

hear Special Agent Peters on the phone. "We found Ava Woods. She's alive."

They had been looking for me. And they had found me. I only wished they had been looking for the others first, then they wouldn't have had to look for me at all.

FIFTY-TWO

VAL

In the overly air-conditioned hallway of Los Angeles County General Hospital, I met up with Peters. His demeanor was one of puzzlement and frustration.

"The Tates still aren't talking?"

He shook his head in resignation. "Both lawyered up—father and son, not saying a word."

"And those rounded up at the surgery center?"

"So far, nobody's speaking up. But they're all in interrogation. Hopefully, someone breaks soon. With time, I think at least one of them will. Between the Douglases' testimony and the evidence found at the surgery center, I don't think a single person will avoid jail time."

It wasn't surprising. They had been incredibly cautious every step of the way with the Douglas family. They knew how to circumvent IRS reporting and clean the motel room so that the Douglases could evade talking to us.

According to the testimonies from Jack and May, it seemed Henry Tate had suggested they go into hiding to protect them from people who were more dangerous. Did Henry actually care?

But as I suspected, Henry Tate's compassionate facade was just that. He and his son acted as if they were clueless about their arrests, feigning ignorance about any connection to human trafficking or illegal organ transplants. They were unaware we had May and Jack in protective custody—both of whom had implicated the Tates.

Knowing the Tates were involved in Scarlett's transplant and subsequent burial, we planned to run more tests to determine if they had left any of their DNA behind—either on Scarlett or on the sheet she had been wrapped in. If we could find any physical evidence, it would discredit their claims of having nothing to do with Scarlett's death or her transplant. A competent lawyer could minimize their involvement, assuming no one else turned against them. But the Douglases' testimony would significantly help our case, even if the Tates argued they were ignorant of the true extent of harm inflicted on their victims. And those victims were undoubtedly suffering.

"Any word yet on the conditions of the four teens?" I asked, trying to keep my voice steady.

Peters nodded and said solemnly, "It's grim, really grim. Of all the things I've seen in this job... and I've seen some horrific things as you can imagine. Some of them have a chance of survival. Others, not likely."

It was nothing short of a miracle we'd found Ava, Mia, Tina, Ethan, and Abby alive. The extent of the harm inflicted upon them and how they had been kept alive since their disappearances remained a mystery. The medical team that arrived recommended against moving the teens while they were being examined. So, the dedicated doctors worked tirelessly through the night, conducting comprehensive physicals on the four victims.

Judging from the look in Peters' eyes and the tremor in his voice, I could tell the situation was bad. However, it was better to know the truth before I went in to speak with Ava Woods and embarked on my journey home—a promise I had made to Kieran. I needed to understand the condition of the victims and whether our efforts to halt the organ-trafficking ring had managed to save any of the missing individuals.

"We should sit down for this," I suggested, pointing toward the kitchenette the nurses had given us full use of. He nodded in agreement, and we both made our way to the dimly lit room. After grabbing a couple of coffees, we found an empty table.

Seated across from me, Peters began, "You and I have been doing this job for a long time. We've seen the worst of what humanity does to one another, but you need to brace yourself for this."

A barrage of thoughts rushed through my mind about what could have happened to those kids. I was all too aware that people were capable of unimaginable horrors. Having been captured by one of those people myself, I was annoyed at the lack of progress in catching the Bear. Despite the frustration, I found some solace in knowing we had apprehended some of the culprits responsible for the terrible fate of those four children.

"Give it to me," I urged him.

"Tina... she's been missing the longest. Her sister claims about two months while..." He paused, exhaled, then continued, "She's been in a medically induced coma, likely for nearly the entire time she's been missing, based on the bedsores and infections, and extent of procedures."

My stomach twisted. An awful picture of what they had done to Tina was beginning to take shape.

"They conducted X-rays of her body and did a visual inspection. She has multiple surgical incisions. One of her kidneys was removed, seventy percent of her liver is gone, and multiple sections of skin and fat cells were removed from her body."

They had kept her alive just to continue harvesting her

organs. I shoved my coffee away, realizing I couldn't stomach it now. My last meal was threatening to come right back up too.

"Will she survive?" I managed to ask.

"Technically, yes. But they're running some tests. Based on the number of surgical incisions, the doctors believe they may have performed a liver transplant, let it grow back after about two months, and then harvested it again—a process most people can't handle. In the legal world of organ transplantation, a liver donor can only donate once. They think they took Tina's liver twice." He paused and said, "Has the DNA come back yet?"

"Not yet." The anticipation was unbearable. Any day now, we would hear whether Tina was the kidney donor for Scarlett Douglas.

I had viewed photographs of the victims, and I was painfully aware that the atrocities committed against them were beyond horrific. Yet, hearing the reality verbalized made the horror all too real. I shook my head in disbelief, struggling to process it. "And Mia?" I asked, recalling her image—a bandage obscuring her eyes.

"Mia, like the other three, is in a medically induced coma and she hasn't woken up. They've all been fed through tubes. At least they pumped them full of pain medication," Peters said, his voice heavy with a sorrow that acted as a chilling precursor to what he about to reveal. "Mia had both eyes removed, and multiple skin and fat cells are missing, and she has multiple scars. We think they took her liver, kidney, and spleen."

"Survival likelihood?" I asked, bracing myself for the response.

"The doctor thinks if she's taken out of the coma and off the life support machine, she might survive, she might not. She's got a nasty infection and her body has been through a lot. If she does survive, her life is forever changed."

I shook my head, struggling to digest this information.

"Why let them have infections? They can't use the bodies if they're infected, right?"

"You're right, but it sounds like the infections are relatively new. Perhaps they were just waiting to treat her in case they needed other organs, like her heart."

"And the family, the next of kin? Have they been contacted?"

"They're looking into it but haven't found anyone yet. We plan to interview Ava. She's in fairly good condition."

"And Abby?" I had to know, but feared the answer.

"Abby had skin, fat, a kidney, and the majority of her liver removed. The most shocking part is her heart is missing; she's been on an artificial heart for quite some time."

The people who did this were monsters. There was no other word for it. "And Ethan?"

"He had only been missing for a little over a week. He's missing a kidney, but other than that, he's in decent shape."

As I processed this information, it appeared that we might lose Mia and Abby, but Tina and Ethan might have a chance of survival. I stared at Peters, who gave a resigned shrug. "The only family we've been able to contact so far is Tina's sister. We told her that Tina, if she survives, will have a very, very rough road ahead. They're still not sure about the condition of her liver. If it can't repair itself, she won't survive."

Barbarians.

"Ready to go talk to Ava?" he asked.

I paused, taking a deep breath. "Give me a minute. You're right. I've seen a lot, but this... it's beyond comprehension."

"Inhuman," he murmured.

After a few deep breaths, I told Peters I was ready to speak with Ava. She was the only one who had looked for the victims, aside from Tina's sister. At least we were able to reassure Ava that all the people involved in the surgery center were now in custody, including the Tates.

The FBI had their own long road ahead in untangling the web that had led to the formation of the organ transplant business. It was too early to determine who would face prosecution, who would go free, and who would betray the true puppet masters—if there were any beyond those at the center.

"Okay, let's go." As we headed toward the elevator, my phone rang. It was Brady. Perhaps he had information about Tina Torres' DNA. "Hey, Brady. Have the DNA results for Tina come back?"

"No, Val, that's not why I'm calling."

I raised my hand to signal to Peters I needed a moment. "What is it, Brady?"

"It's your mom."

My heart pounded. Had the Bear gotten to her? "What about my mom?"

"Val, she's had a stroke. She's in the hospital."

My heart nearly stopped. "How bad? When did this happen?"

"She was having tea with friends, about thirty minutes ago, they recognized the signs. They called nine-one-one right away."

"And her condition? Will she be okay?"

"They say it's too soon to know."

"I'll book the next flight home."

"I'm sorry, Val. I'm at the hospital now. I'll call you with updates as soon as there are any."

Tears welled up in my eyes. It was all too much. The Bear, my captivity, the organ transplant victims, and now my mom. I wasn't sure I could handle much more. Was it the exhaustion causing my fear of a meltdown? I had hardly gotten a wink of sleep since I'd landed in LA.

Peters noted my reaction. "Do you need to go? I can talk to Ava. I'll fill you in on the case as we learn more. It sounds like you need to leave."

"I have to go," I affirmed. "But I want to meet Ava before I leave, just to see that she's okay."

In this whole chaotic ordeal, I needed somebody to be okay. Seeing a kind-hearted person like Ava might just be what I needed to pull myself together.

"Okay." Peters led the way into the room.

A woman in her thirties with dark hair and wearing gray sweatpants was packing up her things.

"Ava," Peters greeted her.

She glanced up and responded with a smile. "Hi, Agent Peters."

"This is my colleague, Agent Costa. She's been aiding the investigation. She was the one who alerted us to the organ trafficking. She's here from Northern California."

Ava's eyes were filling with tears. "Thank you so much for finding them. For finding me."

The truth was awful, but I decided to let Peters divulge the details if she really wanted to know. "Thank you for caring about Ethan, Mia, and Abby. They were fortunate to have you in their lives." My voice faltered, knowing that at least two of them no longer had a future.

"I just wished we could've found them sooner."

"The organization covered their tracks well—until now. But many of them are now in custody."

"Good. How are the kids?" she asked, her eyes filled with hope.

My stomach flipped and flopped. "I have to leave due to a family emergency, but Agent Peters will fill you in. It was very nice to meet you."

As I waved goodbye, I found myself uttering a prayer for the first time in twenty years, hoping that my mother and those poor kids would be okay.

FIFTY-THREE

VAL

One week later

Over the past week, I had felt more emotion than I had in the past twenty years. It had been a series of tumultuous events, beginning with our race against time to find the missing teenagers. We'd managed to rescue them, but the victory was bittersweet. Two of them, Mia and Abby, did not survive. Their injuries were so severe, their young bodies couldn't handle it. The truth was, no one's body could.

The most heartbreaking part was the absence of their families. Neither Mia's nor Abby's families could be found, and no one stepped forward to claim their bodies. When Ava learned this harsh reality, she took it upon herself to claim them. The community rallied around her, gathering funds to provide proper burial services for the two young women who'd lost their lives at the hands of monsters. These vile people who failed to see the potential and worth in the young lives they'd taken.

Tina was still in the hospital, her sister steadfast by her side, praying for her recovery. But the second liver donation was healing rather slowly, and the doctors were unsure if she'd fully recover. At least she had her family by her side. Ethan, on the other hand, had fully recovered and was ready to be released from the hospital, but there was no one to release him to.

His family, who was supposed to love and protect him, was the reason he'd run away in the first place. He pleaded with the social worker not to contact his parents. Knowing his history, and despite Ava's minimal finances, she offered Ethan a solution. She had an extra room and needed someone to help take care of her cat, Mr. Flowers. She offered Ethan this job in exchange for room and board, with the condition that he abided by the rules of her home.

The stark contrast between Ava and those who'd caused so much harm was glaring. Ava, who did everything she could to help people she didn't even know—befriend them, take care of them, and ensure they weren't forgotten—compared to greedy criminals who saw them only as a payday.

In this life, the light and the dark tended to balance out, but every once in a while, I liked to believe that the light was winning. I had to believe that because I didn't think I could survive otherwise.

There was some solace in this entire case, though. We'd learned who had given Scarlett Douglas an illegal transplant that hadn't been a good match, leading to her death, but we liked to think her death may have prevented many more in the future. We'd also succeeded in saving Tina and Ethan, and we'd found Mia and Abby and given them a proper burial—the love they should've had when they'd been alive. The knowledge that these people couldn't take any more children was a consolation, and it would have to be enough to keep us going.

The human trafficking task force was still collecting evidence and building their case. They aimed to ensure every single person involved in the organ-trafficking operation would be sent to prison, hopefully for life.

The DNA results on Scarlett's donor kidney had come back

as a match for Tina. It was such an awful realization, but it confirmed the Douglases' story and would make their testimony in court all the stronger. Jack and May were securely hidden away until they could testify once the case went to trial. As it stood, the Tates were looking at a long time behind bars, as were Dr. Davis and his grisly crew.

Peters suspected there were additional connections to the trafficking ring, as there usually were. They had a full-blown task force on it with a tactical plan in place.

But I had to let it go. It wasn't my job.

I had found the four missing teenagers and uncovered what had happened to Scarlett Douglas. We all have limitations, so for me, that had to be enough.

It was because of Mia, Abby, and Ethan that I realized how crucial it was to be there for family. When I arrived at the hospital to see my mother, I knew I couldn't leave her. I had many lengthy discussions with her doctors and my sister, Maxine, learning that Mom would need months of physical rehabilitation and speech therapy. She couldn't live alone. She needed full-time help.

Maxine, an officer in the Army, had offered to take leave. However, the uncertainty of how long it might take for Mom to recover made it clear that there was only one person for the job: me. It wasn't even a job, really; it was what I knew I needed and wanted to do for the greatest mom in the world.

With her release from the hospital just a few hours away, I was at the house overseeing the installation of a wheelchair ramp and making sure the house was ready for her return. We'd retrofitted one of the downstairs rooms into a bedroom she could stay in since the stairs were no longer a viable option for the foreseeable future. Brady, along with some of the local contractors, had helped with all of it.

It was amazing to see a community come together like that.

Brady walked out onto the porch and said, "Looks like everything is just about ready for Elizabeth."

"Yes, thank you so much."

"Of course. She means a lot to all of us."

After a moment, he asked, "Have you done it?"

I shook my head. Now came the hard part—something I never thought I would do but knew it was what I had to do, what I was meant to do. "I was just about to."

"I'll give you some space. When you're ready, we'll head over to the hospital to pick up your mom," Brady said softly.

"Thanks."

Brady walked back into the house, leaving me alone with my thoughts. I pulled out my phone and thought about how I never would have expected to be making this call.

"Hey, Val, how are things? How is your mom?" Kieran asked.

"We're bringing her home in a little bit," I said, trying to steady my voice.

"It's a tough thing, what she's going through," he said sympathetically.

"It is. And my sister and I have made a decision. We don't want strangers taking care of Mom. We don't want anyone other than family making sure she has everything she needs and makes it to every appointment. Makes sure she gets better."

"Oh?"

Since my hospitalization, I had been counting down to when I could return to work. I'd never imagined that my time with the FBI was over and that I'd never be going back. "I want to be here for my mom. We don't know how long it's going to take before she can walk again. It could be six months, two years —she needs me. So, I'm putting in for my retirement. I'm not coming back." I paused, fighting the lump in my throat. Never did I think I would quit the job I loved, until I was ready to retire.

And not before having caught the Bear.

But I had to do what was right. Mom had been there for us our whole lives. She never asked for anything; she only gave. I never thought I would ever see her so feeble, so weak, so in need of help.

"I understand, Val," Kieran said gently.

I held back tears, feeling as if I was losing my old life. I felt selfish for even thinking that, considering what Mom was going through.

"How are you holding up, Val? You've had a heck of a month."

Truthfully, I felt like I was about to crumble. "I'm still talking to the therapist," I admitted.

"That's good to hear. Your retirement includes benefits, so you won't need to stop."

I wanted to tell him he was a great boss, mentor, and friend, but I couldn't without falling to pieces. "Thank you for everything," was all I could manage.

"We've worked together for a long time, Val. And I gotta say, what you're doing is brave, and I know it's not easy for you. You're an agent through and through, and one of the finest I've ever worked with."

"Thanks, Kieran."

"Don't be a stranger, Val."

"I won't," I assured him and hung up.

I looked around the neighborhood, then down at the porch and the front door of the house I grew up in.

After a deep breath of fresh mountain air, I opened the door. "Hey, Brady, I'm ready." But as soon as the words left my mouth, the tears began to fall. For the first time since my captivity, it all became too much. Brady held me as I cried. After a minute, I composed myself and whispered a shaky, "Sorry..."

Brady stepped back, and said, "You know, sometimes we can't choose our path—sometimes it chooses us. Think of this as a beginning to something new. And hey, you know we can always use someone with your skills at the sheriff's department. Actually, I just got a call from the sheriff. One of the deputies in Hectorville just got a call about a suspicious death," Brady said, trying to suppress a smile.

Suspicious deaths shouldn't have made me feel better about retiring, but if I was going to be around anyways, I supposed I could help out when I wasn't taking care of Mom. Who knew, maybe Brady was right. Maybe this wasn't an ending at all, but a whole new beginning.

A LETTER FROM H.K. CHRISTIE

Dear reader,

Thank you for reading *Gone by Dawn*. I hope you enjoyed reading it as much as I loved writing it. If you did enjoy it, and want to keep up to date with all my latest releases, you can sign up to my author mailing list, where you'll be the first to hear about upcoming novels and other author news. Your email address will never be shared and you can unsubscribe at any time.

www.bookouture.com/h-k-christie

If you're interested in exploring more of my books, or you'd simply like to say hello, visit my website and drop me a message. You can also sign up for my H.K. Christie Reader Club, where you'll be the first to hear about new releases, giveaways, promotions, and a free eBook of *Crashing Down*, the prequel to the Martina Monroe crime thriller series. I love to hear from readers! You can also follow me and reach out on social media.

Thank you,

H.K. Christie

KEEP IN TOUCH WITH H.K. CHRISTIE

www.authorhkchristie.com

 facebook.com/AuthorHKChristie
instagram.com/authorhkchristie

ACKNOWLEDGMENTS

Val is a character who was created from a place of deep admiration. As I've reached a point in my life where the cycle of care becomes ever more present, I've been inspired by the strength and grace of a few dear friends who have had to navigate the complexities of caring for aging parents while balancing the demands of young children, careers, and their own health. Their strength and resilience have blown me away. Val's relationship with her mother, and her hometown, is a tribute to one particularly *incredible* woman in my life, who has shown me the way love can manifest in acts of service, sacrifice, and loyalty.

Many thanks to my editor, Billi-Dee Jones, and the team at Bookouture for helping bring Val to life.

And, of course, a big thank you to Charlie, for all his looks of encouragement and reminders to take breaks. If it weren't for him, I'd be in my office all day working as opposed to catering to all of his desires such as snuggles, scratches, treats, and long, meandering walks. To the mister, thank you, as always, for supporting and encouraging me—and of course the celebratory tequila.

Last but not least, I'd like to thank all of my readers. It's because of you I'm able to continue writing stories.

PUBLISHING TEAM

Turning a manuscript into a book requires the efforts of many people. The publishing team at Bookouture would like to acknowledge everyone who contributed to this publication.

Audio
Alba Proko
Sinead O'Connor
Melissa Tran

Commercial
Lauren Morrissette
Hannah Richmond
Imogen Allport

Cover design
The Brewster Project

Data and analysis
Mark Alder
Mohamed Bussuri

Editorial
Billi-Dee Jones
Ria Clare

Made in the USA
Thornton, CO
09/04/24 12:09:34